THE EARL THAT GOT AWAY

"What do you usually wear when you row?" she asked. He was ruining his good shirt.

"I don't think I should say?"

"Why not? Now I am more curious than ever."

He grinned. "If the weather allows, I usually end up discarding my shirt when I get too hot."

"Oh." The image of Basil shirtless flashed in her mind and suddenly she was overheated, too. Warmth flushed through her body and her cheeks were burning. Her reaction had nothing to do with overexerting herself.

"Isn't it beautiful out here on the river?" Basil asked. "Are you enjoying the view?"

She licked her lips. "I am very much enjoying the view."

Also by Diana Quincy

The Sirens in Silk series
THE DUKE GETS DESPERATE

The Clandestine Affairs series
HER NIGHT WITH THE DUKE
THE VISCOUNT MADE ME DO IT
THE MARQUESS MAKES HIS MOVE

The Rebellious Brides series
SPY FALL
A LICENSE TO WED
FROM LONDON WITH LOVE
THE DUKE WHO RAVISHED ME

The Accidental Peers series
COMPROMISING WILLA
SEDUCING CHARLOTTE
TEMPTING BELLA
ENGAGING THE EARL

The Atlas Catesby Mysteries series
MURDER IN MAYFAIR
MURDER IN BLOOMSBURY
MURDER AT THE OPERA

ATTENTION: ORGANIZATIONS AND CORPORATIONS
HarperCollins books may be purchased for educational, business, or sales promotional use. For information, please e-mail the Special Markets Department at SPsales@harpercollins.com.

DIANA QUINCY

THE EARL THAT GOT AWAY

Sirens in Silk

An Imprint of HarperCollinsPublishers

Without limiting the exclusive rights of any author, contributor, or the publisher of this publication, any unauthorized use of this publication to train generative artificial intelligence (AI) technologies is expressly prohibited. HarperCollins also exercise their rights under Article 4(3) of the Digital Single Market Directive 2019/790 and expressly reserve this publication from the text and data mining exception.

This is a work of fiction. Names, characters, places, and incidents are products of the author's imagination or are used fictitiously and are not to be construed as real. Any resemblance to actual events, locales, organizations, or persons, living or dead, is entirely coincidental.

THE EARL THAT GOT AWAY. Copyright © 2025 by Dora Mekouar. All rights reserved. Printed in the United States of America. No part of this book may be used or reproduced in any manner whatsoever without written permission except in the case of brief quotations embodied in critical articles and reviews. For information, address HarperCollins Publishers, 195 Broadway, New York, NY 10007. In Europe, HarperCollins Publishers, Macken House, 39/40 Mayor Street Upper, Dublin 1, D01 C9W8, Ireland.

hc.com

First Avon Books mass market printing: September 2025

Print Edition ISBN: 978-0-06-324756-7
Digital Edition ISBN: 978-0-06-324752-9

Cover design by Amy Halperin
Cover illustration by Victor Gadino
Cover images © Getty Images/iStock

Avon, Avon & logo, and Avon Books & logo are registered trademarks of HarperCollins Publishers in the United States of America and other countries.

HarperCollins is a registered trademark of HarperCollins Publishers in the United States of America and other countries.

FIRST EDITION

25 26 27 28 29   BVGM   10 9 8 7 6 5 4 3 2 1

> If you purchased this book without a cover, you should be aware that this book is stolen property. It was reported as "unsold and destroyed" to the publisher, and neither the author nor the publisher has received any payment for this "stripped book."

*To Joanna Shupe.
For all the things,
especially the ones that have
nothing to do with writing.*

THE EARL THAT GOT AWAY

PART ONE

The Earl That Got Away

CHAPTER ONE

Yorkshire, England
1887

"You are next," Auntie Majida murmured in Arabic. "*Inshallah*, God willing, we will find you a very nice husband."

Naila Darwish resisted the urge to roll her eyes. If she had a dollar for every time Auntie talked about finding her a husband, she'd be independently wealthy. "I doubt that's going to happen."

Auntie Majida was not easily deterred. "*Laish let?* Why not?"

"You know why." Naila fiddled with the stack of thin gold bangles adorning her wrist, her finger circling the single pearl adornment on one bracelet. "Because I've already had my chance."

"You had your chance?" Auntie Majida tsked dismissively. "*Hakki fathee.* Stop with the empty talk."

"Why? It's the truth." At twenty-seven, Naila was an old maid by any standard. "I did not seize the opportunity when offered."

"That boy was a stranger," Auntie said impatiently. "We didn't even know if he was *ibn il nas*, the son of respectable people. You were *jahla*, a silly young girl who didn't know better."

Maybe, but eight years later, Naila still hadn't outgrown the ache in her chest whenever she thought of his devastated expression when she ended things. The disbelief in his hollow eyes, the grim flat set of his mouth. She might as well have sliced his chest open and plucked out his beating heart.

Her penance was to spend her life sitting on the sidelines watching others find the joy in life that she'd carelessly tossed away. That's why she was seated beside her aunt in her usual wallflower position while her sister twirled across the dance floor in the arms of her betrothed, a handsome duke with dark golden hair and an aristocratic profile. It was hard to believe that in two short weeks Raya would become a duchess and the mistress of Castle Tremayne.

The evening's prewedding festivities were taking place in the castle's Great Hall, a cavernous chamber with stone walls, mammoth windows and soaring ceilings. The Darwish family contingent had sailed from Brooklyn, arriving two weeks earlier. Some of the Arab relatives who came for the wedding found Tremayne disappointingly dreary and rundown. But not Naila. She was enchanted. Anyone with an appreciation for construction and design could see that the castle was an architectural masterpiece.

The duke escorted Raya off the dance floor. Her sister, a vision in white, was radiant, her happiness more vibrant than a thousand burning candles. Would Naila know the same joy if she'd been brave enough to follow her heart?

Instead, she'd relegated herself to being a supporting player in other people's lives. The aunt who looked after her older sister's children. The person the family automatically turned to when an elderly relative required care or companionship. How had she, a girl who once craved excitement and adventure, settled for such a tedious life?

Naila sighed and tilted her head upward, inspecting the intricate stained-glass designs adorning generous arched windows. At least she had her study of architecture to distract her. Otherwise, she'd die of boredom. Or remorse. Fortunately, with its great old castles and country houses, England was the perfect place to indulge her passion.

Auntie scanned the crowded Great Hall. "Maybe there is a widower in his forties who will need a wife to take care of his children."

"That sounds delightful," Naila said under her breath.

"*Shatra.*" Missing the sarcasm in Naila's voice, Auntie nodded approvingly. "Smart girl. An older man with money and a good family is worth everything."

Auntie did not believe in romantic love, but

Naila knew better. The bridal couple approached, Raya wearing a beatific smile while her betrothed beamed like a man who couldn't believe his good fortune.

"Auntie Majida must dance with me," the duke proclaimed with a twinkle in his eye.

The older woman flushed and fluttered her sparse lashes. *"Malaya minuck.* Don't be silly," she said, clearly delighted to be singled out.

Naila watched the interaction in astonishment. Up until that moment, she'd been certain Auntie Majida was uncharmable.

"Take Naila," the older woman said.

"What?" Now it was Naila's turn to flush. "Oh no, that's not necessary."

"Naila never dances." Their elder sister, Nadine, appeared. "But I am an excellent dancer. Everyone says I am graceful enough to be a ballerina. I took lessons when I was young."

"It shall be my pleasure to dance with Mrs. Habib," the Duke of Strickland said, gallant as ever. "As long as Miss Darwish will consent to dance with Hawksworth."

Naila glanced around. "Who?"

"That's an excellent idea!" Raya said. "The Earl of Hawksworth is one of Strick's oldest friends."

The duke tapped the sleeve of a wide-shouldered man in a perfectly tailored black evening suit standing with his back to them talking with a guest. The man turned to face them.

"May I introduce the Earl of Hawksworth?" the duke said.

The earl's eyes met Naila's. Deep lines framed a steely gaze and a jaw cut so sharp it could do bodily harm. Naila's heart seized as she tumbled into the past, staring into the face that had haunted her for almost a decade.

"Hawk," the duke said, "this is Miss Naila Darwish, my intended's lovely sister."

The world came to an abrupt halt. All movement in the ballroom—the dancing couples, chattering guests and roaming servants proffering refreshments—froze in place. Everything, that is, except for Naila's plummeting stomach.

Basil.

His eyes widened, joy lighting them ever so briefly. For a fleeting unguarded moment, they were them again, connected, invincible, their hearts melded. Hope and possibility blossomed between them. But then a cold mask slid into place on Basil's face, and a stranger, absent of all warmth, inhabited the man she'd once adored.

Still adored.

"We have met." Time had deepened Basil's voice, seasoning it. But those cut-glass tones were still sharp enough to stab her heart.

"You have?" Both Raya and Strickland spoke in unison.

"Many years ago." His gaze slid away from Naila. "In Philadelphia."

"Philadelphia?" The duke's brows rose. He looked from Basil to Naila and back again. "This is—?" His mouth fell open. "What are the chances?"

"You are already acquainted?" Raya exclaimed with obvious delight. "It truly is a small world."

"Unbelievably so," Strickland muttered.

Nadine stared at Naila. "You met an earl when you visited Philadelphia?"

Stricken, Naila did not answer. Her lungs were paralyzed. After all these years, Basil Trevelyn had become more of a dream than an actual person. Yet the beautiful man standing before her, vibrant and alive, his wide shoulders filling out tailored evening clothes, was *achingly* real.

Strickland recovered himself enough to introduce Majida. "And this is the young ladies' aunt, Mrs. Kassab."

"We have also met." Cynicism laced Basil's words. He dipped his chin. "Ma'am."

Auntie Majida narrowed her eyes at him. "Isn't this the boy from Philadelphia?" she asked Naila in Arabic. In English, she said to Basil, "What does it mean? Earl?"

His eyes were gray ice. "It's simply a title. One that is not as high as a duke."

Raya interjected. "But an impressive and important noble title, nonetheless," she explained. "Among the highest in the land."

Majida ran an assessing glance over Basil. "Highest?"

"I assure you that I am the same man." Scorn iced his words.

Disbelief spun through Naila. How was this happening? Surely the chances of running into the love of her life in a far-flung English castle were as remote as being crowned queen of England. And how was it possible for Basil to be an earl? That was one of England's highest titles. She wasn't overly familiar with how nobility worked but she knew titles were inherited and Basil's father wasn't an earl. Nor were any of his uncles.

The musicians struck a chord. Strick's glance bounced between Basil and Naila before he offered his arm to Nadine. "That is our cue," he said to her. "Shall we?"

Nadine beamed. "If you insist."

"And Hawk will dance with Naila," Raya said cheerfully, somehow missing the thick undercurrent of tension congealing around them. "Go on, you two."

Basil hesitated before offering his arm. What choice did he have? To refuse would be unthinkably rude. "Miss Darwish."

A hint of derision laced the way he spoke her name. Naila didn't blame Basil for despising her. A truly loyal woman, a person of courage and substance, could never be persuaded to abandon the man who owned her heart. She'd bitterly regretted her decision every single day since sending Basil away.

For years, Naila had dreamed of seeing him again, yearned for a chance to set things right. But now that Basil stood before her in the flesh, her first instinct was to flee. Anything to avoid the tumult inside her. And the faint mockery in his eyes.

"Naila." Nadine turned away from Otis, the footman who'd brought her a note. "Malik is feeling sick. He's insisting that his auntie Naila tuck him into bed."

"That can wait," Raya said, clearly annoyed. "Naila is about to dance."

"She doesn't even like to waltz." Nadine looked to Naila. "Do you?"

Fidgeting with the gold bangles on her wrist, Naila avoided Basil's gaze. Yet again, when it came to him, she opted for the coward's way out. "I will go see to Malik," she said. "If you will excuse me."

"Naila—" Raya started.

"Perfect," Nadine said brightly before turning to the duke. "I am ready to dance."

Naila didn't look Basil's way, but as she hurried to attend to her nephew, she felt his disdain burning through the back of her embroidered silk gown.

Chapter Two

Before
Philadelphia

"Are we in good company?" Auntie Majida asked Cousin Hamda in Arabic as they surveyed the couples dancing in the assembly room.

Naila tapped her foot to the beat of the music, not giving a fig whether they were in respectable company. She was thrilled to be at a party and couldn't wait to dance.

Hamda, a brisk, no-nonsense woman, bristled. "Of course, Majida. Do you think I'd bring you around people who are lower than us?"

"Why are you getting upset?" Majida sniffed. "I was just asking. I wouldn't want to expose Naila to bad people when her parents trusted me to bring her with me to visit you."

Hamda's face reddened. "You insult me by suggesting I would subject a young, unmarried girl to bad people?"

Naila barely heard the bickering between the older ladies. She was accustomed to their squabbling about the smallest perceived insult. Majida and Hamda were cousins who'd grown up together until Hamda married and moved to Philadelphia decades ago.

Naila sighed. It was warm in the hall and she was bored. She'd been in Philadelphia for three days with little entertainment. Thankfully, her cousin Eyad's employer invited them to this amusement. But no one had asked her to dance yet.

She tried to catch Eyad's eye across the dance floor in hopes that he'd come rescue her from the quarreling aunties. But her cousin was too busy chatting with a group of young men to notice.

"Your blood is so thick," Hamda was saying to Majida, accusing her of being obnoxiously heavy-handed.

Majida's eyes rounded. "That is how to talk to your guest?"

Naila's gaze locked on the half-open door to the terrace. A cool breeze across her overheated skin would be very welcome. She edged away while the wrangling aunties were too preoccupied to notice.

Once she was close enough to the exit, she slipped outside. Freedom! It was delicious. She hurried down the stairs into the garden where it would be harder to be detected. The air was cool and fresh, the scent of roses wafting through the air. The sound of masculine laughter from deep in the garden grew louder. Naila quickly stepped behind a rose-covered lattice. The last thing she needed was the ridiculous scandal that would surely erupt if she ended up in the garden alone with strange men.

The rich floral scent filled her nostrils as she watched the garden denizens approach. It was an older couple, the man with a shock of white hair, accompanied by a woman whose dark curls were streaked with silver. They looked around before stealing a quick kiss.

Naila smiled. She rarely saw old married couples openly dote on each other. Whenever Baba, who was naturally affectionate, tried to pull Mama in for a kiss, she blushed and pushed him away, chastising Baba for being a silly old man.

Naila tracked the couple until they disappeared into the ballroom. That's when a match struck close by.

Very close by.

Naila froze. She was so focused on remaining out of sight that she hadn't realized she wasn't alone. Taking a breath, she turned toward the sound of the match. Playful dark eyes, illuminated by the flame, sparkled back at her.

"Oh!" she said.

He inhaled as he lit his cigarette. "My apologies," he spoke in a clipped British accent. "I didn't mean to startle you."

He wasn't American. Relief slid through her. The chances of Auntie Hamda's family being acquainted with an Englishman were almost nil. Word of Naila's solo garden encounter with this *inglese*—this very handsome-seeming *inglese* from what she could tell—was unlikely to reach them.

She relaxed a fraction. Even as her eyes adjusted to the low light, she could barely make out his features beyond the high forehead and aristocratic nose, the smooth, flexible lips puckering around the cigarette.

"Favor a fag?" he asked.

She tore her eyes away from his supple mouth. "A what?"

"I guess you Americans call them cigarettes." She registered the amusement in his voice. Was he insulting her by offering her a smoke?

"Do respectable young ladies in England enjoy cigarettes?" she asked.

He chuckled. "Not in public. But I am rather certain that those who do indulge do so while hiding out in dark gardens."

Naila had snuck a cigarette or two. Sometimes, she and her cousins crept to the rooftop to share a pilfered cigarette at the family row house on Henry Street. That was one advantage of having a large extended family. There were eighteen cousins on Baba's side of the family and thirteen on Mama's, too many bodies for the adults to notice when a handful of cousins vanished for a little while.

Naila considered the *inglese*'s offer. So far, Philadelphia was completely boring and she was in the mood for adventure. "Maybe just one."

He smiled, baring a mouthful of nice-looking teeth. Naila felt a little warm inside. She took the proffered cigarette and watched him strike another match, this one just for her. She placed the cigarette between her lips and noted how his eyes focused on her mouth as she inhaled long and slow, lighting the cigarette.

"Ah," he remarked. "Not a novice then." He pursed his lips and blew, extinguishing the flame. Naila could barely tear her eyes away from his mouth. His accent made him seem much more worldly and dashing than American boys with their flat intonations, even though she knew how a person sounded had nothing to do with either of those things.

"You're a surprise," he remarked.

"You don't know me at all." She blew out a smooth column of smoke, feeling very daring and grown-up. "Everything about me should come as a surprise."

"You are quite right. Allow me to introduce myself. My name is Basil. May I have the pleasure of knowing yours?"

"Could you have a more English name?"

"I could be called Sebastian, I suppose."

He had a sense of humor. She liked that. "My name is Naila."

"A lovely name for a lovely lady. And unusual. I cannot say I've heard it before."

"Because it's Arab. My parents emigrated from

Palestine." She waited for him to react. To look down on her, but interest lit his eyes.

"In the Levant? How fascinating."

His voice, so elegant and debonair, slid along her skin like a velvet glove. "I've never been there," she told him. "I was born in Brooklyn."

"In New York? I haven't had the pleasure of seeing New York as of yet. I am visiting my uncle."

"Your uncle lives in Philadelphia?"

"Yes. He is the proprietor of a business concern here." He tilted his head back and exhaled, smoke billowing out of his rounded lips. "I might take it over, as he has no children."

She studied his noble profile, the defined nose and sharply hewn chin. "You would settle here? In America?"

"Why not?" His eyes sparkled when he looked at her. "I am learning there are many enticements here."

Her cheeks heated. *He was flirting with her.* Naila was accustomed to boys back home in Little Syria running after her. But they were just that—boys. The *inglese* was a full-grown man. A thrill coursed through Naila at the realization that her feminine appeal extended beyond neighborhood youths.

"Why would you move here?" She tapped the ashes off her cigarette. "I should think an *inglese* like you would have a country mansion to return to."

THE EARL THAT GOT AWAY

"*Inglese*?" he repeated, a question in his eyes.

Naila blushed. She hadn't intended to call him that to his face. "It means *Englishman* in Arabic." She dropped her gaze. "My apologies."

"Don't be sorry." He blew a column of smoke toward the blue-black sky. "I'm flattered that you already have a pet name for me."

Her cheeks burned hotter. Thank goodness it was dark so he couldn't see how red her face surely was.

"Alas," he continued, his teeth gleaming in the low light of the garden, "I am not a lord, nor a duke nor an earl. It is peers of the realm, or men of significant wealth, who possess the grand manor houses that you speak of. I am just an ordinary person."

Ordinary. Ha! If this was what all men in England were like, she'd book her passage there first thing tomorrow. It was odd to be sitting behind the trellis talking to a man she barely knew. And yet, weirdly, Basil didn't seem like a stranger. Something in her recognized him, which made no sense at all.

"Why were you hiding behind the roses?" she asked, drawing on her cigarette.

"Same as you, I suspect. I didn't want to embarrass the clandestine couple."

"It is a relief that they did not see us."

He eyed her billowing skirts. "It's a wonder they missed you in that rather vivid orange gown."

She grinned. "The dressmaker said it was tangerine. I adore bright colors. Tangerine most of all."

"It suits you. A vibrant color for a vibrant woman."

She wondered if that meant he thought she was too much. She shrugged. He was a stranger. What did she care what he thought of her? "How lovely was that older couple? Imagine being married that long and still sneaking kisses."

"It would be lovely, I suppose, if they were actually wed."

"What?"

"They are not married," he informed her.

"How scandalous!" she returned with mock horror.

"You do not know the half of it." His eyes crinkled at the corners. "I should clarify. They are not wed to each other."

Now she was truly scandalized. "Are you saying—?"

"That they appear to be conducting an illicit affair? Yes. Each is married to someone else."

She'd never encountered anything so deliciously shocking in real life. She wasn't sure whether to believe him. "How do you know?"

He laughed. A deep rumbling sound. "The gentleman is a business associate of my uncle. I have met his wife and the woman with him this evening was not her."

"Why would anyone sneak intimacies in the garden?"

His gaze dropped to her lips. "I can definitely see the appeal."

Naila's breath caught. Her blood simmered in her veins. Something was happening. The air thickened with the heat arcing between them, sparks that had nothing to do with her cigarette. More than a few boys back in Little Syria had tried to steal a kiss from Naila. But this was the first time in her life that she was actually tempted to let a man take liberties.

"Are you flirting with me?" she asked, pretending to be accustomed to drawing the interest of appealing strangers.

"American girls are very direct." His gaze dipped to her mouth yet again. "It is a very attractive trait."

Nervous, Naila licked her lips. Wanting churned deep in her belly. She'd never understood how a girl could just throw away her reputation by getting mixed up with a boy. But now she did. It was like her body took on a mind of its own, leaving her brain with no say in the matter.

Alarm shot through her. Naila stamped out her cigarette and stood abruptly. "I must go!" she said and fled back to the safety of ballroom.

Chapter Three

Now
England

Naila was so changed that Hawk barely recognized her.

The sparkle was absent from her midnight eyes, the blush long gone from her cheeks. This version of Naila Darwish, with her terse mouth and sallow complexion, possessed none of the radiance of the bold, orange gown–wearing beauty who had captivated him in Philadelphia.

This Naila cloaked herself in a drab dark gown that the girl he'd known would never be caught dead in. Despite the unflattering dress, he still got a sense of the lavish body he'd worshipped. Naila possessed curves that went on forever, with abundant breasts and swaying hips that made a man weak in the knees.

And hard in other places.

Yet, she wasn't the same. This Naila was drained of all vivacity. She was almost lifeless, so quiet and bland that she easily blended into the background. His Naila could never be a wallflower. Without even trying, she outshone every person in the room.

A part of Hawk, the less charitable, more aggrieved part—the place in his soul that still resented her decision—felt a pang of satisfaction. By the looks of it, Naila had done Hawk a favor, her abandonment sparing him a lifetime chained to a colorless mouse.

"I do wish Naila had danced with you," Raya said.

"Hmm?" Hawk glanced down at his dance partner, so lost in thought he almost forgot he'd escorted Naila's sister to the dance floor. "Ah, yes."

"She is an excellent dancer."

"Is that so?" he murmured politely, smoothly guiding Raya along the crowded dance floor. Hawk possessed firsthand knowledge of Naila's dancing skills. They'd waltzed once at a party hosted by his uncle in America. He could still feel the soft curve of her back where he'd held her. His fingers tingled at the memory.

"Oh, yes, but she rarely dances now."

"Why is that?" Hawk hated himself for wanting to know. Was it because Naila was miserable without him? Did she miss Hawk as much as he missed her? *Used to miss her.* Any feelings he once had for Naila Darwish were in the past.

They had to be.

There was a time when he'd have done anything for her. Before he inherited the earldom, he had nothing to offer but himself and his determination to make something of his future. But that hadn't been enough. *He* hadn't been enough.

"I don't really know why Naila doesn't like to dance anymore," Raya admitted. "I am surprised that you and my sister are previously acquainted. How did you meet?"

"Through mutual family friends in Philadelphia. I was contemplating taking over my uncle's manufacturing concern. He has no children."

"A business?" Surprise lit her eyes. He noticed they weren't as dark as Naila's. And nowhere near as mesmerizing. "But you're an earl."

"Quite by accident."

Her forehead wrinkled. "How does one accidentally fall into an earldom?"

"I inherited from my father's cousin." Hawk was not well acquainted with his friend's future wife, having met the woman only a handful of times. But he appreciated her directness. "He and his three sons all perished together in a boating accident."

"How perfectly awful!"

"A terrible tragedy that meant the title fell to me."

"That must have been quite a shock."

"It was. But it was my duty to step up and lead the family." There'd been a lot to learn, but Hawk welcomed the distraction. He might not have survived Naila's desertion otherwise. She'd stolen not only his heart, but also his honor and all of his hopes and expectations for the future.

"Is it not also your duty to take a wife?" Amusement glinted in her gaze. "There seem to be plenty of women here who would be delighted to help you fulfill that obligation."

He briefly wondered if Naila had mentioned him to her sister, but immediately dismissed the notion. Raya hadn't even known Hawk and Naila were acquainted until this evening. That's how little he meant to Naila. He was likely just a glancing memory.

Raya surveyed the crowded dance floor. "Every young unmarried lady is staring at us right now."

"What of your sister?" He strived to keep a note of general disinterest in his voice. "Now that you are betrothed, I imagine she will think of marriage."

"Naila? Who knows? She's had offers, but she rejected all of them."

"Is that so?" Maybe she made a habit of rebuffing suitors. Who else had she sent away?

"Naila is far more interested in old buildings than new suitors," Raya said. "Once she sees to our nephew, she'll probably sneak off to explore the castle. My sister is enthralled by architecture."

"Still?" Memories of long strolls with Naila, exploring the structures in various Philadelphia neighborhoods, jolted through him.

"You know that about Naila?" She contemplated him. "Just how well acquainted were the two of you?"

"Not very." He cursed to himself. The last thing he needed was gossip that tied him to Naila. Pivoting, he offered up a tempting distraction. "I am, as it happens, in search of a wife."

Interest glinted her gaze. "What sort of woman would you like for a countess?"

"Why do you ask?" An image of Naila, as she'd once been, vibrant and laughing, fearless and daring, popped into his head. "Do you have someone in mind?"

"I won't know until you tell me what qualities you require in a wife."

"Very well," he said. "Above all, she must be of firm character."

"A man who appreciates a woman who knows her own mind?" she said approvingly. "That is rare."

"It shouldn't be."

"On that we agree." They took another twirl. "I suppose she has to be an aristocrat."

"It might be easier to adjust to her role as countess if she is. But that's not an absolute requirement. What I absolutely abhor is a woman who shrinks away from difficult decisions."

She smiled. "I shall be on the lookout for an appropriately strong-minded woman."

"I'd be much obliged." If she offered up her sister, maybe he would do the rejecting this time.

"If word gets out that you are looking for a

bride, it will be a favored topic of conversation in the fortnight leading up to the wedding."

"Surely not." He made a show of frowning even as relief flowed through him. His acquaintanceship with her sister now seemed like the last thing on Raya's mind.

NAILA STUDIED HERSELF in the full-length mirror. "Are the upper sleeves too puffy?"

"No, that's considered the style." Nadine bit into an apple. "Since when do you care about fashion?"

Since seeing Inglese again. Even though his obvious disdain for her during their brief encounter was as thick as the fog that engulfed the castle most mornings.

"Naila always looks polished." Raya lounged across the bed in the guest chamber assigned to Naila. "The orange color of that gown flatters your complexion."

Naila ran a hand over her cheek. "Do you think so?" Her skin was duller than it used to be, her eyes even seemed smaller. What did Inglese see when he looked at her now?

Nadine slumped comfortably in a faded stuffed chair by the unlit hearth. "Since when do you wear bright colors?"

Naila turned, examining her reflection over her shoulder to see how she looked from the back. "Since Mama and I went to the dressmaker before this trip and she insisted I add some color."

"As much as I hate to admit it, Mama's right," Raya said. "Vivid colors brighten your face."

"That's true," Nadine said between mouthfuls of apple. "All you wear is brown, gray, white and black. Entirely *boring*."

"I like muted tones," Naila protested. She reached for a set of gold hairpins her mother had purchased for her and clipped one into her hair. Too showy. She pulled it out.

"You used to wear bright colors all the time," Raya pointed out. "I remember when orange was your favorite color."

"It was *tangerine*. Anyhow, people's tastes change." Rainbow colors made Naila feel like an impostor now. They were a reminder of a braver way of living. Of a time when she'd been happy and full of hope for the future. She hadn't married Inglese, but she'd mourned the loss of him as a widow might.

"Those gold hairpins are pretty," Nadine said. "Mama should have bought me a pair too. I am a married woman. I need to look respectable."

Naila faced her sisters. "Should I wear this dress to supper or the blue gown that I tried on before?"

"I like the blue," Nadine said.

"Orange," Raya said at the same time. "Mama

would insist on the orange. The brighter the better."

"Well, she's not here," Naila responded. Their mother rarely left Brooklyn. She'd been plagued by debilitating seasickness during her immigrant voyage from Palestine to New York Harbor nearly three decades ago.

Naila had placated Mama by having the colorful gowns made for her, but she never intended to wear them in England. Yet, after seeing Basil again, a part of her yearned to be more like the version of herself that had once besotted him.

"Raya, did the duke say anything about how gracefully I dance?" Nadine never went long before bringing the conversation back to herself. "He told me he enjoyed our waltz immensely."

"No." Raya's amused glance met Naila's in the mirror. "But I am sure he was impressed."

"This old castle is so drafty." Crossing her arms over her chest, Nadine shivered and gazed at the barren hearth. "Why aren't the fires running?"

"Put a shawl on," Raya advised. "We can't light every fire all day long. We must economize."

Nadine grimaced. "What good is it to inherit a castle if you're cold all the time?"

"I'm not cold," Naila said in solidarity with Raya.

Nadine changed the subject. "Raya, how was dancing with the earl?"

Naila pivoted to face Raya. "You danced with Ba . . . um . . . the earl?"

Nadine tossed her apple core aside. "Hawksworth is handsome in a meanish sort of way. That persistent scowl makes him look like he's about to tear someone's head off."

"Hawk was very polite when I danced with him, but he seemed preoccupied." Raya rolled onto her stomach, propping herself up on her elbows. "He says he's looking for a wife."

The breakfast Naila had eaten earlier soured in her stomach. "He told you that?"

Nadine pouted. "How unfortunate that I'm already married."

Raya looked heavenward. "Yes, I'm sure you would have been first on his list."

Naila forced a casual tone. "Did he say if he has anyone in mind?"

"No." Raya's eyes twinkled. "I should set him up with you."

Nadine scoffed. "As if a handsome, rich earl would marry a twenty-seven-year-old spinster." She shot Naila an apologetic look. "I mean no offense, of course."

"Then why do you say things that offend?" Raya snapped.

"I wonder what an earl looks for in a wife," Nadine mused. "I suppose she has to be very beautiful."

"He didn't mention looks." Raya rolled over

and rose from the bed, shaking out her skirts. "It seems character is most important to him."

Naila fidgeted with her bangles, the gold cool against her fingertips. "What did he say to make you think that?"

"He wants someone who knows her own mind. The earl seems to have contempt for women who shrink away from making hard decisions."

Naila froze. The words stung. "Oh."

"I have to go." Raya strode toward the door. "I have some castle accounts to settle."

Nadine rolled her eyes. "Most brides-to-be would be obsessing over their wedding, not their ledgers. How does the duke tolerate your infatuation with business?"

"He not only tolerates my enthusiasm, he loves it." Raya's mouth curved into a knowing smile. "Perhaps a little too much."

Nadine grimaced. "I'm sure I do not want to know what you mean by that."

Laughing, Raya turned to Naila. "Which dress have you decided on? The orange or the blue?"

"The brown silk," Naila responded. "There's no use in pretending to be someone I'm not."

Raya and Nadine groaned in unison.

Naila tugged the orange dress off. She suddenly couldn't stand to be in it. There was no going back to the past. No use pretending that she was someone that she wasn't. That part of her life, when she was young and fearless and easily drew the admiration of men, was over, no matter how much she wished that wasn't the case.

"It is not as though I have anything to prove to anyone," she said, leaving the orange silk in a forlorn heap on the floor.

"I'LL MARRY THE earl," Hind, Naila's cousin, announced with a twinkle in her eye. "I am ready and available."

"Don't you think you should wait for him to propose?" Naila asked.

Hind, a few years younger than Naila, was practically a third sister. Her mother died when Hind was a child, which led to the young cousin spending a great deal of time at the Darwish house while her father, Umo Refaat, was at work.

That close bond was why Hind joined Naila, Nadine and Ghassan, Nadine's husband, on the voyage to England. The four of them, along with Auntie Majida, who had come to England with Raya several months earlier, would represent the bride's side of the family at the nuptials. Their brother, Salem, stayed behind in New York to tend to the family linen business.

"The earl is a forbidding person but that is part of his attraction," Hind observed as they entered one of the castle's numerous drawing rooms after supper. The rest of the party consisted of about two dozen people, including Basil and the duke's other friends and family. "Did Hawksworth tell Raya what he's looking for in a wife?"

"He wants a woman who knows her own mind," Naila answered. "Who is firm in her decisions."

Hind winked. "I could definitely stand firm in my decision to marry a man like that."

Unlike Naila. Regret waived through her as she surreptitiously tracked Basil's movements. He stood across the room conversing with a striking, well-dressed couple. The pair's matching vibrant copper hair suggested that they might be related.

"So Hawksworth wants a strong woman?" Hind mused. "Meanwhile, the aunties are busy telling us to act shy and malleable in order to attract a husband. That shows how much the old ladies know."

Naila recalled how wrong Auntie Majida had been about Basil. "Isn't that the truth?"

"Are you acquainted with the woman he's talking to? She's frightfully elegant."

The copper-haired lady was also beautiful, with flawless skin and delicate bone structure. "I don't know who she is." Jealousy flared in Naila's stomach. Not that she had any right. She had given up all claim to Basil eight years ago.

Nadine appeared. "Will you play the piano," she asked Naila, "so that we can all dance?"

"Of course." She welcomed the distraction. "If that is what Raya wants."

"She said you should only play if you care to. And that it's not fair that you never get to dance." Nadine rolled her eyes. "As if you like to dance."

She had once. With Basil. She could still feel the cocoon of his protective embrace, the warm sensation of his large hand flat against her upper back.

Naila crossed over to the piano. As she browsed the sheet music, Raya approached with a man who appeared to be about their age. She introduced him as Mr. Kareem Amar.

"A pleasure." With a slight bow of his head, Mr. Amar pressed a hand flat against his chest in a show of respect and courtesy. He was of average height, with sharp features and dark eyes. His smile was appealing and his manner pleasant.

"Kareem is something like our fifth cousin," Raya told her. "We couldn't quite figure it out. But his grandmother and Auntie Majida share the same great-great-grandparents."

Naila noted Mr. Amar's crisp English accent. "You grew up here?"

He nodded. "I was born in Manchester."

"Kareem is an architect," Raya told Naila. "I thought you two would enjoy meeting since you share a love of old buildings."

He smiled, baring crowded white teeth. "The more ancient the better."

"I envy your living in England," Naila remarked. "There is so much to see here."

"Kareem is working on a project that might interest you," Raya said. "He's cataloging old manor houses before they disappear."

"Disappear?" Naila frowned. "What do you mean?"

"Kareem will have to explain it to you." Raya looked across the room, to where her duke sat with Auntie Majida and Nadine. Their sister spoke animatedly while the duke listened with an expression of polite interest. "I must go and rescue Strick from Nadine."

"Your sister is a force of nature," Mr. Amar remarked after Raya departed. "This castle might very well have fallen into ruin without her management."

"Raya is remarkable," Naila agreed. "What did she mean about the manor houses vanishing?"

"The old aristocratic families are unable to keep them up. They can no longer make a handsome living off the land like they used to. As a result, some of the big houses, many of which are architecturally significant, are being abandoned. It is only a matter of time before they are torn down."

"What?" She couldn't imagine treasures like Castle Tremayne being razed to the ground. "That's terrible!"

"I agree. That is why I am cataloging England's

significant country manors so that they won't be completely lost to history."

"But the actual buildings will be?"

"I fear that will inevitably be the case. Everything, even the family crypts, will be destroyed. We could eventually lose prime examples of the finest Tudor and Palladian architecture."

Naila couldn't imagine such a thing. "Surely something can be done to save them."

"Some aristocrats have wed American heiresses with dowries significant enough to save the crumbling estates."

"That seems to be a fair trade," she remarked. Mr. Amar was very easy to talk to. "The brides become aristocrats and the nobles save their homes?"

"Precisely. And some actually marry for love. So it is said about Lady Randolph Churchill."

"Who is she?"

"She was born Jennie Jerome of New York. When she married the third son of a duke more than a decade ago, her dowry was large enough to begin a major restoration of Blenheim Palace, one of England's grandest country homes."

"More aristocrats need to follow that example."

"You will get no argument from me. I would like to photograph the estates as well, but that is a costly endeavor. I hope to raise funds, perhaps through a generous benefactor, to photograph all of the estates that I catalog."

Nadine came over, interrupting their conversation. "Are you going to play?" she asked impatiently. "We're all waiting."

Naila was so caught up in her exchange with Mr. Amar that she'd forgotten all about providing the evening's music. "If you will excuse me," she said reluctantly to him.

"Of course. I hope we can continue speaking another time?"

She smiled up at him. "I will look forward to it."

Chapter Four

Hawk clenched his teeth when Naila smiled up at her companion.

She was engaged in a very animated conversation with the man Hawk had never seen before. It was the most alive he'd seen her since coming to Castle Tremayne. She wore yet another drab gown, but her companion seemed charmed enough.

"So." Hawk was surprised to find Strick at his side. "That's her."

"Who is that man with Miss Darwish?"

"His name is Kareem Amar. He's an architect. Raya tells me they are very distantly related."

"He's an Arab?"

"Born in England to Arab immigrant parents with a distant familial connection to the Darwishes of New York."

Hawk studied the man. No doubt an architect of Arab origin would be far more acceptable to Naila's family than a penniless Englishman.

"He's cataloging old homes," Strick was saying.

"Hmm." An architect whose work involved historic structures would certainly appeal to Naila.

"So she's the one," Strick remarked.

"What one?"

"Raya's sister is the girl who broke your heart."

Hawk's tone hardened. "Don't be ridiculous."

"You said yourself that you met the lady who stole your heart when you were in Philadelphia."

"You do realize that half of Philadelphia's population is female."

"And did you stare at every one of them the same way you're ogling Miss Darwish?"

Hawk released a long breath. He didn't have the energy to keep up the pretense with his friend. "Is it that obvious?"

"Your regard for her might as well be stamped on your forehead." The duke sipped his drink. "Maybe it isn't as apparent to the rest of our guests. But being in a similar besotted condition, it's easier to recognize the malady in others."

"She has changed a great deal." Hawk kept his eyes on Naila and the architect. "I doubt I would have immediately recognized her had you not reintroduced us yesterday."

"I can see the appeal."

Hawk looked at his friend. "You can?"

"Why do you sound so astonished?"

"Because back when I first knew her, she was radiant. So vibrant and animated that she shined."

"Granted, she's no vivacious debutante, but Naila has a quiet charm to her. From what Raya tells me, she is very well regarded in her community."

Hawk tracked the architect as he took his leave of Naila. She adjusted some music sheets and began to play.

"Raya says Naila is widely respected for her even temper and sound judgment," Strick continued.

"Sound judgment?" Like forsaking him? "Why isn't she married?"

"She's had offers. The oldest sister's husband wanted to marry her first."

"Mr. Habib? Nadine's husband?"

Strick nodded. "When she declined, he wed the elder sister."

"You certainly know a great deal about her."

"Raya talks about her sisters all the time. Who'd have thought that the young lady who broke your heart would turn out to be my betrothed's sister?"

"Broke my heart?" Hawk scoffed despite the twinge in his chest. "I never took you for the melodramatic type."

"You *are* staring at her like a lovesick boy."

"There you are." Raya approached, accompanied by a petite young woman with a robust complexion and a mass of barely contained dark curls. Raya introduced the girl as Hind, one of her Darwish cousins.

"It won't do for the host not to dance," Raya

admonished Strick after the introductions were made. She then turned to Hawk. "I hope you will dance as well."

"That sounds like more of a command than a suggestion," he noted.

"Interpret it as you wish," she responded. "You can have that dance with Naila that was interrupted yesterday."

Unease pulled at his belly. He searched for an excuse. "But Miss Naila is at the piano." Then he offered a diversion. "Perhaps Miss Hind will consent to take a turn with me."

As he'd hoped, the girl flushed with delight, a wide smile adorning her face. "That would be wonderful."

"Then I would be honored," he said gallantly to her, "if you will dance the next dance with me."

Strick offered his arm to Raya. "My love." And then, under his breath, he added, "It's a waltz and I embrace any opportunity to put my arms around my future bride."

That left Hawk alone with the American cousin until the next dance, which meant he had to make conversation. Aristocrats excelled at inconsequential exchanges, but it was a skill that Hawk hadn't quite mastered. The ways of the nobility still felt alien to him. Growing up as the distant cousin to an earl, with no expectations of inheriting the title, he hadn't mingled much in high society.

"How are you enjoying England?" he asked the young girl.

"I am surprised, honestly, by how much I like it," she said perkily. "The countryside is beautiful."

"Are you the only cousin who made the trip?"

"Naila and I are good friends as well as cousins. I thought it would be an adventure to come to England with her."

He could easily envision Naila befriending this cheerful girl. "Do you and your cousin spend a great deal of time together in Brooklyn?"

"When we can. Naila works with one of our cousins at his architecture firm. She spends a great deal of time studying buildings."

As the music drew to an end. Hawk offered his arm to escort her onto the dance floor.

"Do you like the two-step?" she asked.

"Well enough." The truth was that he had no preference for any dance. Or much of anything beyond running the numbers at his estates. That and the serenity and clarity that came with rowing, which he did almost daily when he was in residence at one of his properties.

"Let's go ask Naila to play it for us," Miss Hind said.

His gut twisted, but this time Hawk didn't have a ready excuse to avoid coming face-to-face with Naila. He reluctantly escorted Hind over to the piano just as Naila struck the last note of music. She didn't see them coming until they were at her side. Their gazes locked just for an instant, yet Hawk still experienced the flutter he'd always felt in her presence.

"Naila, will you play a two-step next?" Hind asked.

"If you'd like." Naila set her arms in her lap, the gold bracelets jingling, a sound that always reminded Hawk of her. "Certainly."

"Good evening, Miss Darwish," Hawk said, because there was no polite way not to acknowledge her.

"My lord," she answered with a tight smile before focusing on the piano keys. "A two-step it is."

"Maybe you two can dance next," Hind suggested. "Raya says you missed your turn yesterday."

Naila darted a quick look at him before blinking away. "It would be my pleasure to dance with Ba . . . umm . . . the earl but—"

He interrupted her. "I am called Hawk by those with whom I have a passing acquaintance."

Her eyes widened ever so slightly and then they were politely blank again. She knew as well as Hawk that their intense involvement, however brief, could never be viewed as incidental or inconsequential. But, for the sake of his sanity, Hawk was determined to keep a safe, formal distance firmly between them.

She used to call him Basil. Or Inglese, her pet

name for him in Arabic. But that was a long time ago. It needed to stay in the past.

"Hawk then." She spoke in a clear, calm voice. Yet her face reddened. "As Hind knows, I always play at family gatherings. Who would replace me?"

Hawk sensed her relief at dodging the possibility of being somewhat alone with him. She'd obviously do anything to avoid touching him. Bitterness surged into Hawk's throat. There'd been a time when they could barely keep their hands off each other, the pull between them almost impossible to control.

But she had thrown it all away. And for what? To be a spinster who made music so that others might dance?

Hind balked. "I might not be as accomplished as you at the piano, but I can manage a song or two while you dance."

Hawk wondered if Naila would decline, and hated himself for hoping she wouldn't.

"Well?" Hind looked expectantly at her cousin. "What do you say?"

Naila glanced at Hawk. He held her gaze, willing her not to look away, unable to quell the emotion roiling through him.

"Here you are, Miss Naila." The architect reappeared bearing lemonade. "I thought you might like some refreshment."

She looked away. "How very kind of you." She introduced her new friend. "Mr. Amar, this is the

Earl of Hawksworth and my cousin, Miss Hind Darwish."

Hawk forced himself to exchange pleasantries with the man while Naila adjusted the sheet music.

"Ah, here it is." She kept her attention on the papers before her. "The two-step is coming right up."

She did not look in Hawk's direction again. She played the lively tune while Hawk escorted her cousin onto the dance floor. When Hawk glanced back over in her direction, he saw that the architect had planted himself firmly next to the piano.

Chapter Five

*Before
Philadelphia*

Majida and Hamda both eyed Naila when she rejoined them.

"Where were you?" Majida asked, her permanent frown in place.

"I was hot." She darted a look behind her to see if the stranger had followed her. "I stepped out for some fresh air."

Majida sniffed the air. "What is that odor? Is something burning?"

Naila inched away from her aunt. Why hadn't she realized they'd detect smoke on her? "I don't smell anything."

"Did you go out alone?" Cousin Hamda asked her. "*Habibti*, you can't go outside by yourself. Maybe they let you do that in Brooklyn but here we don't allow *binatna* to go off on their own."

"*Ya khrib-bait-itch*," Majida snapped at her cousin. "May God ruin your house. How dare you insinuate that we don't look after our unmarried girls?"

Hamda's son, Eyad, approached. He was a kind and fun-loving young man a couple of years older than Naila. "Would you like to dance with me, Cousin Naila?"

She happily took his arm. "Thank you for rescuing me," she said when they were out of earshot. "All they do is argue."

He laughed. "They drive each other mad, yet they can't seem to stay away from each other. They write to each other several times a week when you are home in New York."

"I don't understand it." She tried to keep a little distance as Eyad took her into his arms. She didn't want him close enough to smell the cigarette smoke. Happily putting the argumentative aunties and the stranger in the garden out of her mind, she gave herself over to the music. The tune moved through her body. Her legs always seemed to have a mind of their own once the dance notes started. "It was very nice of your employer to include us." Eyad's employer was the evening's host.

"Mr. Linton is a fine man. He has no wife and children so he has embraced me and my family as his own. He dines with us every Thursday."

"That is lovely of your mother to include him."

"When the dance is over, I'll introduce you to Mr. Linton, if you don't mind," Eyad said as the music drew to a close.

"Why would I mind? I enjoy meeting new people."

Eyad led her over to a balding, round-faced older man with ruddy cheeks. A slim young man with chestnut-colored curls stood with him. Naila's eyes widened.

"What a pleasure to meet Eyad's cousin," Mr. Linton said effusively. "Miss Darwish, allow me to introduce my nephew, Basil Trevelyn, who is visiting from England. Basil, this is Miss Darwish of New York."

Naila would always remember the first time she saw Basil in the full light. In the garden shadows, she'd gotten the impression of a handsome man. And he was. But Inglese was much more than that. His laughing eyes met hers and she saw that they were a slate gray. His hair, which had appeared dark, was actually a burnished chestnut. His distantly polite gaze met hers, and yet humor flickered in those polished steel depths.

"How do you do?" In the garden, he'd spoken in low intimate tones. Now his confident rich baritone waved through her like a melody she ached to dance to. "I hope you are you enjoying Philadelphia."

"Very much so." She could feel the flush in her cheeks and hoped it wasn't obvious to the others. "And you?" she asked politely, "how are you enjoying your visit to America?"

He smiled, deep dimples carving into each cheek. "More and more by the moment."

She resisted the urge to grin at him, and instead cast her eyes downward in a show of polite modesty. This was turning into a most entertaining evening.

Eyad sniffed the air. "What is that smoke smell?" He looked toward Naila, recognition dawning.

"That must be me. My apologies," Basil said. "I was out in the garden smoking."

Eyad shot Naila a dubious look. "Ah," he said to Basil, "that explains it."

"Perhaps Miss Darwish will honor me with the next dance?" Basil spoke in a politely distant manner as though they truly were complete strangers. Even though he already felt like a friend.

Naila wanted nothing more. "I would love to dance."

He offered his arm to escort her onto the assembly room floor. Excitement fluttered through her. And when she took his hand, the hair on her arms lifted, the warmth of him sliding along her skin. His other hand settled lightly at her back, strong and firm, encasing her in his protective hold. She closed her eyes at the sensation, her breath hitching. What she'd felt in the garden was no anomaly.

"I thought you were lovely in the garden. But I hope you will permit me to say that you are even more beautiful in the light."

"Thank you." Her cheeks heated. *"Ayounik il hilween."*

"I beg your pardon?"

She flushed even more. "In Arabic, when someone compliments your looks, we say *'Ayounik il hilween,'* which means that the eyes that are looking at me are beautiful."

He blinked. "That is rather lovely."

"Arabic tends to be a flowery language."

"I was worried I'd scared you off in the garden."

"I don't scare that easily," she replied, with more confidence and self-assurance than she felt. Inglese put her off-balance in a way no other boy ever had.

The steel in his eyes gleamed. "I'm very glad to hear it."

They moved to the music. He led her expertly, but it was immediately apparent that Basil was not a natural dancer. Yet, somehow, it felt completely natural to be in this man's arms.

"Thank goodness you are here," she said. "I was beginning to be very bored by Philadelphia."

Amusement lit his face. "Do you always say exactly what is on your mind?"

"To my mother's everlasting regret," she returned.

"I much prefer a woman who speaks her mind."

"Do you? My mother is certain men prefer quiet, docile girls."

"Not this man," he said guiding her through an extravagant twirl along the floorboards.

"Oh!" she said, delighted. "Even though you are not a natural dancer, you still move wonderfully."

His brow lifted. "I cannot parse whether that's a compliment or an insult."

"It is not an insult," she reassured him. "Natural dancers feel the music in their body. It moves through them."

"I cannot say that happens to me."

"But you still lead beautifully, a learned skill, which is much more difficult than having it come naturally."

"You certainly have the ability to twist things around so that perceived insults become compliments."

"Why, Mr. Trevelyn, I do believe you are fishing for a compliment."

"Not at all." He smiled. "I am merely seeking to clarify your position."

She returned his smile. "I do hope I will see you again," she said. "Otherwise I'm bound to be dreadfully bored."

"I live to entertain," he said. "And fortunately, I believe my uncle mentioned dining at your aunt's home this Thursday evening. He says it is a standing engagement he has with your family."

"Yes, that's right!" Delight slid through her at the idea of seeing Basil again. "Eyad mentioned that Mr. Linton comes to dinner every week."

"I wasn't exactly looking forward to going," he said, "but now I cannot wait."

She grinned up at him. "Neither can I."

Chapter Six

Now
England

There were daisies everywhere.

The cheerful blooms dotting the landscape lifted Naila's spirits, making her glad she'd allowed Raya, Nadine and Hind to persuade her to join their walk. It helped get her mind off Basil.

No. *Not Basil.* He was Hawk now. She had to stop thinking about the earl in familiar terms. At this point, they were nothing but strangers. Even worse than strangers. They'd once been intimately connected; now they could barely stand to acknowledge each other.

The four women strolled past beautiful cone-shaped purple flowers springing up from the wild grasses and enormous leafy trees with expansive branches. Rabbits scurry-hopped not too far from them. Naila inhaled the crisp air. The English countryside certainly was a long way from Brooklyn.

"Hawk must be past thirty," Hind said to Raya. "What hasn't he married yet?"

"That is the great mystery." Raya adjusted her straw hat. "Strick says some woman in America broke his heart. Hawk spent some time in Philadelphia a few years ago."

Naila's stomach cramped. Hawk had told people about her? How much had he revealed?

"That's where Naila met him." Nadine cut Naila a sidelong glance. "Did you hear anything about Hawk courting a lady when you knew him in Philadelphia?"

"No." Naila kept her focus on the path ahead of her. "Nothing."

"Are you sure?" Nadine pressed. "There must have been a lot of gossip about him. It's not often one meets an English earl."

"He wasn't an earl back then."

"Why not?"

Raya bent to pluck a violet wildflower. "Hawk inherited unexpectedly when his father's cousin died." She brought the bloom to her nose to inhale its scent. "It was apparently quite a surprise."

"My goodness." Nadine's eyes rounded. "That girl who turned him down in Philadelphia, whoever she is, must feel like a complete *habla* now. What a fool."

Regret pooled in Naila's belly. And it had nothing to do with Hawk's money and title. For at least the hundredth time, she thought about what a fool she'd been to abandon the love of her life.

"Should we start back?" Raya asked. "I have a meeting with the steward soon."

"Oh, do let's walk some more," Naila protested. She relished being away from the castle, which felt suffocating with Hawk in such close proximity. Her nerves were jangled from the ever-present possibility of running into him every time she turned one of the castle's numerous corners.

Nadine yawned. "No more walking for me. I am tired. I could use a nap."

Hind was Naila's last hope. "Let's walk for just a little longer," she urged her cousin.

Although Hind looked like she wanted to return with the others, she relented. "Okay, but let's not walk too much farther."

"We won't," Naila promised. They parted with Raya and Nadine and continued on their way.

"Since when do you like to walk so much?" Hind asked as they entered a copse of trees.

Since I need to avoid Hawk. "We don't have views like this in Brooklyn. Look how pretty the daisies and those purple flowers are."

"Views?" Hind screwed up her face. "It all looks the same to me. Grass, grass and more grass. With some flowers and trees thrown in."

"You're clearly not a country girl."

Hind laughed good-naturedly. "That's for certain."

Naila looped her arm through her younger cousin's. Hind was nineteen now and more of a friend than the young cousin who'd needed looking after for so many years. With her innate sweetness and gaiety, Hind's presence was a balm at a time when seeing Hawk again had upended everything. She had a perpetual knot in her stomach.

"I'm so glad you're here to keep me company," she told her cousin.

"You have Nadine," Hind pointed out.

"Very amusing." They both knew that Naila's eldest sister wasn't exactly a source of support for anyone.

"What about Raya?"

"Raya is busy running the castle's operations," Naila said. "Besides, what little spare time she has I am sure she'd prefer to devote to her duke."

Footsteps sounded, followed by the snap of breaking twigs. Hawk emerged from the trees like a dream come to life in a navy tailcoat and worn brown boots. He stopped short when he spotted them but quickly recovered. "Good afternoon, ladies. This is an unexpected surprise."

Hind's face lit up. "A nice surprise, I hope."

To her astonishment, Naila realized that Hind was flirting. She suppressed a sudden, violent urge to pinch her cousin's arm.

Hawk smiled at Hind. "A very nice surprise, indeed."

Naila felt a sting of desire deep in her belly. Hawk had always had that effect on her. Even though, at the moment, his smile was for Hind alone. Naila might as well be just another blade of grass in the meadow.

"What brings you two this far from the castle?" he asked.

"We could ask the same of you," Hind bantered, her manner cheerful and engaging.

"I enjoy a long walk in the country. It gives me time to think."

Hind tilted her head coquettishly. "In America, we say, 'A penny for your thoughts.'"

Amusement lit his eyes. "Your penny would be wasted. My thoughts aren't at all interesting."

"We enjoy long walks, too," Hind said. "The daisies and those purple flowers are beautiful."

Naila suppressed an urge to snort. Hind liked long walks in the country about as much as Naila enjoyed visiting the dentist.

Hawk dipped his chin. "One cannot help but appreciate a lady with a love of nature."

Hind batted her eyelashes. "I was just mentioning to Naila how there are no views like this in Brooklyn."

"Yes," Naila said dryly, "she certainly was."

"Won't you join us?" Hind asked the earl. Naila discreetly elbowed her cousin but it was too late.

"It would be my pleasure." He turned to walk

with them, Hawk on one side of Hind, Naila on the other.

"What do you call those purple flowers, the cone-shaped ones?" Hind asked Hawk.

"I believe you are referring to the lupines," he told her.

Hind proceeded to ask several questions about the various plants they encountered, which Hawk patiently answered. Naila knew her cousin had zero interest in nature, but she kept that to herself. Slowly, she allowed herself to fall behind until she trailed them.

But her attempt to put more distance between her and Hawk immediately proved to be a poor decision. Because now Naila had an unrestricted view of his strong masculine form. And she could not help but to admire the view.

Broad shoulders perfectly filled out his coat. Long legs encased in boots took sure confident strides; the muscles in his athletic thighs were visible just below the hem of his coat. Need wound through Naila, sharpening in her belly. A reminder that she'd missed this man not only emotionally, but also physically. Her body craved him as potently as ever.

Up ahead, Hind was posing questions to Hawk. "What is it like to be an earl?"

"It is very strange," he answered. "People treat you very differently once they learn you have a title."

"I can imagine."

"Before I had the title, people judged me for me. And sometimes found me lacking."

"I cannot imagine that," Hind said.

"I assure you that it is the truth," he said. "But now, every marriage-minded mama is throwing their daughters into my path, hoping to make a marital connection to a man with a title. They have no interest in my character."

"That would be tiresome."

"It is, but I'm hardly in a position to complain. I understand that I am privileged and many would very much like to be in my position."

They came to a hilly area. Hawk paused. "Are you ladies fatigued?" He half turned to include Naila in his question without actually looking at her. "Shall we turn back?"

"Yes," Naila replied immediately. "I am tired." Anything to be free of the agony of being in Hawk's presence while he treated her like an inconsequential acquaintance.

"Oh no!" Hind protested. "Do let's continue. I am so enjoying our walk."

Naila suppressed another snort. Hind was savoring Hawk's attentions, not the country air.

He paused. "If Miss Darwish has overexerted herself, we really should turn back."

Naila's spine stiffened. He made her sound like an old lady, as if she were a spinster chaperoning a young courting couple.

"I assure you," she said tartly, "that I am not overtaxed."

His brows went up. Probably at her tone. But Naila didn't care. "Very well," he said carefully. "Shall we continue?"

They were interrupted by the soft rumble of an oncoming open carriage drawn by two horses. At the reins was Mr. Guy Vaughan, a friend of the duke's, with his sister beside him. Frances Vaughan was the frightfully elegant woman with the same vibrant copper hair as her brother who'd been in conversation with Hawk the other evening. Raya had introduced them later that same night.

"Good day," Mr. Vaughan called out, pulling the carriage to a stop when he reached them.

They all exchanged greetings before Mr. Vaughan ran an appraising eye over Hawk and Hind, who stood by his side. Naila remained a few steps behind them. "On an excursion?"

Hawk shot his friend a stinging look. "I came upon the Misses Darwish on a walk and decided to accompany them."

"How gallant of you," Mr. Vaughan said with a glint in his eye.

"We are on our way to Castle Tremayne now for luncheon," Miss Vaughan told the walkers. She and her brother lived close by and were not staying at the castle as many of the other wedding guests were.

"Would one of you young ladies like a ride back?" her brother asked. "We have room enough for one more."

"No, thank you." Hind responded quickly, shooting a shy glance Hawk's way. "I am very much enjoying our walk."

"Take Miss Naila," Hawk said. "She just said that she is tired."

Miss Vaughan smiled at Naila. "Do say you'll come, Miss Darwish. I could use some feminine company."

Jealousy curled in Naila's stomach. There was a time when Hawk would have done just about anything to prolong their walks. Now he couldn't wait to be rid of her.

"Yes," Naila said. "I would appreciate a ride back."

Before she knew it, Hawk's hands were on her waist, strong, firm and decisive, lifting her into the carriage. Her breath caught at the feel of his strength and the sensation of his hands on her body. The scent of him, shaving soap and traces of outdoor exertion, floated over her. Miss Vaughan scooted closer to her brother to make room.

Hawk tapped on the carriage frame. "We shall see you back at the castle."

Guy's eyes sparkled. "Do enjoy the rest of your walk."

As they pulled away, Naila could still feel

the sensation of Hawk's warm, powerful grasp. Had his hands lingered on her waist a fraction longer than necessary? She shook the thought away. She'd obviously imagined it.

"How are you enjoying England, Miss Darwish?" Guy inquired as the carriage rumbled away from Hawk and Hind.

"It is a beautiful country. And the castle is remarkable, a prime example of medieval architecture."

"Are you interested in architecture?" Frances asked.

"Very much so. I've apprenticed with my cousin, who is an architect."

"Apprenticed?" Frances regarded her with interest. "Do you design buildings?"

"No. I am more a student of the principles and different styles of architecture. I often research the design elements for my cousin before he begins a commission."

"My goodness," Frances said with what seemed like admiration, "you and your sister are most enterprising."

"What kind of buildings do you most admire?" Guy asked.

"Just about everything here," she said with a laugh. "In America, everything is so new. In England, your country houses are such a treat for me, especially the older styles that we Americans don't see much of."

"My home is quite old." Guy adjusted the reins, guiding the horses over bumpy terrain. "But if you wish to visit truly ancient properties, then you'll want to visit Briar Hall."

"What is Briar Hall?"

"It's an Elizabethan-style country manor house in Lincolnshire."

"Oh, I would love to see it." Being able to visit a structure that was built more than two centuries ago offered an authenticity that she'd never be able to match at home.

"Then we must convince Hawk to invite us all."

Her mind stumbled. "Hawk?"

Guy nodded. "Yes, Briar Hall is one of his country houses."

"I would not want to bother him." It was too painful to contemplate visiting one of Hawk's properties, a place where they might have lived together, where their children's shouts and laughter should echo through the halls.

"He has several more properties," Frances told her. "The earldom of Hawksworth is quite vast."

Guy chuckled. "That's why so many debutantes have their eye on him."

Frances adjusted her parasol so that it shaded both women. "Raya says Hawk has announced his intention to wed."

"Might he have his eye on Miss Darwish?" her brother asked.

Naila's face heated. "I'm sure that's not—"

"Miss Hind Darwish," he clarified.

Naila's stomach turned, the bumpy ride heightening the nauseous sensation.

"Do you think so?" Frances pondered this. "Miss Hind does appear to possess a sunny nature and she is certainly very pretty."

"I imagine that a man who marries a cheerful woman can expect to see many happy days," Guy remarked. "What do you think, Miss Darwish?"

"Any man who weds my beautiful young cousin would be very fortunate." The thought of Hawk and Hind together was a knife twisting in her gut. But she would never say anything hateful about her cousin. "There is no one with a kinder heart."

"That sounds like an endorsement," Guy noted. "I assume you would approve such a match? And your family as well?"

"I cannot speak for my uncle Refaat, Hind's father." She spoke truthfully despite the sorrow in her heart. "But I do believe that Hind would make an ideal wife."

"It is settled then," Guy said cheerfully. "We should do everything in our power to ensure Hawk's happiness."

"Do you not think you are moving rather quickly?" Frances asked her brother. "We do not know whether the earl tends to court Miss Hind."

"You might be right," he acknowledged. "I am

just so eager to see Hawk happy after all he has been through."

Naila couldn't resist asking. "What he has been through?"

"Hawk hasn't revealed himself to me," he answered, "but I suspect there was a woman in Philadelphia who broke his heart."

"You don't know that," his sister interjected.

"What I am certain about is that Hawk returned from America a much more somber and cynical man. He's almost a different person now. It is hard to describe."

The lump in Naila's throat ached at this confirmation of just how badly she'd hurt Basil. The cold stranger of today was nothing like the man she'd known. Even now, if she closed her eyes, she could still see Basil's warm smile and feel the adoration in his earnest gaze.

"Hawk was but a boy when he went to America." Frances adjusted her skirts. "Maybe he just grew up and, as a man, is a more serious person than the boy you used to know."

"Possibly," Guy said. "But somehow I don't think so."

Frances turned to Naila. "Wouldn't you agree, Miss Darwish, that growing up alters people?"

It had certainly changed her. But it hadn't altered her desires, just her expectations.

"I do agree on both points," Naila said diplomatically. "I think we are shaped by both maturity and by life's setbacks and disappointments."

"A very sensible answer," Guy pronounced.

His words stung. The old Naila, the impulsive, joy-seeking person she used to be, would balk at being called sensible. Even if that was exactly what she was now. Practical. Reasonable. Logical.

Unremarkable.

Naila lacked the life experiences that make a person truly interesting. She was ordinary, unexceptional, an example of what happened when youthful promise did not live up to future expectation. No wonder Hawk barely noticed her now.

Naila scarcely recognized herself.

Chapter Seven

Before
Philadelphia

"Eat," Mrs. Shaheen encouraged Basil. "Eat more."

"It's very delicious, ma'am." Basil slid his empty plate forward for Eyad's mother to refill. She piled his plate high with a second serving of rice, lamb and vegetables. "May I ask what is in this?"

"It's called *maklouba*," Naila said. She was seated at the opposite end of the table from him. He'd have liked to sit closer to her, of course, but instead he was surrounded by Eyad and his brothers, a distance Basil thought might have been purposely engineered. Naila's young male cousins appeared very protective of her. "Which means upside down."

"How does it get that shape?" he asked, mostly just to be able to continue speaking with her. The *maklouba* had been in the round shape of a cake when first presented at the table.

"We cook it in a pot and then flip it upside down for serving," Naila explained.

"It have lamb and seasoned rice," Mrs. Shaheen explained in her heavy Arabic accent. "And fried vegetables, eggplant, cauliflower and carrots."

Supper with Naila's relatives turned out to be like nothing in Basil's previous experience. His main reason for coming was to see Naila again but, to his surprise, he was enjoying the communal assembly.

There were a dozen people seated around the table including Eyad's parents and siblings, Basil and his uncle Edward, and Naila and her aunt. The others were assorted cousins. The older people were lively and animated and knew how to tell a good story.

"The first time I ate a pancake, I thought it was the most terrible thing I'd ever tasted," said Mr. Shaheen, Eyad's father. "It was soggy and sweet. I couldn't understand how Americans could eat that."

Mr. Shaheen was called Abu Eyad and Mrs. Shaheen was Um Eyad. Naila later explained that translated to "Father of Eyad" and "Mother of Eyad." It was how Arabs respectfully referred to adults, by referring to them as the parent of their eldest son.

"What if the eldest child is a daughter?" he'd asked.

"My parents were Um and Abu Nadine, the name of my eldest sister, until they had a son," she explained. "Then they became Um and Abu

Salem, which is my brother's name. I don't think Nadine ever got over the demotion," she said with a playful smile. "But that is the way of the world. Girls always get pushed aside."

His heart fluttered whenever she smiled at him. And he could not imagine anyone ever pushing Naila aside. She was born to be the center of attention, the axis around which everything else revolved. He was thrilled to be in her orbit.

Mr. Shaheen pushed a plate of liver and onions in Basil's direction. "Here, have some. It's very good."

Basil wasn't a picky eater but there was nothing in the world that he detested more than liver. He couldn't even stomach the smell. "Thank you, sir. But I have plenty of food on my plate."

The man pushed the serving dish even closer to Basil. "But it's liver," he insisted. "Very good." He began to spoon the organ meat onto Basil's plate.

To his relief, Uncle Edward interjected. "Basil doesn't care for liver."

"*Shoo?* What?" Mr. Shaheen scrunched up his face. "Who doesn't like liver?"

"I'll take his share," one of the cousins said, sliding his plate across the table. To Basil's immense relief.

He fared better with dessert, a milk and rice pudding served alongside hot tea flavored with mint.

"This is very delicious," he commented after sipping the steaming beverage.

"Hot tea with mint is my most favorite drink in the whole world," Naila said from across the way. She took a drink and sighed with complete, unfettered pleasure. Basil couldn't take his eyes off her. But he pretended to, given that he was under the collective watchful eye of her male cousins.

After supper, the men brought out instruments, a small hand drum called a *tabla*, and a pear-shaped stringed instrument that produced a deep mellow sound. Eyad said it was called an oud. The evening was spent drinking mint tea and listening to the upbeat music.

Someone brought out a water pipe, which Basil had never tried before. He took a few turns when the pipe came to him, enjoying the soothing gurgle of the water as he inhaled, and the camaraderie that came along with sharing the ritual with the others. The men he sat with laughed and made jokes, asking Basil when he intended to marry because at twenty-two, he was already very old.

Some of the cousins got up to dance. They lined up and held hands, the men at the front of the line, with Naila and Um Eyad bringing up the rear. Hands clasped and shoulders aligned, they moved counterclockwise, doing synchronized dance steps with their feet. Eyad, who led the line, was clearly the most talented dancer, moving with flourish and setting the energy for the rest of the dancers. Basil found himself tapping his foot to the beat.

Mostly, he couldn't stop staring at Naila. She danced with an abandon that mesmerized him. Her cheeks were flushed and some of her hair fell from the loose bun at her nape. He imagined curling those dark strands around his fingers.

One of the older men encouraged him to get up and dance. Basil welcomed the opportunity because Naila was at the end of the line. He rose, eager to join her, to feel her hand against his. But just as he reached her, the cousins at the head of the line all gave Basil a hard look. Naila herself refused to take his hand, even though he'd danced a waltz with her before.

"Up here," Eyad called to him in a voice that was equal parts polite and steely. "You break in with the men. Not with the young ladies. Naila does not hold hands with men."

Basil flushed. "My apologies." He'd waltzed with Naila, which struck him as more intimate than holding her hand. But he obeyed the rules of *debke* by joining the men as instructed. His rhythm wasn't great but he was nonetheless soon swept up in the dance, stomping his foot somewhat awkwardly until he started to get into the swing of things.

Out of the corner of his eye, he watched Naila

laugh as they all perspired and grew breathless from their exertions. And, although disappointed because he hadn't had the opportunity to truly speak with Naila, Basil couldn't remember the last time he'd enjoyed himself as much.

CHAPTER EIGHT

*Before
Philadelphia*

Naila couldn't wait to see Basil again the following week for his uncle's standing Thursday invitation to supper. To her disappointment, Auntie Hamda declined to invite the two men according to schedule.

"*Abe*, Auntie, *abe*," Auntie Hamda tsked when Naila casually asked about it.

"Why is it inappropriate?" Naila widened her eyes to look more innocent.

Auntie Majida made a humming sound of disapproval. "Because he looks at you like a lamb he can't wait to eat."

"What?" Naila feigned surprise, but secretly she was delighted. Inglese was clearly interested in her as a woman. That people around them noticed made it all the more real. It was flattering but also troublesome. The aunties wouldn't let Naila out of their sight even more now that they were both convinced her virtue needed protecting.

"*Salam alaykum.*" Eyad walked through the sitting room and stopped to grab a handful of *bizzer buteekh*, roasted and salted watermelon seeds, which they were snacking on.

"*Alaykum u salam.*" The three of them responded to his greeting. *And peace be upon you, too.*

"Guess who I ran into at the ice cream shop?" He settled in a chair. "Mr. Linton's nephew. The one visiting from England."

Majida scowled. "*Aina baitha.*" *He has white eyes.* Meaning his eyes widened so much when he looked at Naila that all one saw were the whites of his eyes.

"Please," she fake scoffed. "He's an elegant Englishman. I'm sure he has no interest in me."

After that, Naila developed a craving for ice cream and insisted on going practically every day. Eyad didn't mind escorting her most of the time, because he was a true ice cream lover. If she wanted to see Basil again, and add some amusement to her trip, she needed to force a chance encounter. After about two weeks of visiting the ice cream shop every day, she finally saw him. She and Eyad were sitting on a bench in the park across the street eating their frozen treats when Basil appeared and went into the shop.

"This is so delicious," she said. "I would like another ice cream."

Eyad frowned. "Another?" She knew her cousin

was probably thinking that she was curvy enough but she didn't care.

"Please," she smiled beseechingly. "Just this once."

"A bunch of people just went in there. The line is so long."

"I won't ask you to bring me for ice cream again for at least a week. *Wallah.* I swear."

"*Yalla.*" He rose. "I'll be right back."

As soon as he disappeared inside the shop, Naila tossed her ice cream out and hurried across the street. She took up a position in a narrow alley outside the ice cream shop and waited. Fortunately, Basil came out before her cousin.

"Hello!" she called out when he walked by.

Basil did a double take when he realized who it was. "Miss Darwish. This is a delight."

She backed farther into the alley so it would be harder to spot them. She smiled brightly. "Good day."

He looked around. "Are you alone?"

"No. Eyad is getting me some ice cream."

"And left you to wait in the alley?"

"No, I was in the park but then I saw you and wanted to say hello."

"I'm very glad that you did. I was disappointed that Uncle did not receive his customary Thursday invitation to dinner."

"As was I." Her heart pounding, she darted a look toward the alley. "I cannot be seen alone with you."

"I understand. I should like to call on you."

"That won't be possible but I will be at the lending library on Cross Street tomorrow at two o'clock." She purposely chose the time both aunties went down for their afternoon naps. "Perhaps I shall see you there."

His brows lifted. "Perhaps you will."

"Excellent." She needed him gone before Eyad returned. "Goodbye now."

He paused. "Erm. Good day," he finally said and continued on his way.

Once Basil departed, she spotted Eyad in the park holding her ice cream and looking around. She crossed over to him.

"Where did you go?" he asked crossly.

"I was looking for the ladies' retiring room."

When he looked around suspiciously, she rubbed a hand over her belly. "I think all of this ice cream is causing me some discomfort."

Eyad, who had no sisters, immediately looked uncomfortable. "I suppose we need to get you home."

She took his arm. "Yes, let's go home."

"You definitely need a break from ice cream."

"Absolutely," she agreed, grateful that she could finally stop eating ice cream. "Tomorrow, I think I'll go to the lending library."

"I DID NOT expect to find you in the architecture section," Basil told Naila the following day.

"That shows how much you know about me," she said with a saucy smile.

His heart leapt a little. This girl had a strange effect on him. She looked very becoming in a pink gown that hugged her curves and set off the rosiness in her cheeks. He was unaccountably happy to see her. "I would like to be able to court you so that I could know you better."

She giggled. "That's impossible."

"Why? Don't you like me?" He knew that she did. Basil possessed enough experience with girls to know when one appreciated the look of him.

"Are you fishing for compliments again?" she teased before lifting her chin. "I like you well enough, but my family will never consent to a foreigner courting me."

"My intentions are honorable." Basil hadn't even realized that he wanted to court this girl, but apparently some instinctive part of him did. It was the only way to see her, to spend time in her enchanting presence. Even though courting inevitably led to marriage, and Basil barely knew Naila, the thought of being bound to this mesmerizing girl for life excited him.

"How many girls have you courted before me?" she asked.

"None."

She shot him a skeptical look. "None?"

It occurred to him that courting in America might not be the same as in England. She might not understand the seriousness of what he'd just said. He briefly considered enlightening her but immediately decided against it. He didn't want to scare her off, even though Naila Darwish did not seem like someone who was easily frightened.

"You still haven't said why I should expect to find you looking at books about architecture," he said.

"Because I am fascinated by building and design."

"You are?" He had not considered what her interests might be, beyond him, but he found himself wanting to know everything about her. "Why?"

"Why?" she repeated, as if the question was ridiculous. "Architecture is functional art. It cannot be art just for art's sake; it must also be practical."

He had no idea what she meant but the way her eyes lit up made his heart speed up. "How do you mean?"

"A building has to work, it has to fulfill an important function. It's everyday art that we walk through and live in and use daily."

"Hmm," he said. "I've never thought of it like that. To me, a building is shelter and as long as there are windows and a door, I'm generally content."

"But structures are so much more than that. Each building must reflect the time it was produced in.

It's a living history of its time. It tells us a great deal about the context of the time when it was constructed."

"Shall we take a walk and discuss architecture?" he asked.

"Oh no," she said. "I cannot leave the bookstore. My maid is outside. If we want to speak privately, we have to remain inside."

He frowned. It wasn't honorable to see Naila behind her family's back. "I wish I could call on you at your aunt's house."

"It's impossible," she said with a firm set of her chin. "Now, do you want to spend what little time we have arguing or should we visit the part of the bookstore that reflects your interests?"

His interests? At twenty-two, Basil was still trying to decide what to do with his life. He liked numbers and calculations. It was satisfying when everything added up, but that was hardly as compelling as Naila's enthusiasm for architecture. "Very well," he finally said. "Follow me."

They strolled along the sections until he found what he was looking for. "Ah." He pulled a book from a high shelf.

She took it from him and flipped through it. "Sailing? You're a sailor?"

"Not exactly. That's a book about maritime pursuits. I'm a rower."

"You like to row people in boats?"

"I was a competitive rower at university. Now I just compete against myself."

"Do you go out on the water a lot?"

"Every chance I get," he said. "Maybe I'll take you one day."

He registered the doubt in her eyes. She expected to keep their acquaintance small, insignificant and hidden away, a forgotten moment in time, when he wanted nothing more than to walk proudly beside her.

She handed the book to him. "Show me what kind of boat you use."

"It's usually a skiff." He paged through until he found a vessel similar to what he used. He went through the pages, showing her the different kinds of boats. He was very aware of her proximity to him. He relished the soft inhalations of her breath, the lemony smell of her soap filling his nostrils. Once in a while her arm brushed against his, and the hair on his arms stood up, the feel of her closeness tingling through him.

Eventually they ended up examining her favorite books. He wanted to know why she liked what she did. It gave him some insight into what motivated her. She pointed out the different elements of varying architectural styles, including her favorites.

"You would love England," he told her after she pointed out several Elizabethan buildings. "Every old estate looks like one of these styles."

"That would be something," she said on a wishful sigh. "But I cannot imagine ever going."

"If we were married, I'd take you." He spoke impulsively, without thinking. But once the words were out, he did not regret saying them. "It is my home. I would want to show it to you."

She lightly punched his arm. "If you keep talking like that, I will have to stop seeing you."

"Like what?" Most women of his acquaintance were thrilled if a man of good family—Basil was distantly related to an earl, which carried a lot of capital back home—and moderate good looks showed a serious interest in them.

"We can only ever be good friends," she said firmly. "I am here just for a few weeks and then I must return to New York and my real life, where certain things are expected of me."

"What sorts of things?"

"I am expected to marry a boy from my community."

"Why?"

"It's too much trouble to explain," she said with a wave of her hand. "For these few weeks, let us resolve to have fun."

He was quickly coming to the realization that he might want more than a few weeks with this gem. But she was obviously skittish, so he resolved to go slow and allow her to set the pace of their acquaintanceship.

"Will I be able to see you again?" he asked. "Outside of a bookstore, I mean."

She smiled. "As it happens, I have a plan."

Relief poured through him. He very much wanted to see her again. "Would you care to enlighten me?"

"I can meet you the day after tomorrow at two o'clock" was all she would say.

As long as he could see her again, that was all Basil needed to know.

Chapter Nine

Now
England

At supper that evening, the conversation veered, as it did so often these days, toward matters of love and marriage.

"I think men have many more opportunities to find a suitable companion. You are all allowed to travel as extensively as you choose," Raya observed. "But unwed young ladies are expected to keep to home and hearth. We must wait to be chosen."

"You did not wait," her duke said from the opposite end of the long table. "You came all the way across an ocean to run me to ground."

"I hardly came for *you*," she returned. "I traveled to England to visit my late cousin and stayed on to manage the castle I inherited."

"Some would say you also managed the duke quite nicely," Guy put in.

"I am not averse to being managed by my future duchess." Strickland raised his wineglass in his betrothed's direction. "In fact, I welcome it."

"You do know that it is unfashionable to be besotted with your wife?" Guy teased them both.

The duke shrugged. "We are doomed to be frightfully unfashionable."

To Naila's surprise, Raya blushed becomingly. This altered version of her sister took some getting used to. Raya normally hid her emotions but when it came to her feelings about the duke, she didn't bother. She managed to seamlessly blend her love of enterprise with her very clear devotion to Strickland.

Naila, who was seated next to Guy, wrinkled her brow. "That makes no sense at all. If you are to be married, you should have high regard for each other."

"I do not make the rules," Guy said. "I merely live by them."

"But you are not wed yet," Strick returned.

"True enough," Guy allowed.

Nibbling on nuts, Naila's gaze drifted down to where Hawk sat near the duke, with an obviously delighted Hind at his side. She could not hear their conversation but they seemed very engaged with each other, speaking quietly together during the early courses.

Auntie Majida sat on the duke's other side, a position of honor. Strickland obviously knew how to win over her ornery aunt. Hawk had never had the chance to do the same. In Philadelphia, Auntie Majida steadfastly refused to speak to him about a possible match between him and Naila.

Hawk entered the conversation. "I respectfully disagree with Miss Darwish's supposition that gentlemen hold all of the power when it comes to making a match."

"*You* certainly do," Guy shot back. "You're an earl with vast holdings. No woman in her right mind would turn you down."

Naila pretended to study her white fish as she flaked the tender flesh with her fork. Anything to avoid seeing Hawk's reaction. Her insides were in turmoil. Grief, regret and longing intermingled, all fused to her bones since leaving the dream of them behind. And being around an indifferent Hawk made it all the worse.

"A man does not want to be desired for his title and fortune," Hawk said. "He wants to be valued for his character. For his potential."

"How much potential does an earl need?" Frances asked. "Some would say acquiring a title is potential fulfilled."

Raya studied Hawk. "Why do you think men do not hold all the power when it comes to relations between men and women?" she asked with obvious curiosity.

"It is true that the gentleman has the great advantage of doing the choosing. But what if the young lady of his choosing rejects him?" Hawk asked. Naila pretended to look his way. It would be the height of rudeness not to when Hawk addressed the table. But she kept her gaze focused on the silver tea set on the sideboard visible just beyond Hawk's shoulder, rather than on his face. "Then the gentleman has given away his heart only to have it stomped upon."

He hadn't glanced in Naila's direction for the entire evening. And did not do so now. He acted as though she didn't exist. Up until this moment, Naila had felt guilty about rejecting Hawk. But now anger kindled in her chest. How dare he behave so callously? She might deserve his antipathy but not his cold dismissal. He treated her like she was lower than the dirt on the bottom of his boot.

"A young lady does not always have the final say when it comes to choosing a husband." She fixed her gaze on Hawk. "It is her family, or her guardian, who makes the final choice."

Now Hawk did give her his full attention, his icy eyes boring into her. "Not if the woman is constant enough."

She held his gaze. "That is easy for a man to say. Young girls are not as free as you are."

Raya looked thoughtful. "I suppose that is the advantage of seeking a wife who knows her own mind."

"Indeed." Hawk held Naila's gaze for another interminable moment before blinking his attention away from her.

The conversation stalled momentarily while the footmen served the main course, a variety of beef and chicken dishes. As Naila replayed her brief exchange with Hawk, something new sprouted within her. An awareness that had been growing in her since Hawk walked back into her life.

It was an urge to defend that young girl who'd made the mistake of her life. And sorrow for all she'd suffered. Naila had flailed herself over Hawk for eight years. And for what? To be ignored by him? To endure his barely disguised contempt?

He'd obviously relegated Naila to the past. Shouldn't she do the same? She'd never been able to put Hawk behind her. Even in his absence, he'd been there, dominating her thoughts. Not a day went by when she didn't regret her choice. But this evening, as she watched Hawk converse with Hind, his decisive profile partially obscured by the gleaming of the candles lining the mahogany table, it dawned on her that Hawk was neither her present nor her future.

How could she expect to find any happiness or satisfaction in her life until she moved on? She could not allow one regrettable decision to define the rest of her life. But after years of flagellating herself, she had no idea how to move forward. The only thing she could think of in that moment was to immerse herself in one of her favorite subjects.

She turned to Guy. "So, Mr. Vaughan, you mentioned that your home is quite old. Will you tell me about it?"

Guy appeared delighted to be asked. "It is called the Grange. It was built about one hundred years ago."

"Do tell me more about its design," she encouraged with a smile.

Hawk couldn't help noticing how raptly Naila listened to whatever Guy was babbling about. The other exchanges at the table made it impossible to hear their conversation, but Naila's eyes glowed with interest.

When had those two become so well acquainted? Something twinged in Hawk's chest when Naila smiled at Guy during their animated exchange. It was as if they were in their own world. The rest of the people at the table might as well not exist. Hawk's hand unwittingly curled into a fist. Maybe they should just get a room.

"Is something wrong, my lord?" Hind's voice broke into his thoughts.

"Not at all." Hawk forced himself to relax his fist, and to otherwise appear at ease. "What could be wrong when I am in the company of the most delightful dinner companion?"

Her cheeks colored. "You are very kind to say so," she said demurely. He wasn't. Not really. Mostly Hawk just played the part of a noble gentleman. He sometimes marveled at the extent to which pretense and obfuscation defined his life. He rarely said what he truly thought. Ambiguity was a useful barrier. A coat of protection. The polar opposite of Philadelphia, when it had never occurred to him to dissemble. Back then, he'd been clear and direct about what he wanted, throwing himself into his campaign to make Naila his wife. He hadn't been able to imagine a future without her at the center of it.

After the debacle with Naila, he had erected scaffolding around his heart to protect him from the inconvenience of deeply held emotions. When he finally took a wife, it would be a practical decision. Hawk would lead with his head. Involving his heart was the way of disaster.

He'd never survive another Philadelphia.

"Is your home very far away from here?" Hind asked.

"Not so very. It's about a day's ride." He told her about Briar Hall, his nearest residence. There were several other houses that he didn't mention. He'd inherited them along with the title, but they didn't belong to him. As the current titleholder, Hawk was merely the caretaker. His job was to preserve the earldom and its assets for the next generation.

One day he'd have to do what was necessary to secure the succession, which meant taking a wife and producing an heir. He surreptitiously studied Naila's cousin. Although she was merry and charming, he had no interest in her as a potential wife. She was far too young for his tastes and, more importantly, she deserved better than a cold husband who would never love her.

Besides, the last thing he needed was another connection to Naila. He couldn't fathom running into her at future family functions. It was bad enough that his dearest friend was marrying her sister. Thank goodness it wouldn't be long before Naila returned to America. He couldn't relax until there was an ocean between them again.

"Given how much you enjoy nature walks, I think you would delight in Briar Hall," he said to the cousin. "We have a varied landscape with much for an admirer of the natural world to appreciate."

"Do you?" she said. "I would love to see more . . . trees and . . . um . . . flowers."

The sound of laughter drew his attention. Naila was clearly amused by something Guy had said.

Hind followed his gaze. "I'm so pleased to see Naila enjoying herself. She rarely allows herself to laugh and have fun."

"Why is that?" he asked.

She shrugged. "I cannot say. But sometimes, when we are in private, she can be wickedly amusing."

He knew that far too well. "I am surprised she hasn't married," he remarked, even though Naila's name shouldn't cross his lips. "Miss

Darwish was quite popular when she visited Philadelphia."

Hawk could still picture her in the garden smoking a cigarette, flashing that irrepressible smile. And then later, when she allowed certain intimacies. He could still taste her lips and feel the dewy silkiness of her most private areas.

"She is still very well liked," Hind assured him. "No one is more sensible."

"Sensible?" That was the last word he'd use to describe the Naila he used to know. She was adventurous, passionate and fearless. At least she had been until the end, when everything changed.

Perhaps he'd never really known her at all.

"Everyone in the family values her advice, judgment and reasoning," Hind said.

As he contemplated this foreign description of Naila, the scowling aunt addressed him from across the table. "How come you be an earl?"

Hawk didn't know how he'd ended up sitting across from the crone. He mostly blamed Naila for their breakup but the old crow came in close second. She'd manipulated a young girl, cheating both Hawk and Naila out of a future together.

"I inherited from my father's cousin," he responded, each word glazed with arctic courtesy.

She regarded him with sharp, beady eyes. "He have no sons?" she asked in her heavily accented English.

"His three sons perished in a carriage accident."

"This no being good." She wagged her index finger. "Bad to be putting all the sons in one carriage. Should be two in each carriage. If one carriage crash, the other ones they being living still."

Hawk didn't know how to respond to that. *I'm sure my cousin is sorry now* would hardly be an appropriate rejoinder. Thankfully, the duke interjected.

"Very wise, Aunt Majida," Strick said approvingly. "It would never occur to me to split my family up like that."

Relieved to be spared further conversation with the old lady, Hawk returned his attention to Hind, trading light conversation through the final courses.

"You actually seem to enjoy the old termagant's company," he said to the duke after supper.

"I am quite fond of her," Strick admitted. "I also fear her. Being on Auntie Majida's bad side would be most unpleasant."

"As I well know," Hawk murmured. Not that the old woman ever gave him a chance to win her approval. His financial status at the time was reason enough for her to completely disregard him. And to convince her niece to do the same.

Strick's attention centered on Guy and Naila. "Those two seem to be getting along well." Guy remained by Naila's side after supper. At the moment, he was using his hands to describe something while Naila listened attentively.

Raya came up and took her betrothed's arm. "We should encourage the match." She wore a deep green silk gown that enhanced her complexion. Naila had also always looked very well in green. "I would love to have my sister just a quick carriage-ride away."

Strick darted a look at Hawk. "I doubt they'd be suited."

"Why do you say that?" Raya asked. "Look how engaged they are with each other. What do you say, Hawk? You are close to Guy and you knew Naila in Philadelphia. Do you think she and Guy would make a good match?"

"I am quite literally the last person you should ask about such matters," he answered. "I've no idea what makes a suitable match."

"You and Hind seem to enjoy each other's company," Raya noted.

"She is most amiable," he said vaguely. He could barely recall what they'd talked about at supper. The girl was a useful diversion but he had no intention of courting her.

"Oh, she truly is," Raya enthused. "We all adore Hind. She is like a little sister to us."

The duke shook his head. "Don't you think you should stop your matchmaking schemes and focus on the match you've made?"

She smiled up at him. "I can think about you and other things at the same time."

"I cannot," the duke said. "All I can think of is making you my wife."

She squeezed his arm. "It won't be long now. The wedding is only four days away."

His eyes smoldered at her. "I cannot wait."

Hawk was truly happy for Strick and Raya. But their happiness reminded him of all he'd lost. And he was already annoyed at the way Naila was hanging on to Guy's every word.

"If you'll excuse me," he said. "I think I'll retire for the evening."

As Hawk made his way to the nearest exit, he brushed past Guy, who took a step back, unknowingly moving into Hawk's path. The two men collided.

"My apologies," Guy said, obviously surprised by how hard Hawk bumped him. "I am sorry."

"As you should be," Hawk growled as he kept walking. "Do stay in your lane."

"What's wrong with it?" She considered the hat's unique shade. "Would you say that color is puce?"

"It looks like a sad, muddy version of pink," he responded. "But if you truly want it, I will avert my eyes and buy it for you."

"It's such a hot day," she said. "Let's have ice cream instead."

"Let's," he said with a wink. "As long as it's not puce-colored."

She laughed and they made their way to the ice cream shop down the street. But Naila's heart stumbled the moment she entered the shop. She spotted her cousin Eyad at a table with friends, their laughter drifting over to her. She ducked out immediately, hoping he hadn't seen her, and walked away as fast as she could.

"What is it?" Basil asked, following her until they were well away from the ice cream shop.

"Eyad is in there," she hissed. "My cousin can't see us."

He made a sound of frustration. "I do wish you'd allow me to call on you properly."

"Aunt Majida will insist on returning to New York if you show any interest in me."

His jaw clenched. "My intentions are honorable."

"We are just enjoying each other's company for the summer." She reminded him again, as she always did when they met. "That is all."

"Naila, I'm trying to court you. Why do you

insist on hiding it?" he demanded to know. "Why won't you allow me to prove myself to your family?"

"Because you won't able to." It was becoming a familiar argument between them. Basil would never understand her family's requirements. "There is nothing you could do to win them over."

"Why not?" he asked. "Why wouldn't I be able to convince your family?"

"It's just the way our culture is," she said, frustrated. "It's hard to explain. Please don't be so serious. Can't we just enjoy ourselves?"

Even though she counted the minutes until they could spend time together, Naila refused to allow herself to develop feelings for Basil. It wasn't easy. Basil was smart and curious and had a wonderful sense of humor. But she'd known from the outset that they were from different worlds. When the summer was over, they would be forced to return to their real lives.

"Are you ashamed of me?" he asked.

"Of course not." She took him in, appreciating every aspect of his physical form, from his ruffled chestnut curls and steely gray eyes to his athletic body. "Any young lady would be proud to walk beside you."

"Anyone but you."

"I suppose I have to prove it to you," she said flirtatiously, hoping to distract him from a problem that had no resolution. She pulled him into the nearest alley, walking until they were out of sight of any passersby.

"Where are we going?"

"Here." She pushed him up against the wall. She was determined not to end their acquaintanceship before they'd kissed at least once. Although she was inexperienced with boys, Naila knew they usually wanted to kiss her. Standing on the tips of her toes, she pressed her lips against Basil's. It was sweet and quick. But not life-altering. "There."

He blinked. "What was that?"

"I have never kissed a boy. That was perfectly pleasant."

His eyes sparked. "That was not a kiss."

Her brows drew together. "It wasn't?"

He swung her around, reversing their positions so that she was the one up against the wall now. Looking deeply into her eyes, he cupped her cheeks in both hands. His thumbs stroked her cheeks with a featherlight touch that sent a shiver of pleasure through her.

Keeping his gaze locked on hers, he slowly lowered his head, building the anticipation between them. An answering heat rose in Naila as she stared back into Basil's eyes. He tilted his head before finally settling his mouth on hers with the lightest of touches. She closed her eyes, all of her focus on the way he was touching her, with lips that were firm yet yielding.

He brushed his lips against hers several times, then kissed her top lip and then the bottom one. He explored the shape of her mouth, as if he were savoring something delicious. Naila's legs melted beneath her.

He nipped at her lips and when her mouth parted in surprise, his tongue gently came into her mouth and touched hers. His tongue immediately pulled back and hers instinctively searched him out. She felt him smile against her lips as his tongue played with hers, the movements shallow, quick and playful. She was drowning and flying at the same time. In the best possible way.

When he pulled back—much too soon—she wanted to cry out in protest. She blinked her eyes open, hazy pleasure thrumming through her. She'd never experienced so much sensation. It was as if her body had just awakened from a lifelong slumber.

"That," he said, his voice low and throaty, "is a kiss."

CHAPTER ELEVEN

Now
England

"How much longer before we get there?" Nadine grumbled as they trudged along the steep side of the hill. "This seems like a lot of trouble just to see a few ruins."

"Not much farther," Kareem said encouragingly. "We are almost there."

It was late afternoon. They were on their way to see what was left of an ancient abbey on Strickland's estate. Their group also included Nadine's husband, Ghassan; their two boys; and Hind and Hawk. The duke and Raya had stayed behind, closeted in a meeting regarding their upcoming nuptials.

As they walked, the group fell into pairs, Naila with Kareem, Nadine and Ghassan. And Hawk with Hind. The two boys walked and chatted with Naila before scurrying ahead.

"How old are your sister's children?" Kareem asked, watching the boys chase each other.

"Malik is six and Abdallah is nine."

"They seem very attached to you."

"As I am to them." Naila determinedly focused on her conversation with Kareem, rather than preoccupying herself with Hawk and Hind's interactions. Putting Hawk in the past meant she must not be affected by his blossoming courtship of her young cousin. It did not escape her notice that Hind was the age she herself had been when Hawk first took an interest in her. Perhaps he preferred younger women.

When they reached the summit, the abbey came into view and Naila forgot about everything but the majestic solid stone structure sprawled before them. It was a breathtaking combination of columns and arches, with a lantern tower that soared high into the sky.

"Oh," Naila breathed. "It's exquisite."

"It is?" Nadine said. "What's so exquisite about it?"

"I thought you might like it," Kareem said to Naila. "Come, let us get closer."

All that was left of the once-grand structure were the outer walls with immense arch-shaped window openings. A shell of a building brightened by a luscious carpet of violet wildflowers.

"Raya must love it here," Naila said. "Purple is her favorite color."

"Why would she care for this place?" Nadine returned as if the very idea was ludicrous. "She has a castle that actually has floors and a roof."

They spread out a blanket and snacked on fruits, cheese and sweetmeats that had been prepared in the Castle Tremayne kitchens. The boys ran wild, looping in and out of what remained of the abbey's corridors and courtyard.

"Shall we explore the lantern tower?" Kareem asked once they'd eaten. "The view from there is really quite special."

"And climb all those stairs?" Nadine said. "I'm content to remain here resting my feet for the walk back." Ghassan decided to stay with his wife while the rest of the group made their way up to the top of the lantern tower to admire the view. From this vantage point, Castle Tremayne rose proudly in the distance, surrounded by the natural splendor of the green landscape and rolling hills. They made their way down again and walked around, the boys darting between them, laughing and shouting, chasing each other.

"Come and play with us, Auntie Naila," Malik cried out to her. "We could play hide and seek."

"Perhaps later," Naila said. "At the moment, I am speaking with Mr. Amar."

Malik pouted but scampered off after his older brother.

"I also feel badly trampling through the flowers," Naila said to Kareem.

"As I understand it, the duke planted these for his future duchess." After a moment, Kareem added, "My wife used to love violet flowers."

"Your wife?" Naila said in surprise. "I didn't realize you were wed."

"My late wife. Few of my more recent acquaintances know about Layalle," he said. "I do not speak of my loss very often."

Naila realized she and Kareem had more in common than a love of architecture. "I am sorry for your loss."

"Thank you." He looked off into the distance. "I wasn't married for long. She fell ill barely a month after the wedding."

"That must have been a terrible shock."

"It was. You can have no idea what it is like to suffer such a loss."

"I have not lost a husband, that is true. But I have some understanding of what it is to lose someone very dear to you."

"Is that so?" He smiled sadly. "I am sorry to know that you have suffered in that way. I would not wish such a tragedy on anyone."

They passed an old stone bench. Malik hopped onto it and launched himself onto Naila's back. "Come play with us now, Auntie!"

Malik's arms tightened around Naila's neck as he rode piggyback. "Malik," she said firmly, trying to loosen the child's grip. "Not now."

"Please," Malik said excitedly, refusing to be dislodged. "Let's play horsey. Just one loop."

"Malik," she said. "I am speaking with Mr. Amar." It was not the thing to roughhouse in polite company. She didn't want Kareem, but mostly Hawk, to view them as heathens from America. Her cheeks burning, she wiggled, trying to displace the boy as gently as possible.

"You heard your aunt," Kareem's voice was stern. "Come down from there."

"Who are you again?" Malik asked.

Hawk appeared out of nowhere. Stepping around Naila, he slipped his hands under the boy's arms and pulled him away, setting him firmly but gently on his feet. "Now run along," he directed the boy.

"Hey!" The boy spun around to see who had displaced him, but whatever he saw in Hawk's face made him clamp his mouth shut and dart off to join his brother.

Before Naila had a chance to thank him, Hawk nodded abruptly and took his leave, striding back to join Hind, who watched him with undisguised admiration.

"WE'VE DECIDED TO change our wedding trip plans," Raya announced.

It was the night before the wedding. The three sisters were sugaring, removing the hair from their bodies using a traditional sugar, lemon and water paste recipe passed down from their ancestors. Arab brides often practiced the hair removal ritual in preparation for their wedding night.

"Change your plans how?" Naila was relieved

the wedding date had finally arrived. After Raya and Strick were married, Hawk would undoubtedly return to his own estate. Only then would she finally be free of him and able to focus on moving forward.

Raya spread the sugar paste over her calf. "Strick and I will go to London for a week and then you all will come join us in town."

Naila used two hands to knead a portion of the taffy-like mixture. "But I thought you were eager to take an extended wedding trip."

"We can do that after you all return to New York. I want to spend time with the family while you're here." Raya grimaced as she ripped the sugar from her calf, yanking out a strip of fine leg hair with it. "I think you will enjoy seeing London."

"Oh, I would." Naila thought of all of the historic structures she'd be able to visit in town. "Are Nadine, Hind and the rest of us to remain at Castle Tremayne before traveling to London to join you?"

Nadine released an exasperated sigh. "How boring to be stuck all the way out here in the middle of nowhere," she grumbled. "Why can't we go to London right after the wedding?"

"Because I'd like to be there to receive you," Raya said. "And to make sure the house is ready for visitors."

Nadine rolled her eyes. "Isn't there anything else we can do instead of staying at this dreary castle? The boys are getting bored."

"There is plenty to do here," Naila protested.

Nadine ignored her. "Is there something else we can do before meeting you in London?" she asked Raya.

"Maybe." Raya spread the paste on her other calf. "I'll think of something."

THE FOLLOWING DAY, Raya married her duke in a small morning ceremony. It was a modest affair with just a handful of friends and family on hand, to be followed by an equally intimate wedding breakfast. The evening wedding ball, to which hundreds were invited, would be the main event celebrating the duke's marriage to his duchess.

Raya was a vision in a silk and lace wedding gown tastefully embellished with *tatreez* of the palest silver, a nod to the bride's Palestinian roots. The *fallahi* cross-stitching featured traditional motifs, the geometric patterns symbolizing eternity and unity. The florals represented growth and nature; the pomegranate flowers denoted life and fertility. Auntie Majida had spent weeks embroidering the designs onto the bodice and hem of Raya's dress. Her hopes and wishes for her niece's future were lovingly and meticulously crafted into the silk fabric.

Naila's chest swelled as she watched Raya exchange vows with her duke. Strick, dressed in dark formal clothes, had eyes only for his bride, who had never been more radiant. Hawk stood to the side, watching the ceremony with a serious expression. He looked impossibly handsome in a burgundy frock coat and snowy waist coat.

Naila sighed inwardly. If only the man had had the decency to lose his good looks. But rather than becoming old and out of shape, he was more appealing than ever. His cheekbones were extra prominent, the cut of his chin sharply defined. His shoulders, broad before, were even wider now, evidence that he hadn't abandoned his daily rowing habit.

But it wasn't Hawk's appearance that had reeled her in all those years ago. Of course, his good looks were a factor. But mostly she had been attracted to the wicked gleam in his eye, the mischievous smile, the repartee that kept Naila on her feet and at her best.

Emotion rose into her throat. For a brief moment, she envisioned herself in Raya's place. What would it be like to publicly pledge herself to the man she loved? For his silver gaze to be one of the first sights greeting her each morning? She imagined basking in Hawk's tender adoration and then swallowed down the soreness in her throat.

It was Majida who had convinced Naila that a foreign man with limited prospects was an unsuitable match for the daughter of a prosperous Arab New York merchant. *A man should have at least as much as you*, she said, *if not more*. And Naila, young and naive enough to assume that great love was as common as falafel in New York's Little Syria, had foolishly listened.

And she'd paid dearly for it. She snuck another peek at Hawk and found him looking in her direction. An electric charge jolted through her as their gazes locked.

She tumbled into those metallic gray eyes, once so full of compassion and sultry need, but now unreadable. Longing, urgent and physical, streaked through her. It was as if she and Hawk were having a silent conversation. About what could have been. About the road not taken. And the happiness that could have, *should have*, been theirs.

Naila blinked back tears. She'd thrown away so much.

Hawk continued to watch her as though they were alone in the room. A muscle ticked in his jaw. Why wouldn't he look away? Why couldn't she? Naila didn't want to break the spell. There was no doubt that Hawk saw her now. And she relished his undivided attention.

Murmurs of congratulations sounded around her and Auntie Majida's keening voice tore through the air. Naila reluctantly dragged her attention away from Hawk to find the duke kissing Raya's forehead. Auntie Majida's high-pitched rhythmic sound was an ululation, a celebratory *zaghrouta* that was integral to Arab festivities.

"*Ha hee*," her aunt called out in a high-pitched Arabic tone that sounded from the back of her throat. "Oh groom! Oh bride! Oh you, blue-eyed bead! Protect them from the evil eye!" she called out, ending the *zaghrouta* with rapid side-to-side movements of her tongue, a "lolowee!" sound that all of the Arab relatives joined in on.

Flushed and triumphant, the duke took his bride's hand and faced the assembled wedding guests. "May I present Her Grace, Raya, Duchess of Strickland?"

Just like that, Naila's sister was a married woman.

And, as happy as Naila was for her sister, she'd never felt more alone.

THE STAFF HAD spent days readying Castle Tremayne's Great Hall for the wedding ball. Fresh flowers and hundreds of glittering candles would greet the guests.

Naila was in her bedchamber getting ready for the ball when Nadine came in.

She stared at Naila. "You're wearing the orange gown to Raya's wedding ball?"

"It's what Mama and I picked out." Naila studied herself in the mirror. For the first time in quite a while, she'd put some real effort into her appearance. Her hair was upswept with thick tendrils framing her face. Dangly gold earrings sparkled from her ears. She thought she looked quite well. Vivid shades really were much more flattering to her skin tone.

"But you hate bright colors," Nadine insisted. "Don't you think subdued colors are more appropriate for a spinster?"

"No," Naila said, a trace of laughter in her voice. "I do not. Not so long ago, you were encouraging me to wear bright colors."

Nadine shot Naila a dubious look. "But wearing such a bright color could detract from the bride."

It occurred to Naila that Nadine might be more comfortable with a wallflower younger sister who remained in the background. She pushed thin, gold bangles onto her wrist. "Raya doesn't mind. She encouraged me to wear this gown."

Naila was determined to cast off the melancholy that had gripped her during the exchange of vows. She didn't intend to spend her entire life pining for what could have been. It was past time to throw off her mourning, to fully embrace life again. Raya's wedding ball was the perfect place to take charge of this next phase of her life, the one in which Hawk and their broken secret betrothal no longer took center stage in her thoughts and actions.

"What has gotten into you?" Nadine's forehead wrinkled. "Why do you seem so . . . I don't know . . . happy?"

Not *happy* precisely. More like determined to get on with her life. "Our sister got married this morning. She's a duchess now. If that is not an occasion for celebration, then I don't know what is," Naila said. "Is there something you need?"

"I wanted to borrow that pair of gold hair clips that Mama bought you."

"I'm already wearing them." Naila shifted, giving her sister a better view of her hairstyle. "They are part of the updo."

"Well, if I can't borrow your hair pins, I supposed I'll have to find something else to dress my hair." Nadine turned to go but then paused. "Will you tuck Malik into bed this evening? He specifically asked for you."

Naila slipped two gold rings onto her fingers. "I'll stop in to say good night but I cannot stay and tuck him in."

"Why not?" Nadine asked.

"Because your children go to bed late and I intend to be at the ball."

"Doing what?"

"I plan to dance all night."

"What?" Nadine stared at her. "What has come over you? It's as if you are a completely different person than the girl who came to England just a few weeks ago."

Naila assessed herself in the mirror. The gold in her hair sparkled, winking at her. She smiled at her sister. "Maybe I am."

Nadine rolled her eyes. "Don't forget to stop in and see the kids before you go to the ball."

"Don't worry." Naila adored her nephews. "I won't forget."

Hawk took another glass of champagne and poured it down his throat, wondering how long courtesy demanded that he remain at the wedding ball.

"You'll have to stay at least until after supper," Guy said.

Hawk suppressed a groan because the food wouldn't be served until close to midnight.

Guy sipped his drink. "Strick looks happy."

"He does," Hawk concurred. "In fact, I don't think he's ever looked happier." Elegant in black evening clothes, the duke stood across the room with his new duchess, his face glowing and animated.

"Shouldn't you be dancing?" Guy asked.

"I have been. I'm taking a break." Hawk had danced with a handful of ladies, including Miss Hind, which was pleasant enough, and also Naila's older sister, Nadine, who couldn't stop talking, mostly about herself. Hawk took care only to dance with each woman once to avoid sparking talk that he favored any particular one of them. They were more than an hour into the ball and Naila had yet to make an appearance.

It had been a mistake to allow himself to fully

look at her during the wedding ceremony. Her lavender gown was a step above her usual uninspiring dresses but not by much. Still, he couldn't help staring at her. He was starting to get a glimpse of her loveliness again. Hawk shook his head against the thought of being drawn back into Naila's orbit. Only a fool would allow that.

"Oh my." Guy whistled low under his breath. "Would you look at that?"

Hawk followed his friend's gaze. When he realized what Guy was reacting to, his eyes widened and he swallowed hard.

Naila had arrived.

And what an entrance it was. Gone was her customary frumpy attire, replaced by a vibrant tangerine silk that brightened her eyes and gave her skin a luminosity that heightened her beauty. The gown emphasized her beautiful curves in a way her dowdy dresses never could, the generous neckline showcasing ample breasts that he'd once had the honor of feeling against his palm.

And his tongue.

"I never realized," Guy said in breathless wonder, "that our Miss Naila is a beauty!"

Chapter Twelve

Hawk suppressed a primal urge to pummel Guy even as he understood his reaction.

This proud and confident version of Naila was hard to look away from.

"If you'll excuse me," Guy said. "I believe I have found my next dance partner."

As much as he wanted to trip his friend, hopefully causing him fall hard on his nose, Hawk nodded politely and watched Guy do what Hawk restrained himself from doing. His friend immediately approached Naila and before long, the two were waltzing.

Grabbing another glass of champagne, Hawk spent the next half hour watching Naila dance with a succession of partners, which included the architect, who danced with her twice. She'd clearly decided to cast off her wallflower ways along with the shapeless gowns.

The appreciation that other men in the room had for her was palpable. It was as if Naila had suddenly come alive again after a long season of hibernation. As soon one partner escorted her off the dance floor, another would appear in his place. A part of Hawk felt fortunate to witness her spectacular metamorphosis. The other part, the jealous part, clenched his teeth until they ached every time a new dance partner put his hands on her.

Seeing Naila this evening rekindled the exhilaration he'd once felt in her presence. Naila danced as if alive with joy and optimism, like there wasn't a single obstacle that she couldn't overcome. Her vibrations were contagious. When a man took a woman like that into his arms, he felt there was nothing he couldn't accomplish with such a brilliant creature by his side.

Strickland came up beside him. "Perhaps it will be your turn next."

Hawk forced his attention away from Naila. "Congratulations again, my friend. How does it feel to be a married man?"

"Like all is finally right with the world," the duke responded with a sigh of contentment.

"I wish you much happiness." Hawk returned his focus to Naila—his gaze inadvertently dropping to the seductive sway of her abundant hips—as Guy escorted her off the dance floor for the second time.

Strickland was watching, too. "Your little wallflower has come out of her shell."

Hawk bottomed out his champagne. "She is not *my* anything." *Unfortunately.*

"She could be."

"Have you forgotten that I already attempted to make her mine? She resoundingly declined."

"That was a long time ago, when you were a young man with no prospects."

Bitter acid rose in his throat. "I would not want Naila to wed me because I am an earl."

"Your title and fortune will win over her family. I gather that you alone were always acceptable to her."

"What are you two talking about?" the bride asked as she joined them. The new duchess was resplendent in her white gown threaded with silver.

"We're discussing how beautiful my bride is." Strickland pulled her close to his side. "And what a fortunate man I am."

"Pray don't forget it," she said cheekily.

Hawk inclined his chin. "I wish you every happiness, Duchess."

She gave him a rueful smile. "I don't think I will ever become accustomed to being called duchess."

"If the duke ever gives you any trouble, you must call upon me," Hawk said gallantly. "I am ever at your service."

"Well," she said hesitantly, "there is something you can do for me."

"Is there?" he said with surprise. "You must name it."

"Strickland and I are going up to one of his

hunting lodges for a week before joining my relatives in London," she told him. "Rather than leaving my family members behind here at Castle Tremayne for that week, I hoped you might consider inviting them to Briar Hall for two or three nights since your estate isn't far from London."

"You want me to host a house party?" Hawk smothered an immediate urge to quash her plan. The last thing he needed was more time with Naila. His sense of well-being required that he be as far from Naila as possible in order to regain his hard-earned equilibrium. He did not care for the sensations—jealousy and banked fury, desire and possessiveness—that swept through him this evening as he watched a succession of men put their paws on Naila.

And yet.

The idea of keeping Naila close, of showing her his beloved Briar Hall, of having her under his roof, held a dangerous appeal. And that alarmed him. His carefully honed instinct for self-preservation, which he'd wrapped around him like a cloak since Philadelphia, was quickly unraveling.

"You want Hawk to host your relatives?" Strickland asked his bride. "Whatever for?"

"It would be a nice surprise for Naila," Raya said. "She is entranced by Elizabethan architecture and I'm told that Briar Hall is an excellent example of that style of home. I hate to overstep but—"

"I think it is an excellent idea," Strickland interjected. "Hawk can personally give Naila a tour of his property."

Hawk resisted the urge to scowl at his friend. "Are you trying to play matchmaker?" he growled, the question flying out of his mouth before he could censor it, like he did with most of his thoughts.

Comprehension lit Raya's face. "Oh . . . I had not thought of that. But Hind really is a lovely girl. This visit will give you a chance to get better acquainted with my cousin."

Studiously avoiding Hawk's gaze, Strickland said, "I don't think Hind is a good match for the earl."

Her forehead crinkled. "Then what are you saying?"

"I think perhaps an older woman might suit him more—"

Hawk decided to interject before Strickland ventured into dangerous territory. There was no telling how much wine and champagne his friend had imbibed. Who knew what could fly out of his mouth next? "It would be my pleasure to host the Darwishes at Briar Hall," he said.

"Lovely!" Raya clapped her hands together. "Auntie Majida has elected to stay behind. She's perfectly content here and one of the staff will bring her to London in a week's time."

Hawk wondered if he should take the old woman's decision not to visit Briar Hall as a personal affront. A part of him wanted her to see his home, to fully comprehend the scope of what she'd persuaded Naila to give up. But the other part was relieved not to have to entertain the old battle-ax.

"Afterward," Raya continued, "if you'd like, you could come to London with them."

"A honeymoon with the relatives," Strickland said, the words rich with sarcasm. "What more could a newlywed man ask for?"

"What an excellent idea," Hawk said pointedly. Weary of Strick's innuendos about Naila, he welcomed the opportunity to get under his friend's skin. Besides, escorting his guests to town was a courtesy he'd normally extend to foreign visitors. "I would love to join you all in London. The more the merrier."

Strick scowled at him. "Said no bridegroom ever."

After the ducal couple wandered away, Hawk made his escape, slipping out to the terrace for a cigarette. He didn't smoke much these days but something about seeing Naila dance as though she were the bride made him crave one.

He found an old stone bench deep in a quiet part of the outer garden and lit up. Inhaling deeply, he savored the stillness, relieved to have a moment of peace away from the crush. As he exhaled, long and slow, the faraway sounds of music and laughter drifted out to him, mingling with the sounds of the night, the chirp of insects, birds calling out to one another.

His ears honed in on a new sound. The delicate jingle of bracelets. A calling card like no other that summoned the past and could belong to only one person. She appeared, a dream but real, a rustle of orange silk in a cloud of delicate perfume. Naila, more appealing than ever, halted when she spotted him.

He felt sure she would have preferred to pretend not to see him. But surprise lit her luminous face when their gazes met and there was no pretending that they weren't alone in a garden as they'd been all those years ago.

After a moment, during which she seemed to come to an understanding with herself, humor lit her eyes. "Fancy meeting you here, *Inglese*."

Englishman. Something pulled in his chest. How many years had it been since someone had called him that?

"Looking for a smoke?" he asked.

She glanced over her shoulder before meeting his gaze. "It has been a very long time since I've smoked with a strange man in the garden."

"Ah, only this time I am not a stranger."

"Aren't you?" she asked mildly.

Her offhand remark stung because it highlighted the chasm between them. Which was her doing. Not his.

She settled next to him on the bench. The clean woody notes of her perfume coated his nostrils. "Are you going to offer me a cigarette?"

"This is the only one I currently have in my possession," he informed her. "But you are most welcome share it with me."

Her full dark brows lifted. "You would do that?"

"It would be ungentlemanly of me not to."

She accepted the cigarette from him. Holding the fag between delicate fingers, she closed her rose-tinted lips around its tip and inhaled long and slow. "It has been forever since I've had a cigarette."

"Why is that?"

Her eyes glittered at him. "Because it has been a very long time since I've been in a garden with you."

His heart skipped a beat. "Ah, so you did not make a habit of it after I left America."

"I did not," she said simply.

"Why have you abandoned your dance partners this evening?"

"The same reason as you, I suspect. I escaped into the garden for a reprieve. It has been a long time since I've danced so much."

"Why is that?" He was genuinely curious. "You used to adore it."

She met his gaze. "I didn't feel like dancing after you went away."

Being this close to her, *really* talking to her, was like a knife through his heart. And yet he craved any crumb of interaction with her. "That wasn't my doing."

"No." She swallowed, the intricate cords of her throat stirring beneath vulnerable skin. "It wasn't."

He felt a stab of guilt. For what? For holding her accountable for wrecking him?

"I am glad to have a moment to speak with you." She passed the cigarette back to him. "To say a proper goodbye."

"A proper goodbye?" He took the cigarette and put it to his lips, mindful that just moments ago, her mouth touched the same spot. "How do you mean?"

"Raya and the duke depart for their wedding trip tomorrow. I assume that you will be leaving as well, along with the other guests."

"Your sister has other plans for us." He returned the cigarette, lightly grazing her fingers. Touching her, no matter how slight, still blasted through his blood like wildfire. He was dismayed that his body's primal reaction to her hadn't diminished. At all. He rubbed the afflicted arm. "I gather she didn't tell you."

Her brows came together. "Raya has other plans? For us?" Even in the low light, he could detect her blush. "How so?"

"She has asked me to escort your family to Briar Hall, my primary country estate, for two or three days before you journey on to London." He watched carefully for her reaction.

Alarm lit her face. "Whatever for?"

"As a special surprise to you, from what I gather. She asked me to give you a tour of my home." He could easily picture Naila at the place where she might have been mistress. "Briar Hall is a prime example of Elizabethan architecture."

Her midnight eyes lit up, but then the glow in them dimmed. "But it is too much of an imposition."

"Not at all," he assured her. And then, because he must, for the life of him, resist falling into her thrall again, no matter what it cost, he added, "Besides, Miss Hind indicated an interest in the nature walks we can offer at Briar Hall. I am keen to show them to her."

"I see." Hawk thought he detected a hint of sarcasm, although he couldn't be sure. "Yes, Hind is very fond of walking in the wild. Will you ask Mr. Amar, as well?"

"Mr. Amar?"

"Kareem is an architect. He's expressed an interest in seeing Briar Hall."

Ah. She'd answered his opening shot with a cut of her own, and it hit exactly as she intended. Jealousy flooded him.

"Then I shall also ask your friend Mr. Amar to join us," he said stiffly. "If it pleases you."

"Yes," she said. "It does please me. Very much."

"Then it will no doubt delight the new duchess," he responded, "and I am ever at her service."

She did not look impressed. "You've become so polite," she mused. "So proper."

Coming from Naila, it was not a compliment. "You knew me a long time ago. I am a different person now."

She thought for a moment. "And yet here you are, still hiding away in the garden smoking cigarettes."

He couldn't help but smile. "As are you." She was different, the Naila of this evening. It took him a moment to put his finger on it. To realize this conversation was like talking to a grown-up version of the girl he had met in Philadelphia. The one who laughed easily, who glowed from within.

And, just as quickly, he remembered that this grown woman before him was an even more potent incarnation of the Naila who'd captured his heart and then trampled it. She'd destroyed him once. He couldn't give her the opportunity to do it again.

He rose. "If you will excuse me."

She looked up, surprised. "But you haven't finished your cigarette."

"It is yours to enjoy." He spun away from her and walked as quickly as his legs would take him without breaking into a full-blown run.

Chapter Thirteen

Before
Philadelphia

"You can swim, I hope," Basil said as he helped Naila into the boat.

"I can swim but I have never been boating," she said. "And swimming involves staying close to shore. Unlike boating."

Naila was generally a little skittish on the water but she would do just about anything for Basil, including following him over a waterfall if he asked.

He helped her get settled at one end of the little boat and then sat to take control of the oars. "Ready?" he asked, sensing her trepidation. "Do you trust me?"

"With my life apparently," she said with a nervous laugh. "What happens if the oars fall into the water and we're stranded far from land?"

"Not to worry," he said cheerfully. "The blades are held in place by oarlocks so they cannot slip into the water."

"That's a relief." She held tightly to the side of

the small boat, which felt like it could capsize at any moment. "And you are good at rowing?"

"Reasonably so," he assured her.

"That is not very convincing."

"I'm a very strong rower." He unbuttoned his sporting blazer. "I row almost daily when I am home."

"You enjoy the water that much?"

"I like the peacefulness of it once I find a rhythm."

"Hmm." She was too apprehensive to feel serene, especially as he started to row in strong vigorous strokes, taking them farther and farther from land. A least the water was calm. For now. "What if the water becomes choppy?"

He chuckled, his eyes crinkling. "I see there are limits to your trust in me. Are you certain you know how to swim?"

"Why do you keep asking?" she half-snapped. "Am I going to need to swim for my survival before this adventure is over?"

His smile melted, replaced by an expression of tender concern. "If you are truly worried, we can return to shore. I don't wish to make you uncomfortable."

"No." She gripped the sides of the boat even harder. "If you enjoy rowing so much, I want to experience it with you."

"Don't worry then about the water," he told her. "There used to be rapids here but the city built a dam that makes this part of the river placid and perfect for rowing."

"That's a relief."

They quieted for a while, listening to the sounds of the oars swishing through the water. Basil rowed in strong, smooth strokes and she became mesmerized watching him in motion. After several minutes he paused to remove his blazer. She could almost see the play of the muscles in his arms and legs with each stroke. She watched his capable hands grip the oars, the power with which he propelled them forward. He was perspiring from his efforts, beads of sweat gathered on his brow and dampened his shirt under his arms.

"What do you usually wear when you row?" she asked. He was ruining his good shirt.

"I don't think I should say?"

"Why not? Now I am more curious than ever."

He grinned. "If the weather allows, I usually end up discarding my shirt when I get too hot."

"Oh." The image of Basil shirtless flashed in her mind and suddenly she was overheated, too. Warmth flushed through her body and her cheeks were burning. Her reaction had nothing to do with overexerting herself.

"Isn't it beautiful out here on the river?" Basil asked. "Are you enjoying the view?"

She licked her lips. "I am very much enjoying the view."

He stilled as he studied her face. "You are a naughty girl."

"What can I say?" she returned. "I never thought watching you row could be so . . . inspiring."

The cords in his throat moved. "If you keep talking like that, I shall have to come over there and truly inspire you."

She wondered what he would look like without any clothes on. "You should feel free to remove your shirt," she said with forced nonchalance.

His brows shot up. "I beg your pardon?"

"I wouldn't want you to get heatstroke."

"I am shocked, Miss Darwish," he teased her, "that you would make such a scandalous suggestion."

"I am just worried about your health," she said saucily.

"Is that all?" he pressed. "Maybe you are eager to know me . . . more fully."

"I am curious," she admitted. "I've never seen a man without a shirt on. Baba and my brother, Salem, are always fully clothed in my presence. But if I have insulted you—"

"You have not." He tore off his necktie and pulled the white shirt over his head.

The breath whooshed out of her lungs. Barechested, he was even more beautiful. And she immediately saw that the daily rowing had developed the muscles in his arms and chest. Even his stomach was flat and rippled.

"Oh my." If she'd had a fan, she would have used it to cool herself. She wondered what his biceps felt like. "Can I touch you?"

He shook his head. "If you lay hands on me, this boat will most definitely capsize."

"It might be worth it," she murmured.

"I'll tell you what. You come over here and I'll teach you how to row."

That seemed like a poor consolation prize for not being able to touch him but she agreed anyway, scooting over to sit on his bench. He sat behind her, not touching but close enough so that she could feel his body heat.

"First," he murmured in her ear, a hand soft at her spine, "you must keep your back straight."

Naila straightened, a shiver running through her body.

His hand feathered along her wrist. "Your arms and lower body will power the oar."

He showed her how to grip the oars.

"Like this?" The words were breathy.

"Perfect," he complimented, his breath warm on her skin. "Now push your feet against the foot plate. It will give your stroke more power."

She braced her feet as he instructed.

"Now pull." He showed her the stroke, his hands over hers on the oars. "Where the oar enters the water is very important. As is the finish, where the oar leaves the water. Both are factors in maintaining speed and keeping the boat stable."

His hands fell from hers as she got into a rhythm, backward and forward, moving in the way he'd shown her.

"Excellent," he said. "You're a natural."

Within a few minutes, she was exhausted, her muscles screaming with pain. But she kept at it because she wanted to show off for him.

"You have excellent endurance," he remarked.

When he sensed she'd tired, he put his hands over hers and joined in the rowing, back and forth together in a way that exhilarated Naila. His front up against her back, they moved as one. She felt his power with every stroke and her body strummed from the sensation of moving in rhythm with him.

He picked up the pace, rowing faster and with more intensity, the boat cutting through the water at a fast clip. She kept her eyes on what she could see of him, at the way his muscles worked with each stroke, his abdomen contracting against her back with each movement.

Completely beguiled, Naila forgot all about her fear of the water. Leaning back into Basil, she sighed. "I hope this afternoon never ends."

He rowed faster and faster.

Chapter Fourteen

Now
England

Dismay filled Naila as she stared up at the dilapidated manor. "I simply cannot stand to see significant houses fall into disrepair. Surely something can be done."

Along the way to Briar Hall, Kareem suggested they stop at this nearby property that he'd recently cataloged. Most of the glass in the windows was gone. Wild weeds twined around once-grand columns at the home's entrance. Inside, grass grew through the floorboards.

"Trenton Hall was abandoned by Viscount Hastings more than twenty years ago," Kareem told their group. "He lacked the funds to keep it running."

"Why are we stopping to see a falling-down house?" Nadine complained. "Houses in America are new and in excellent shape. I much prefer that."

"Can we go upstairs?" Malik asked as his older brother ran around the property.

"No, you may not," Ghassan said firmly. He

trailed after the boys to make sure they didn't get into trouble.

Hind peered into one of the window openings. "How expensive is the upkeep on these houses?"

"A grand house like this requires many servants," Hawk told her. "And fewer young people want to go into service at grand houses. Many have moved to cities to find work."

"It is unfortunate," Kareem said, "but more and more of these houses will eventually be demolished."

"That's horrible." Naila couldn't bear the thought of these historic treasures being destroyed. "Surely something can be done to save them. Didn't you say that English nobles are wedding American heiresses?"

"Indeed," answered Guy, who'd decided to join the house party at Briar Hall. "The young ladies gain a title and nobles get an infusion of American dollars to keep their estates running."

Naila ran a hand over a peeling front column. "There must be a way to encourage more of that. If only there was a guide or something similar to match wealthy heiresses with impoverished lords."

"Some things are beyond saving," Hawk said. "We have no choice but to let them die."

"That might be your viewpoint," Naila said hotly, "but it is not mine. It is nothing short of criminal for centuries of significant architectural history to be lost because indolent lords are unable to adapt with the times."

A muscle twitched in Hawk's cheek. "It is easy for outsiders to judge impoverished lords, but the reality is that country life in England is not as profitable as it used to be."

Naila could tell that she'd irritated Hawk. But she didn't care. "Then maybe it's time for people to start thinking differently."

Hawk's brows shot up. "I suppose you imagine that you, an American with a passing interest in architecture, will find the answer when a solution has eluded the very people who live this life?"

Guy's chuckle cut through the rising tension. "I, for one, admire Miss Darwish's can-do spirit."

"Thank you," Naila said to him. "We Americans are an enterprising lot. And Arabs have invented many important things."

"A potent combination," Guy murmured.

Nadine rolled her eyes. "Now you sound like Baba. You must excuse her," she said to Hawk and Guy. "My father always talked of Arab accomplishments in history."

Hawk regarded Naila with open curiosity. "What sorts of inventions are Arabs responsible for?"

"Too many to count. Take a man like Ibn Firnas. Centuries ago, he created a flying machine made of silk and feathers and jumped off a mountain."

"But there are no flying machines today," Nadine pointed out. "So what good was that?"

"There might be one day. And it will be thanks to the vision and foresight of Ibn Firnas. And Arabs created the first hospital and the first library."

"That is impressive," Hawk said, "but I fail to see how any of that will help save homes like Trenton Hall."

"The ancient Arabs saw a need for hospitals and libraries and found a way to fill the need."

"And you propose to do the same for abandoned country homes?"

"We must save these homes *before* they are abandoned and fall into complete disrepair."

"Really Naila!" Nadine admonished. "The earl obviously knows more about the state of affairs here than you."

"Maybe," Naila said as the group headed back to the carriages. She thought of how Raya had found a way to make Castle Tremayne solvent again. And how their Arab ancestors came up with solutions for the key problems of their day. If Naila racked her brain, surely she too could find a way to save these majestic homes.

Naila's first glimpse of Briar Hall would forever be frozen in her memory.

Hawk's home was easily the most magnificent dwelling she'd ever laid eyes on. It was mammoth in size, the rectangular main part of the

The Earl That Got Away

house flanked by several towers, but that is not what took her breath away.

Briar Hall's entire facade was covered by walls of glass that reflected the sunlight, a gleaming palace that looked magical in this bucolic setting. Naila had never seen anything like it. Beholding Briar Hall was like looking at a sculpture, a piece of art to be admired. As with Castle Tremayne, it was hard to fathom that people actually lived in this breathtaking place.

"Welcome to Briar Hall," Hawk said when they alighted from their carriages. Pride shone in his face. And it was no wonder. What must it be like to be master of this spectacular domain?

"My goodness." Hind gasped, staring up at the glimmering palace. "There are more windows than walls."

"That is by design," Hawk explained. "Briar Hall was built at a time when glass was very precious. It was a luxury and showcased the wealth of the people who lived here."

A few feet away, Kareem came up alongside Naila. "It's one of the most significant pieces of architecture in this part of the kingdom."

The sheer beauty of Briar Hall made Naila's throat ache. "I have no words."

Kareem chuckled. "I was also rendered speechless the first time I saw it."

"I've never seen anything like it." The thought that other gems like Briar Hall were being lost because their owners couldn't afford to keep them up sent a fresh wave of devastation through her.

"Because there isn't anything like it." He smiled at her in companionable understanding. "Briar Hall is known as one of the most innovative houses of the Tudor period."

Guy smirked. "Is it any wonder that all of the unmarried young ladies of good birth are clamoring to be mistress of Briar Hall?"

Hind batted her lashes at Hawk. "Any girl with good sense would be fortunate to call Briar Hall her home." As always, Hind spoke with a playfulness that many people found endearing, but, in this instance, Naila did not.

Yet everyone else in their party seemed to, most cracking smiles or having a quiet chuckle. Even Hawk smiled indulgently at her young cousin. The kindly expression on his face made Naila's gut pang. There was a time when Hawk had held her with such high esteem that he barely noticed anyone or anything else.

"I am blessed to be the caretaker of Briar Hall for future generations," he acknowledged. "One day my son will oversee this great place." He dashed a look in Naila's direction before quickly looking away. "And then my grandson after him."

The thought that this glorious place might have been Naila's home was inconceivable. "What a privilege it must be to live here, to be able to experience and admire this place every day," she said. "It would be like living inside a masterpiece."

"It will be even more special when I am able to share Briar Hall with a wife and family," Hawk remarked and she wondered if he spoke of what might have been had she been brave enough to accept his proposal in Philadelphia. Or what might still be if he decided to install Hind as mistress of Briar Hall.

Guy darted an amused glance in Hind's direction. "All of this talk of marriage makes me wonder if we should expect to hear wedding bells soon?"

Hawk ignored the comment. "You all must be fatigued from the journey."

He led the way into his home, where maids and manservants stood at the ready. "You will be shown to your chambers. We can reconvene later for supper."

"I am exhausted," Nadine said, happily following a maid, trailed by Ghassan and the boys.

A maid named Joan was assigned to direct Naila to her guest chamber. As she followed Joan through a myriad of long corridors, Naila absorbed her surroundings. The marbled and plastered interior of the house was as impressive as the outside, with high ceilings and immense tapestries covering the walls. They went up so many flights of stairs that Naila started to wonder whether Hawk had banished her to the farthest reaches of the house.

When they finally reached their destination, Naila's breath caught. She'd been assigned a room in one of the towers. Light poured in from the vast immense windows on the room's two exterior walls. Detailed plasterwork adorned the walls.

"Oh!" She turned in a circle, taking it all in. "What an extraordinary space!"

"Yes, miss," Joan replied. "The tower chambers are reserved for his lordship's most prestigious guests."

"They are?" Hawk had put her in one of the finest chambers? Or was her room assignment the work of his staff?

While Joan unpacked Naila's bags and put away her clothes, Naila stared out the massive windows. One wall of windows provided vistas of the estate's rolling grassy hills and forested expanses. The other overlooked the roof, which was one floor below. The stone-covered rooftop, flat and walkable, was ornamented with pots overflowing with plants, garden statuary and benches where people could take their leisure. It looked like the perfect place to spend some quiet time.

"Where is the access to the roof?" she asked Joan.

"It's down one flight of stairs, miss. There's a window there that also serves as the door to the roof."

"Do people often visit the rooftop?"

"On occasion his lord will invite guests to see the views from there, but the tower chambers provide the very best sights of the landscape."

Naila sighed. "I could look at these views all day long."

"Oh, miss," Joan said from behind her. "What a beautiful gown, if you don't mind my saying."

Naila saw that the maid had unpacked her tangerine gown. "Some say it is too bright, but tangerine is my favorite color."

The maid smiled. "Then you are in the perfect chamber."

It took Naila a moment to understand what Joan meant, but then it hit her. Her eyes widened. The bed linens, tapestries and floor coverings were all various shades of orange, from vibrant corals to the palest apricot. What a delightful coincidence!

If it was a coincidence.

"Are these colors very commonly used here at Briar Hall?" she asked.

"I wouldn't say so, miss. This is known as the Orange Room."

Naila didn't know what to think. Hawk didn't seem at all interested in pleasing her, yet he'd put her in one of the best rooms at Briar Hall?

Joan put away the last of Naila's things. "There is fresh water in the basin, if you'd like to wash up, miss. If there is nothing else, I'll return in an hour's time to help you dress for supper."

Naila thanked the maid and studied the room more closely after she departed. She took in the details of the tapestries, scenes from a forest with frolicking animals. The pieces must be worth a fortune. She glanced out one of the enormous windows and saw that there were two men on the roof.

That's when she spotted Hawk.

He'd discarded his frock coat, waist coat and necktie, which left him in only dark trousers and a white shirt. It took her a moment to realize it was him because she was accustomed to seeing him in far more formal attire.

He stood on the roof engaged in an animated discussion with what looked to be a member of his staff. The man wore a suit, but its quality and style suggested he was of the working class. Hawk pointed to various things, his arm stretching long. The two men walked over and examined one of the statues. Hawk ran a hand over it and seemed to issue some sort of instruction. Crossing his arms over his chest, he laughed at something his companion said.

Naila was riveted. She hadn't seen Hawk look so open and unguarded since Philadelphia. When she'd already thought of him as her husband. Naila's face warmed at the memory of his fingers gliding along her skin, and of the sensation of his mouth, hot and wet, against her neck and . . . other places. Recalling the encounter still stirred her body. Need throbbed deep in her belly, reigniting physical cravings she'd spent years trying to suppress.

The Hawk chatting freely on the roof was the man she recognized, the one she'd loved with everything in her. The good-tempered smile and relaxed posture, the easy flow of conversation. He was far different from the stiff courteous man she'd become acquainted with over the past few weeks.

The Earl of Hawksworth was formal and polite. His words were spoken with an edge and an underlying note of derision. He was so emotionally distant that there might as well still be a full ocean between them. He'd certainly run from their garden encounter at Castle Tremayne so quickly that you'd think the cigarette had lit his trousers on fire.

But watching the man conversing easily on the roof was like seeing her Inglese again. The urge to go to him, to speak with the old Basil at least one more time, overwhelmed her. Without giving herself time to think too deeply, Naila went to him.

"LET'S GET THESE looked at as soon as possible," Hawk instructed his steward. A section of the roof appeared to be leaking.

"Very good, my lord." Waller had come with the house when Hawk inherited his title. The two men had developed an instant rapport. Waller's experience and long history at Briar Hall were instrumental in helping Hawk gain a detailed understanding of how to run a massive estate. "I'll have the roofers look at it first thing in the morning."

Hawk remained on the roof once Waller left him. He gazed deep into the distance, surveying his estate. The reality that he was master of these vast grounds continually astonished him.

Naila was equally smitten with Briar Hall. He'd seen it the moment they arrived. There was no missing the wonder, the sheer enchantment, that overcame her when she saw his home. He sensed that she experienced Briar Hall the same way he had when he'd first seen it as a young boy. Back then he was an awestruck distant relation with no expectation of one day inheriting this treasure.

He cut a glance up at the tower and wondered what she thought of the Orange Room. Not long after he'd taken possession of Briar Hall, a storm had knocked out some of the tower windows. The chamber's furnishings were damaged. When it came time to refurbish the chamber with furniture and rugs from other parts of the manor, the housekeeper asked what color the room should be. He automatically said orange, still thinking of Naila even after she'd forsaken him.

Gazing up at the tower's wall of windows,

he wondered if Naila had noticed the color. He would have enjoyed seeing her reaction to it. And then, almost as if he'd conjured her up, Naila's voice sounded behind him.

"The view is spectacular from here. But I have an even better vantage point from my room."

He turned to face her. Her cheeks were rosy, her dark eyes flashing with the vitality that had overwhelmed him from the moment he met her. He still hadn't recovered. She wore another becoming gown, this one in robin's-egg blue, which set off her soft olive skin. He quashed a primal urge to touch her, to take her, to make her his again. But all he said was "I take it that means you approve of your accommodations?"

"How could I not?" She came closer. "A closet at Briar Hall would be nicer than most rooms."

"Have we put you in a closet?"

"I'm in a tower room. I thought you might know something about that."

"I run a vast portfolio. Many duties, such as room assignments, fall to my staff." It was a lie, of course. He'd hand selected the room for her. Even before she appeared in England, he always thought of her when he entered that chamber. Which is why he normally avoided the place.

"My chamber is decorated in shades of orange."

"Don't you mean tangerine?"

Her mouth curled. "Yes, tangerine."

"What do you think of Briar Hall?"

"I cannot find the right words to describe how marvelous it is."

It could have been yours. *If only you'd believed in me.* In us. The old resentment flared, a sharp simmer in his gut. For some reason, having Naila here made him more bitter. It drove home just how close he'd come to having everything a man could want. If she'd been constant, they might be on this rooftop today with their children, admonishing them to be careful.

His silence seemed to unnerve her. "I . . . um . . . just want thank you for putting me in such a beautiful room."

"Not at all." He felt the ignoble desire to hurt her as she'd wounded him. "You must consider your new rank in the world."

Her finely arched brows drew together. "I don't follow."

"You may not have an actual title, but the sister of a newly minted duchess must be treated with special consideration."

She had a dubious look on her face. "You gave me a good room because Raya is now a duchess?"

"Only partially. Strick is a duke. The highest rank in the kingdom. Only royalty is more elevated." The baser part of him relished the way her face fell, but mostly he wanted to flail himself for hurting her, no matter what she'd done to him. "Besides, Strick is one of my closest friends. It is only right that I honor him by treating his American in-laws with utmost courtesy and consideration."

She studied his face for a moment. He half-expected her to scoff, to challenge the ridiculosity of his words. They both knew he'd put her in the tower because it was one of his finest chambers and was furnished in her favorite shades. Despite himself, he'd wanted to make her happy. He almost wished she would call him out for the liar he was. Instead, she just nodded and he saw that she had decided to play his game.

"I shall be sure to tell their graces just how accommodating you've been." She paused, then added, "My lord."

Chapter Fifteen

After a restless night, Hawk woke early and went down to the lake at dawn to row as he did almost every morning. His guests were still asleep. He'd be back before they all came down for breakfast.

He rowed hard, his blades cutting through the still water, the rhythmic splashing coming at regular intervals. Here, out on the water, his troubles receded. He barely felt the pain in his muscles as he repeated the same motion again and again. He customarily rowed for about an hour a day, but since Naila's arrival at Briar Hall, he'd increased his time on the water, his sessions extending well over two hours.

Perspiration streamed down his torso as his muscles worked. His entire body was involved in the motion of rowing: His legs braced him, his back and shoulders worked in tandem with his arms, his belly contracted with every stroke. He paused long enough to remove his shirt. He was out here alone where no one would see him, save the groundskeeper who was, by now, accustomed to seeing the master out on the lake at all hours.

Yet, no matter how long and strenuously he exerted himself, Hawk couldn't escape thoughts of Naila. Having her here, in the home they might have shared together, was tearing him apart inside. He'd told himself that he had recovered from their break. But seeing her again, having her as a guest in his home, proved what an idiot he was to think he could ever get over Naila. Only a fool would pine away for a woman who'd deserted him.

But here he was.

He tightened his grip on the oars and cut through the water at a faster pace, trying to find the sense of serenity he could usually find on the water, if only Naila would stop intruding on his mind.

NAILA WALKED ALONG the lake. It was early and, as far as she could tell, no one at the hall was awake except for the servants, who were already busy at their tasks. She'd walked for well over an hour, exploring Briar Hall's extensive grounds.

She was surprised to hear the sound of swishing water. Peering out over the lake, she spotted him almost immediately. Hawk was rowing a small boat at a quick pace. Her mouth went dry. He wasn't wearing a shirt. She immediately fell back in time, to the afternoon when Hawk had first taken her out on the water. When she'd boldly asked him to remove his shirt.

His physique had been fine back then but Hawk's body had thickened, losing any lanky boyishness. He possessed the form of a grown man and seasoned athlete. The toned muscles in his arms flexed each time the oars dipped into the water. She stepped back against a tree, hiding in the shadows of the branches so that he wouldn't see her.

She was breathing heavily, and her body tingled as though he were touching her. Her heart raced as she watched him move through the water, mesmerized by the way his lean muscles worked, his skin moist and glistening. She remembered all too well what it felt like to have his body move against hers. She stifled a sob that was equal parts regret and need.

Her body had been denied for too long. She ached for physical connection after having lived too many years without it. She missed being touched by Hawk. He had awakened her body in Philadelphia. She'd been starved for bodily pleasures since.

If only she didn't know what she was missing. Maybe being in the dark would make this longing more bearable.

He released the oars, the boat skimming along the water's surface until it eased to a stop, water ripples ringing out from the boat. He reached for his shirt and mopped his face with it. And then dragged the white cloth over the contours of his chest and under his arms.

Naila devoured the sight of him, relishing this opportunity to stare at him. Something tickled her nose. Alarm rippled through her. She tried to contain the coming sneeze to the point where it ended up sounding like a muffled squeak rather than a full-out achoo.

Out on the water, Hawk suddenly stilled. His body alerted to the sound. He looked around, scanning the trees. Naila shrank back against the trunk and prayed he would not spot her. Her heart stopped when his stare seemed to fix on her. His face was a blur but she could feel the intensity of his searching gaze. She froze, holding her breath, willing herself to die on the spot if he actually spotted her.

After what seemed like an eternity, Hawk tossed his bunched-up shirt aside. Then he reached for the oars and began to move, powering the small boat down the lake and away from her.

Relief poured through Naila. She watched him row, her eyes never leaving Hawk, until he was out of sight. And even then, she stayed where she was for several more minutes before rising and putting herself to rights. Then she started back to the Hall, bracing for what was to come, and willing herself not to flush when she saw Hawk at breakfast.

Chapter Sixteen

Before
Philadelphia

At their next clandestine meeting several days later, Basil and Naila explored a neighborhood of new houses and then went for the ice cream they'd been unable to get at their previous visit to the ice cream shop.

Basil adored being in Naila's company and, even though she made an effort to keep things between them light and fun, he was completely smitten. She pretended their acquaintanceship was nothing more than a summer flirtation, but he was convinced that she was fooling herself. That kiss, which he couldn't stop thinking about, couldn't stop reliving, proved that she was not indifferent to him. Her feelings were there. Now all Basil had to do was convince her to take a chance on him.

Ice cream in hand, they found an isolated spot in a nearby park to settle down. The icy cold treat slid down his throat, a balm against the Philadelphia heat.

During these interludes, they never ran out of things to say. They talked about everything—her childhood in New York and his in London, her interest in architecture, and his plans to make something of himself.

"How will you know what you want to do?" she asked as she dipped a spoon in her ice cream.

"I am still evaluating my options. I don't stand to inherit anything of significance from my father." He had never talked with a young woman so openly. Naila was a true friend. Although his feelings for her far exceeded the boundaries of friendship. "A distant cousin stands to inherit a fortune because his father is the Earl of Hawksworth, but I must fend for myself."

"I am sure you can accomplish anything you put your mind to," she said confidently.

He was buoyed by her faith in him. Naila made him feel like he was capable of doing anything. "My uncle has offered me his manufacturing enterprise. He thinks it has great promise. Uncle tells me Philadelphia is your country's industrial leader."

"I don't know much about that, but I do know Philadelphia is well known for its weaving textiles."

He was enjoying Naila's company, as always, but she seemed a bit distracted. "What is going on?" he asked. "Is there something on your mind?"

A little frown wrinkled the skin between her delicately arched brows. "I am bracing myself to tell you some dreadful news."

"What is it?"

"Auntie Majida is talking about going home next week."

He inhaled sharply. "So soon?"

"We both knew this was inevitable," she said glumly.

"But it's too soon."

"I know." She sighed. "But what can we do?"

"I can come and call on you in New York," he said. "I can assure your father of my intentions."

She shook her head. "Why won't you listen to me?" Her eyes glistened. "I have always told you there is no future for us."

"Don't cry." He couldn't bear to see her upset. "I will think of something. I promise."

"I so want to believe you."

"Then do," he said with a confidence he did not feel. "Come now, finish your ice cream."

She did as he asked. A drop of the cool confection dotted her lip. He could not help himself. He leaned over to capture it with his mouth. Her lips were sweet and lemony. She tasted like the future they could have if they held on tight enough.

He gathered her closer. "Don't give up," he said against her lips. "Hold on."

"I don't know if I can," she said, a catch in her voice.

"Then I will hold on for both of us." He could no longer imagine a life without her. "I promise."

And then he kissed her again.

Chapter Seventeen

Now
England

They were staying at Briar Hall for only three nights before traveling on to London. Naila did her best to avoid Hawk as much as was politely possible.

On their second day at Briar Hall, they toured the grounds, exploring the herb gardens and orchards before Hawk's staff laid out a generous picnic. Hawk, Guy and Ghassan spent a great deal of time talking with one another. And when the men weren't together, Hawk escorted Hind. They were often laughing.

Naila walked with the children while they explored the grounds. She also spent time with Kareem. They'd explored the gallery and other parts of the house, with Kareem pointing out some of the unique Elizabethan architectural details. It was during one of these explorations that they ran into Hawk in the music room.

"I do beg your pardon, my lord," Kareem said

when they entered the room to find Hawk sitting by a generous window with a book on his lap.

Hawk rose and reached for his discarded morning coat. "Not at all."

"I hope you don't mind that Miss Darwish and I were exploring Briar Hall. As an architect, I am naturally fascinated by this magnificent house."

"You are my guests. You must explore to your heart's content." His eyes skimmed over Naila. "Good afternoon, Miss Darwish."

She dipped her chin. "Lord Hawksworth." She deliberately used his formal title, keeping the necessary distance between them. She had had enough of his behavior, of how he ran hot and cold with her. She must endure one more night in this house and then they'd be off to London. And away from him.

"Have you two been spending a great deal of time inspecting the house?" Hawk asked, a slight edge in his voice.

"Do you mind if we explore the house or would you prefer that we keep to our chambers?" she asked, matching the edge in his voice.

Her less-than-polite tone prompted Kareem to look at her in surprise.

"I don't mind at all," Hawk replied. "If you two would like a formal tour of the house then it would be my pleasure to show it to you. After luncheon, why don't we convene in the front hall and everyone who is interested can come along."

"That is a very generous offer, my lord," Kareem said. "We would not wish to inconvenience you."

"Not at all. As I said, it will be my pleasure. I enjoy sharing my house with visitors."

The tour began directly after the afternoon meal. Everyone came along except for Guy, who'd departed for London that morning.

Hawk led them through several well-appointed drawing rooms and the high great chamber which was used for balls and other entertainment. Like Naila's room, many of the bedchambers had color themes; they visited the Blue and Green Rooms. The muniment room held centuries of official Briar Hall records and documents in small wooden drawers that lined the walls. Even the kitchens were impressive, bright, with high ceilings, several worktables and sunlight streaming through the expansive windows.

"And this is my study," Hawk said leading them into a room full of dark woods and leather. "This is where I attend to most estate business."

Naila inhaled the scents of the chamber. Old books, lemon polish, old leather. And the faintest hint of Hawk's shaving soap. She could easily imagine him spending hours in this room, applying himself to running his estate.

Tears stung her eyes but they were tears of pride. She'd always known that Hawk had potential, that he would make something of himself in this world. True, he had inherited his title and lands, but she remembered Raya saying that Hawk ran his vast estate masterfully. That he'd inherited a poorly run estate and spent the past several years making the estate profitable.

Hind surveyed the room with wide eyes. "There are so many rooms. It's a wonder you don't get lost."

Hawk smiled at her. "I must confess that I did lose my way a time or two when I first began living here."

Kareem stared for a bit at the mahogany shelves lining one wall. Then he crossed over to carefully examine them. Naila wondered what he was doing.

"Are we done yet?" Abdallah, Nadine's eldest son, whispered loudly to his mother. "This is boring."

"Hush!" Nadine gave him the death stare. "Where are your manners?"

Over at the bookshelves, Kareem turned to Hawk. "Is there a secret chamber behind this bookshelf, my lord?"

"Very astute," said Hawk, who'd been watching Kareem study the bookstacks. "And yes, there is a secret passage through there."

Nadine's boys perked up. "There is?" Abdallah asked. "Can we see it?"

"*May* we see it?" Ghassan corrected the boy.

"May we?" The boy bounced on his heels. "May we?"

"Of course." Hawk went over to release the hidden latch, swinging the door open.

"Fascinating," Kareem said, before stepping through the portal. The boys scrambled in after him, followed by their parents and Hind.

"Have a care," Hawk said to Ghassan. "The boys should not go as far as the stairs. It is dark and unsafe."

Ghassan nodded. "I will keep them away from there."

That left Naila alone with Hawk. She was about to follow when her eye caught on something on the desk. A gold fountain pen. A prototype created by an inventor named William Purvis that contained a reservoir within the writing implement, eliminating the need to use a separate ink pot.

The pen wasn't widely available but her cousin Eyad knew the inventor and had been able to get the prototype. Naila had gifted the pen to Hawk. *I love it*, he'd said, *as I love you*. It was the first time he'd declared his love.

"Miss Darwish?" Hawk's voice jolted her back to the present. She blinked her eyes away from the pen to meet Hawk's gaze.

She felt lightheaded. "You kept it."

"What?" he asked, his voice politely abrupt. "Kept what?"

"The pen I gave you." Her voice trembled a little. "You've kept it all these years."

His demeanor softened. "Are you really so surprised?"

She was. "I thought you would have purged yourself of anything that reminded you of me after we parted."

"It was the last piece of you that I had," he said. "The only part."

"That isn't true," she returned without thinking. *You had my heart all these years.*

"I beg your pardon?" he said.

"I am so glad that you retained this token of our . . . friendship. I'm so pleased to have seen you again."

He scrutinized her face. "Naila?" His voice was low, intimate. "What are you saying?"

She could not go into the future without settling this part of her past. "We have unfinished business."

He swallowed hard. "We do?"

"Yes," she said firmly. Maybe he was afraid to venture into this emotional minefield but it had to be done. "It must be dealt with before either of us can properly look to the future."

"I still don't quite take your meaning," he said carefully.

"I am saying that we needed to see each other again in order to properly take our leave of each other," she said, "to part as friends."

Chapter Eighteen

"Part as friends?" Hawk repeated. They could never be friends. He'd once told her as much. Didn't she see that? He could either love her or hate her. He could never countenance anything as neutral as being her friend.

A scream sounded from the secret room, echoing through the study. Alarm shot through Hawk. He darted into the secret passage. The screaming got louder, piercing his ears. He heard footsteps and realized that Naila was behind him.

"That's Nadine screaming," she said anxiously. "I do hope that nothing has happened to one of the boys."

They reached the stairwell that Hawk had instructed them to avoid.

"It's Hind," Nadine screamed. "She fell down the stairs. She wanted to see what was down there."

Hawk quickly made his way down the rickety steps, followed closely by Kareem. He cursed to himself. He should never have allowed the group into the secret passage without leading the way. Harm had come to one of his guests because he'd allowed himself to be distracted by Naila. Now her young cousin might be seriously injured while under his care and protection.

"Ghassan, maybe you should take the boys back to the main part of the house," he heard Naila instruct her brother-in-law. "It is probably best for them to be away."

Dread trickled through Hawk. There was no telling what they would find at the bottom of the steps, no way of knowing how badly hurt Hind was. The girl was in a crumpled heap at the bottom of the stairs.

"She isn't conscious," Kareem said.

"We need to get her some help." Hawk scooped Hind into his arms and carried her up the stairs. Nadine continued to scream as he carried the senseless girl back into his study.

Crossing over to the leather sofa, he gently set her down. "Ring the bell," he directed Naila. "Summon the footman."

Pale-faced, she rushed to do as he asked, tugging urgently on the bell pull.

The footman appeared within a minute or two. "Summon the doctor immediately," Hawk barked. "Do not return without him."

"Yes, my lord." The footman hurried away.

"Why did this happen?" Nadine moaned, sinking into a chair. "I'll be blamed if Hind is seriously hurt."

Hawk and Naila knelt beside Hind, examining her colorless visage.

"She must have hit her head," Naila said.

He nodded. "That would explain why she is senseless."

Concern lined the planes of her face. "We won't know how bad it is until she reawakens."

Guilt tugging at him, he reached for Naila's hand and squeezed. "She will be all right. She has to be."

She looked into his eyes. "I pray that you are right."

"I'll move her into a guest chamber. She'll be more comfortable in a bed."

She set a staying hand on his forearm. "We should wait. If she has broken something, moving her could make the injury worse."

"You have the right of it, of course." He admired how she managed to keep her wits about her in such a dire situation.

Naila rose and went to her sister. Kareem stood by Nadine, trying to comfort her.

"Nadine," Naila coaxed in gentle tones, "there is nothing to be done for Hind now. Why don't you go to your bedchamber and rest until we have news?"

"I am the eldest sister," Nadine pouted. "I should be in charge, not you."

"Quite right," she said soothingly. "That is all the more reason for you to be ready and rested for when Hind wakes up. She will need you then."

"That sounds reasonable," Kareem said. "Don't you think so Um Abdallah?"

"And I promise to come find you as soon as the doctor examines Hind," Naila reassured her. "That is when we will know what we are dealing with."

"Maybe you are right." Nadine heaved herself up from the chair. "I am very tired. You have no idea how exhausting it is to have children. You are so fortunate that all you have to think about is yourself."

Intense dislike slammed through Hawk. He didn't care for the way Nadine talked down to her sister. Naila was ten times the woman her elder sister could ever hope to be. He'd noted the way Naila deftly managed the elder sister's conceits while also looking after her nephews and all of her other family members. The Darwishes might not realize it, but Naila was central to their family. It began to dawn on him that she might actually be the heart of the family.

Once Kareem ushered Nadine out, Naila returned to her cousin, dropping to her knees beside the girl. She gently stroked Hind's hand. "You are going to be fine," she said soothingly to her cousin's inert form. "Everything will be well."

Emotion swelled in Hawk's chest as he watched Naila tend to the girl. The lulling sound of her voice had a calming effect on him as well.

Witnessing her quiet capability prompted him to begin to see her in a new light. He'd been so busy comparing the subdued, more mature version of Naila to the lively young girl he met in Philadelphia that he'd failed to appreciate the woman she was now.

Instead of losing that young girl, Naila had incorporated her into the person she'd become. The vivacious girl he once knew was still there—he'd certainly gotten a glimpse of her at Strickland's wedding ball—but this Naila harnessed all the best parts of her into the self-possessed woman before him now. A formidable woman who exuded calm, quiet power and restraint.

"Can I get you anything?" he asked her, his voice tender.

She looked up. "Me?" she said with some surprise. "No, thank you. I just wish the doctor was already here."

He grimaced. "As do I." Where the hell was the doctor?

She contemplated the expression on his face. "You mustn't blame yourself."

"How can I not?" Guilt stabbed at him. "I should have led the way in the secret passage."

"You warned everyone about the stairs."

"I should have been there. But I allowed myself to be distracted."

Understanding lit her face. "Then I suppose we are both to blame."

"You are blameless."

A hint of a wistful smile touched her full lips. "We both know that is not true." She turned away to refocus on her cousin. She stroked the girl's forehead, and the thin gold bracelets on her wrist jingled. And then he saw it. His eyes widened.

"The bracelet." His voice was hoarse. "That's the one I gave you."

"Yes." She fingered the small pearl on the bracelet.

"You kept it. After all these years."

She nodded. "I wear it every day."

"Why?" He couldn't help asking.

She avoided his gaze. "It is precious to me."

He stared at her low-cast eyes. Thick, fringed dark lashes fanned the satiny skin of her cheekbones. His throat constricted as he silently willed her to look at him so that he could see the true answer in her eyes.

"You were precious to me when I gave it to you," he said. *And remain so.*

She nodded faintly, still not looking at him. "Those were the happiest days of my life."

"And of mine." He answered honestly before he could censor himself.

"I'm sorry," she said faintly.

"For what?"

"For so many things." The cords of her throat moved. "That I didn't hold on tighter. That I didn't come to find you sooner."

"Find me?" He frowned, completely confused. "When did you look for me?"

"But you were already gone." Anguish coated her words. "It was too late."

"When was this?" he pressed. "I don't understand."

Hind's sudden moan cut through the air. Naila whipped her attention to the girl, her conversation with Hawk completely forgotten.

"Habiti?" she asked urgently. "Can you hear me?"

"You're practically yelling in my ear," Hind grumbled, her eyelids fluttering. "I'm not deaf."

Naila laughed, exchanging a relieved look with Hawk. "How do you feel?"

"Like someone dropped a heavy rock on my head," Hind murmured before drifting off.

"She woke up," Hawk said. "Surely that's an encouraging sign."

"But she's out again." Naila's forehead crinkled. "That's worrisome, don't you think?"

The sound of approaching footsteps sounded in the corridor. "Maybe that's the doctor," he said, rising. Dr. Hughes appeared on the threshold. Hawk went to him and explained how Hind was injured.

"She was awake," Naila added when Hawk finished. "Just for a moment and then she fell asleep."

"I see," Dr. Hughes said. "Let's have a look." He examined Hind quickly and then supervised the footmen as they moved the girl to a guest chamber. Hawk and Naila waited anxiously in the corridor for news of the girl's condition.

"Do you trust this doctor?" Naila asked.

"I do. I've had some dealings with him," he reassured her. "Miss Hind is in good hands."

She nervously played with her bracelets. "That is good to hear."

Hawk's eye caught again on the bracelet he'd given her years ago. The one she'd worn every day since. What did it mean? And when had she come looking for him? He wanted nothing more than to continue their discussion. But now was not the right time. His focus needed to be on the young woman who'd been injured under his roof.

"We should probably send word to Strickland and the duchess," he said.

Naila nodded. "Raya would want to know if Hind is seriously hurt. But let's wait to hear what the doctor says before we decide anything."

"Hopefully, we'll have word soon." Sitting on a padded bench, they waited together outside of Hind's chamber. It felt good to be on the same team as Naila. This moment of détente was far better than harboring years of resentment, which sapped a great deal of his energy. They both stood when the door to Hind's chamber opened.

"I conducted a full examination," Dr. Hughes told them.

"And?" Hawk said.

"It appears she has suffered a commotion of the brain."

"How serious is it?" Naila asked. "Can we expect a complete recovery?"

"I expect so. Fortunately, she is awake and talking," the doctor said. "She suffered a mild sprain of her wrist, but that should heal quickly. Naturally, she should not be moved for at least a fortnight. She requires complete rest and quiet."

They thanked the doctor and went to find Nadine to share what they'd learned. "Auntie Majida should be brought from Castle Tremayne to be with Hind," Naila told Hawk as they made their way to brief her sister.

"Must she?" Hawk asked. "Will she be a help or a hindrance?"

"I realize you are not fond of Auntie Majida, but she is wise and has a great deal of knowledge about traditional ways to treat injuries. Hind would benefit from her guidance and wisdom."

"Wisdom?" The old lady was responsible for tearing them apart. "You think her wise?"

"Perhaps not in all things," she said, tacitly acknowledging his point. "But her presence will be good for Hind. They are especially close because Auntie Majida is a childless widow and Hind grew up without a mother."

"Very well. If that is what you want." It hadn't

occurred to him that the termagant was capable of nurturing anyone. "I shall personally go to Castle Tremayne and bring her to be by Hind's bedside. If you approve of this plan."

"I do," she said gratefully. "Thank you."

They entered the sitting room to find Nadine, Ghassan and Kareem waiting for word of Hind's condition. Naila briefed them on what the doctor had said.

"Since we are to remove to London tomorrow," she concluded, "I propose that you all go on ahead. I'll stay here to help Auntie Majida look after Hind."

"She will be most fortunate to have you to look after her," Kareem said warmly.

"It is thoughtful of you to offer to stay," Ghassan added. "I think what you propose is the best plan of action."

"Well, I don't," his wife retorted. "Why should Naila stay back instead of me?"

"Naila is good at nursing people," her husband said. "You see how well she soothes the boys when they are ill."

"You are all acting as if she is Florence Nightingale," Nadine snapped. "I am the eldest sister. If anyone should stay behind to care for Hind, it should be me."

"Come now, Nadine." Ghassan barely suppressed a sigh. "Do you really want to look after Hind while she recuperates?"

"Well, of course, why shouldn't I?" she said indignantly. "I *am* the only mother here."

"Very well." Naila relented. "While you remain here with Hind and Auntie Majida, I suppose the rest of us will travel on to London."

"You are all welcome to stay here at Briar Hall throughout Miss Hind's recovery," Hawk told them. He didn't relish the idea of being left with Nadine and the old aunt.

Besides, the thought of Naila leaving Briar Hall, never to return, cut through him like an ax.

"You are welcome to remain here," Hawk told Naila as her party prepared to depart for London.

"That's very kind," Naila said to him. They were back to speaking politely now that the immediate crisis with Miss Hind was past. Even though he longed to ask her why she treasured his bracelet so much that she wore it every day, he decided it was best for his own sanity and survival to leave the matter alone. The last thing he needed was to be entangled with her again in any way.

Besides, maybe her wearing the bracelet had nothing to do with old feelings. Perhaps she just liked the design. He'd never know. They both seemed to tacitly agree to leave the difficult questions unanswered, rather than excavate turbulent emotions that were best left buried.

"Raya will be expecting us," Naila said. "I want to tell her about Hind's injury in person."

"You are welcome to return after you speak with Raya."

"The entire Darwish clan can't remain underfoot at Briar Hall until Hind recovers," she said. "That could take weeks."

He wouldn't beg. "As you wish." Besides, she was right. It was better—*safer*—for Naila to be away from him and Briar Hall.

"Thank you for agreeing to bring Auntie Majida here."

"Of course." He dreaded the journey but he would do it gladly. "I shall leave shortly after you all depart. Your sister will be with Miss Hind until I can bring your aunt back."

Naila paused. "Just one more thing."

"Yes?"

"Please keep in mind that Arab aunties can be a touch . . . um . . . dramatic."

"I shall keep that in mind."

"Hawk," she began.

"Yes?" he asked.

"I want to tell you—" she stopped abruptly and Hawk saw that Kareem had joined them.

"My lord, Miss Darwish, I hope I am not interrupting," he said.

"Not at all," Hawk lied.

"Goodbye, my lord," she said. "I wish you a pleasant journey."

"But wait." Hawk stepped toward her. "What were you going to say?"

She paused. "Nothing of great importance," she finally answered. "Good day and thank you."

When Hawk turned and left, Naila tried to pretend it didn't matter. She'd wanted him to know the full truth. But maybe it was better to leave things as they were. Taking a breath, she turned to Kareem. "Are you sure you won't join us in London?" Kareem's aunt lived in the nearby village and he was going to visit her.

"I will be happy to see you there in a few weeks' time," he answered. "But it will be good to spend time with my aunt and cousins."

The boys scrambled into the carriage, followed by their father.

"Very well. Enjoy your visit." She climbed into the carriage, sitting beside Malik. Ghassan and his elder son, Abdallah, sat across from them.

As the boys chattered away, she stared out the window, watching Briar Hall get smaller and smaller. She would likely never see Hawk's estate again. And who knew when, or if, she might encounter Hawk once more. It was for the best if she did not see him in the future. That was the only way to truly put him in the past. She wondered if he was thrilled to have more time in Hind's company without the entire family about.

But there'd been that glimmer of something between them after Hind's accident. He'd almost been tender with her. A part of her seemed to even sense his admiration. How would Hawk react if he knew the full story?

"Auntie Naila, do you want to play a word game with us?" Malik asked.

"Hmm?" she said absently.

"A word game," Abdallah said. "Will you play?"

"Of course I want to play," she said. "Who gets to start?"

She turned away from Briar Hall and tried to ignore the heaviness bearing down on her heart.

AFTER NAILA'S PARTY departed, Hawk went up to the roof to check on the repairs before departing for Castle Tremayne to retrieve Naila's aunt.

He came in through the landing and paused, staring up in the direction of the tower room, the chamber Naila had stayed in. What would she have said to him if Kareem hadn't interrupted? He wasn't sure. It just felt like they had unfinished business. Their interactions after Hind's accident kindled a tenderness in him. But now that he'd had a moment to reflect on the matter, he decided it was probably wiser to leave those emotions unexplored.

Still, he went up the stairs and strode into the Orange Room. Joan came in behind him.

"My apologies, my lord," the maid said uncomfortably. "I didn't realize you were in here. I've come to clean the Orange Room now that the guests have gone."

He should leave Joan to her work, but the pull to spend a moment alone in the chamber where Naila had slept just hours ago overwhelmed him. "There are some things I need to check in here, if you could return later."

"Yes, my lord." If Joan thought his request was odd, she gave no indication.

After she closed the door behind her, Hawk stood in the middle of the chamber and inhaled deeply. He could still feel Naila's presence in this space, the slightest trace of her unique scent, soap and warm skin and notes of something indescribable that was unique to her.

Yearning overwhelmed him. He wanted her as badly as he had eight years ago. Perhaps even more so, which he hadn't thought possible. The bed linens were still in disarray from where she'd slept. He touched the linens and was unaccountably disappointed to find they were, naturally, no longer warm from her body.

What did she wear when she slept? Was her night rail sheer enough to reveal her considerable physical assets? Sitting on the bed, he closed his eyes, envisioning those sweet round globes tipped with caramel nipples. He could still taste them, could still feel their pertness against his tongue.

He laid back, engulfing himself with her scent. His cock thickened and lengthened. No woman had ever aroused him as completely as Naila.

Even now, after all these years. She didn't even have to be physically present to get him hard.

Unbuttoning the flap of his trousers, he imagined touching her body, the breasts so abundant that one of his hands couldn't contain one beautiful swell. He freed his cock, wrapping his fingers around it.

What a present you are, he'd said to her as he'd cupped one large tit with both hands, before sucking her beautiful swollen nipple into his mouth. She'd bucked her hips and cried out when he put his mouth to her. Naila's reactions during lovemaking were just as bold and free as the young woman he'd fallen deeply, and irretrievably, in love with.

He worked his cock in firm strokes, his thoughts recalling the sway of plush hips, the softness of her belly, the saucy smile that hinted of heaven. Since Naila, he'd only favored women with abundant bodies.

Being with her was like being with more of a woman; everything was amplified, bigger tits and a more generous ass. But the best thing about making love to Naila was feeling so close to her, as if they were inseparable, and being immersed in all of that softness and warmth. His strokes accelerated along his cock as he remembered touching her intimately, feeling Naila's juices on his fingers, tasting her against his skin.

Tension shot up the backs of his legs and rocketed through him. The tension snapped, an exquisite relief flooded him. Hawk cried out Naila's name as he came, a guttural outburst, just as he spasmed and spilled himself onto the bed linens.

He lay there for several minutes, breathing hard, his heart pumping, a sense of euphoria engulfing his arms and legs, his torso, every part of him. His wits slowly returned. What a mess he was in. He'd been obsessed with her all along, even when he'd pretended to put her in the past.

He realized now that, even in her absence, Naila had been the driving force behind many of his actions. He built his properties into model estates because he was still trying to prove himself worthy of her. He'd never married because he couldn't get Naila out of his system. But she was the path to ruin. Loving Naila had the power to destroy him. Again.

She was returning to America in a matter of weeks. Or she would marry one of her kind. Kareem was obviously sniffing after her and she seemed to return his interest. The family certainly supported the match. His hand fisted.

The thought of the architect with Naila made him want to annihilate everything in his path. He forced himself to unclench his fist. He needed to shake his Naila obsession once and for all. *But how?*

He rose to clean up and make himself presentable before leaving the chamber, shutting the door firmly behind him. He passed Joan as he trotted down the steps. "Please clean the tower chamber as thoroughly as possible," he instructed.

He longed to erase all traces of Naila from Briar Hall. If only a thorough cleaning could wipe her from his mind. And from his body's memory of her.

Chapter Nineteen

Naila's aunt fell to her knees, wailing inconsolably.

Aghast, Hawk stared down at the old lady. "She does speak English, does she not?"

"Yes, my lord," Philips, Strickland's butler, intoned. "She certainly does."

He felt slightly panicky. "Then why is she reacting as though the young lady has met a fate worse than death?"

"Mrs. Kassab tends to be rather . . . erm . . . effusive about all manner of things."

"I can see that." Hawk had no experience managing extreme emotional outbursts. The English excelled at pretending feelings did not exist.

He'd arrived at Castle Tremayne minutes ago to collect Naila's aunt, hoping to deliver her to Miss Hind's bedside at Briar Hall by that evening. But the moment he told Mrs. Kassab about the girl's accident, she crumpled to the floor, a stream of incomprehensible Arabic laments pouring out of her.

The butler motioned for two footmen to help Auntie Majida up. They guided her, still moaning, to the nearest chair. All three men looked expectantly at Hawk until he realized, belatedly, that they were waiting for him to take control.

He straightened his spine, reminding himself that he was an earl, a grown man in possession of himself, and not the young boy who'd allowed himself to be bullied by a fearsome scold. Although, at the moment, Auntie Majida looked like a broken old woman that no one could possibly be afraid of.

He cleared his throat. "Thank you," he said to the servants. "That will be all."

Once they were alone, Hawk produced a handkerchief for the old woman. She accepted it and mopped her tears with gusto.

"The doctor expects that Miss Hind will make a complete recovery," he repeated, in case she'd missed it the first time. "Miss Naila thought it best that I bring you to Miss Hind's bedside."

"*Yalla*," she said, pushing up from the chair.

He knew from his summer with Naila that *yalla* could mean all kinds of things, from "let's go" to "hurry" to a verbal shrug. It all depended on the intonation and circumstance.

"I must go to Hind," she added.

He marveled that the termagant seemed to have recovered herself as quickly as she'd burst into tears. The shift was like a violent summer storm that vanishes as swiftly as it appears.

An hour later, they were on the road, the old

lady having packed and presented herself at the carriage within twenty minutes. Here was the part of this endeavor Hawk dreaded most, spending three hours in a confined space sitting across from the woman who'd cheated him out of happiness.

She snored softly, having closed her eyes after twenty minutes of polite silence. He studied her as she slept, the multiple webs of fine lines marking every surface of her face. The brown aging spots. The perpetual frown she wore even in sleep. What had this woman seen in her lifetime?

"You don't like me." She startled him by opening her eyes to stare straight into his.

Hawk was too polite to agree but also wasn't about to deny the truth. "It shouldn't be too long now before we reach Briar Hall."

"I told her to forget you," she said matter-of-factly in heavily accented English. "But she no listen."

The carriage felt suffocatingly small. He needed air. Talking about personal matters with the woman who helped ruin his life was the last thing he could stomach. It was bad enough that being around Naila resurrected feelings in him that were best kept buried.

And then it hit him. *Naila hadn't forgotten him?* What did the old lady mean by that?

"Did Miss Naila tell you that she hasn't forgotten me?"

She shrugged. "She did her duty."

"I know all about duty," he said bitterly. He was an earl, responsible for vast lands and servants and tenants. His *life* was duty.

"Man's duty is different from girl's duty," she said. "If she go against her family and you turn out to be bad, what happens to her? She has no life. No good."

"What kind of life does she have now?" he shot back. "A life in service to others? Looking after other people's children? Nursing sick relatives? Playing the piano so that others might dance? Is that a good life?"

"She's a good girl," she answered, as if that's all that mattered.

"Doesn't she deserve better? She could be married and have children of her own."

She shrugged. "Her *naseeb* didn't be coming yet."

"Her what?"

"The man destiny send for to be her husband," she explained. "Her *naseeb*."

The words scalded him. "Maybe he already came but you sent him away."

She scrutinized him. He shifted uncomfortably under her beady gaze. It felt like she could see right through to the inside of him. "You still be wanting her."

He stiffened. "I didn't say that."

She scowled. More than usual. "Why you wanting her for? Naila, she too old now. You be needing young girl, like Hind. She give you healthy sons."

"I wasn't good enough for Naila, but now I'm good enough for her cousin?" He waited for the old lady to admit to being a fortune hunter. "This wasn't about Naila marrying her own kind, was it? It was all about the money."

She didn't bother to deny it. Nor did she appear affronted. "How much money you having?"

"Plenty. I gather being wealthy makes a man acceptable?" Contempt laced each syllable. "Does Mr. Amar have enough money to satisfy you?"

"Kareem is not rich," she said. "But he be good match for Naila. He educated and from a good Arab family."

"I see." Not that he'd needed it, but here was confirmation that the family championed such a match.

"Naila is daughter of good family," she continued. "We don't be giving her to boy with no future. In Philadelphia, we don't know you. We don't know your family. We know nothing about you. If you turn out to be bad husband, what happen to our daughter? If you have no money, what happen to our daughter? She have hard life."

He looked away from her. Staring out the window at the countryside rolling by them. It wasn't so different, was it, from the English way of doing things? Young ladies married for money and security. For titles, too. He knew that firsthand.

In England, everyone knew he came from a well-established family because he was a distant cousin to an earl. In America, they'd have no one to ask, no way of knowing for sure. They could have inquired of his uncle in Philadelphia, but how many uncles would speak poorly of their relation?

Would Auntie Majida have reacted differently had they known his family? Before he could ask her, a quiet snore rumbled through the carriage. She'd fallen back asleep. Guilt certainly wasn't keeping the old lady awake. Auntie Majida sounded so sure, so secure in the decision she'd forced upon Naila.

For the first time in many years, Hawk began to consider the situation differently. The old lady had done what she thought was right by her niece. He might even be able to forgive her, not that she seemed to care what he thought. He understood now that Auntie Majida truly believed she'd done her best.

His gut panged. But Naila should have known better.

Chapter Twenty

Before
Philadelphia

Naila stared at the bracelet on her wrist, admiring the way the gold caught the sun. She ran a finger over its single pearl adornment. "It's the most beautiful thing anyone has ever given me."

"You like it then?" Basil asked. "I wanted to get something that matches your other bracelets."

It fit perfectly with her thin gold bangles. She gave him a shy look. "Thank you."

He smiled broadly. "It was my pleasure." He looked happy, excited even, despite the fact that she was going back to New York in a few days.

She sniffed. "If I didn't know better, I'd think you are happy to be rid of me."

He pulled her to him. Her body immediately alerted to the feel of her softness against the sharper planes of his athletic form. "I won't let you go."

She sighed, burying her face into his neck, inhaling the scents of him—shaving soap on warm skin. "I wish we could stay like this always."

"We can," he insisted.

"But how?" She was unable to bear the thought of saying goodbye to him in a few days. The idea of a looming future without Basil, of returning to her old life in New York, felt empty and pointless.

"I will take care of everything. I have been asking your cousin Eyad about your people's ways. I will approach your father with the utmost respect and care."

Alarm rippled through her. "You've told Eyad?"

"No, I've just asked questions about your family's customs and ways of doing things."

"It won't matter how much you learn. We don't accept outsiders for marriage."

"There has to be a way. It might be difficult in the beginning but we will make it through."

Clinging to him, Naila almost believed it could be true. To think otherwise was too devastating to contemplate. The bracelet on her wrist made a future together feel real somehow. Was the impossible really possible? Could she have Basil and her family?

She pressed herself against him, wanting to meld herself to him so that no one could ever pry them apart. She felt the manly part of him harden against her belly.

"Naila." His voice was low and rough.

"You feel so good," she said wistfully. "When

you hold me like this I believe we can be together forever."

He gently put her away from him. "We can be. I know I should wait until I have your father's permission but—"

She peered into his grave face. "Yes?"

He took both of her hands in his. She was not a small woman but her hands looked impossibly delicate compared to his. "Will you, Miss Naila Darwish, do me the great honor of agreeing to be my wife?"

"You know it's impossible," she cried, her heart breaking. "Why would you push me on this?"

"Because what we have is worth fighting for. I love you. With all my heart." His eyes locked with hers. "But maybe you don't feel the same?"

She hadn't wanted to let herself admit it. Even as she'd warned Basil not to get too attached, she'd fallen deeply and irretrievably in love with the man. "I do love you," she admitted, coming to an important realization. "I can't imagine my life without you in it."

"I'll be by your side every step of the way," he said urgently. "If it takes a lifetime, I will win over your family. When they see how right we are for each other, they will accept our marriage."

He gave her such strength. Naila did feel she could do just about anything with Basil by her side. Surely her family wouldn't banish her for following her heart. They couldn't stay angry forever.

"Say you'll do it," Basil said. "Promise to stay by my side until we are old and gray. I promise my undying loyalty to you."

She let out a shuddering sigh, still racked with tension and worry about her family's reaction. But she also knew, in that moment, that her life would be meaningless if she let Basil go. "Yes." Her eyes teared. "Yes, yes, yes. I will marry you."

He laughed, swinging her up into his arms, and she was laughing, too, with both relief and excitement. She'd made the decision and she would never change her mind. There was no other way. She finally admitted the truth to herself. She couldn't live without Basil. It wouldn't be easy to convince her family, but she would keep the faith with Basil, no matter how long it took.

He stared into her eyes. "May I kiss my bride to be?"

"Why not?" she said coquettishly. "After all, I am practically your wife."

He swept her up in his arms, kissing her deeply, his tongue exploring her mouth, deep soulful drugging kisses that ratcheted up her body in a way that made her squirm.

Suddenly, she was very afraid. If she lost Basil, she wouldn't be able to go on. But everything was against them. Everyone in their lives would do their best to tear them away from each other.

She wanted to be inside his skin. She wanted

him inside of her. To truly be one together. "Love me like a wife," she whispered into his ear.

He stiffened. "Naila, surely you don't mean—"

"I do. Make me your wife in the way that counts. If we are truly committed to each other, let's go past the point of no return." If she did this with him, she could never lose her courage, they would be truly bonded. Forever.

"Not here. In a park, up against a tree. It wouldn't be right."

She put his hand to her breast. Pressed it there. "Please," she said. "Now."

He led her instead to a soft place hidden in a copse of trees and surrounded by blooming flowers. He laid her gently on the bed of grass and kissed her softly, opening his mouth over hers. Their tongues tangled in a love dance. "You are going to be my wife," he murmured against her lips. "I suppose there's no real harm in anticipating our vows."

"Exactly," she breathed.

His fingers worked their way under her skirts to touch her intimately. She moaned in his mouth, their lips fused. When he entered her, it wasn't the physical pain and discomfort that she focused on, but the exquisite relief at having reached the point of no return.

"It is done now," he said softly as he pushed into her body. "Nothing can part us."

CHAPTER TWENTY-ONE

Now
England

"Why didn't you marry for money?" Naila asked her new brother-in-law, the Duke of Strickland. "You were deep in debt, weren't you?"

The duke chuckled. "Not the question I expected to be asked one week after my nuptials." He sipped his sherry. "I see that my bride isn't the only Darwish with a deep and abiding interest in money."

"I'm not at all interested in money," Naila informed him. "I am interested in what it can do."

Raya sat at a nearby table looking over some ledgers. "Isn't everyone?"

The three of them were in the upstairs sitting room at Strickland House, the duke's lavish townhome three days after Naila's arrival in London. Initial word from Briar Hall was that Hind was improving and Dr. Hughes remained optimistic about her recovery.

Naila paced over to the window, which overlooked one of the city's many tree-lined, tidy squares. She spotted Nadine's boys running and playing while Ghassan sat nearby keeping watch over them.

"These majestic homes that are being demolished are prime examples of period architecture." Naila turned from the window. "History is being lost."

"Times change," Strick said. "That way of life is disappearing."

"But you found a way to make it work," Naila said.

"To be fair, it was your sister's ideas that will take Castle Tremayne into the future."

"Why can't we do something like that for all of these treasures?"

Raya's lips twitched. "I cannot marry every lord in the land."

"You certainly cannot," Strick grumbled.

"There are some American heiresses marrying destitute lords and saving their estates," Naila said. "What if we facilitated more of that?"

Raya jotted something down in one of the ledgers. "In what way?"

Naila took a seat on the sofa across from the duke. "How are these matches made?"

"Word of mouth, I suppose," Strick said. "There are a few matrons in town who are connected to society but have limited resources, who discreetly accept payment for helping American heiresses land a lord."

Naila frowned. "That doesn't seem very efficient. A few women matchmakers are hardly sufficient to save enough of these jewels from being razed to the ground."

Raya closed a ledger. "It's not as if there is some catalog where heiresses can shop for impoverished lords."

Naila contemplated her sister's words. "But what if there was?" Possibility kindled inside her. "What if that's the solution?"

Raya exchanged a puzzled look with her husband. "What did I say?"

"What if there was such a guide? One that listed all the eligible lords in the land?" Naila warmed up to the idea as new elements of the plan came to her. "The catalog could contain information about each noble bachelor's assets and income."

Raya grinned at the duke. "And you accused me of being crass."

But the duke had a considering look on his face. "*Debrett's Peerage* is a social guide that details who's who in society," he said slowly, thinking it out. "Your sister's guide could be a useful accompaniment."

Raya's eyes widened. "You favor this idea?"

"What can I say?" he replied. "My business-minded bride has broadened my thinking."

Raya stared at him. "I can't believe you like the idea."

"You don't?" he returned.

"I don't know." Raya blinked. "I mean . . . I don't disapprove."

He sipped his sherry. "I do tire of seeing these once-grand homes fall into disrepair. If a guide like the one Naila envisions helps alleviate the problem, I don't see the harm."

Too excited to sit still, Naila got up and paced away from them. "I shall call it *An American Heiress's Guide to Landing a Lord*."

Strick chuckled. "Americans can never be accused of being subtle."

"Why be coy?" Naila asked. "This title is direct. No one can be confused about its purpose."

"That is for certain." Raya reached for another ledger. "Are you really going to do this?"

Was she? "Yes, I think so."

"You are definitely going to take London by storm," her sister said. "I can't wait."

"The only question is," Naila said with a frown, "how do I gather all the information that I will need for my book?"

"My sister is a leading society hostess." The duke finished the last of his sherry. "I shall put you in touch with her. Claire is wed to the second son of a marquess. She knows everyone and can direct you to the proper sources."

"That would be marvelous." The more she thought about her plan, the more Naila believed it could actually work. "To do this properly, I think I need to learn more about English customs and how aristocratic society works."

"Guy's sister, Frances, would be able to assist you," Raya said. "She was very helpful to me when I was trying to understand the role of a duchess."

The duke nodded. "Frances's manners are impeccable. She can teach Naila everything she desires to know about society and etiquette."

"I shall ask her then." Naila's mind raced. "And I need to make sure that the homes that are most threatened are featured prominently."

"Kareem can help you with that," Raya said. "Did he accompany you all to Town?"

Naila shook her head. "He has an aunt who lives in the village at Briar Hall. He is visiting with her for a few days."

Raya opened the next ledger. "That's unfortunate."

"But I will write to him asking that he send me a list of the most endangered properties to make sure they are included in my guide."

The duke set his glass down. "And I shall send a note to my sister telling her that we shall all be calling on her soon."

"Thank you." Naila crossed over to the door to immediately go and write to Kareem to tell him of her new venture. She paused. "Strickland, you never said why you didn't marry for money in order to save Castle Tremayne."

"My parents married for money and status. It

was a very unhappy match. They were unsuited. I was determined not to repeat history."

Naila frowned. She hadn't thought of that. "I wouldn't want the people I help match to be unhappy."

Raya looked up from her work. "What if you added each eligible heir's likes and dislikes? That might help couples assess if they would be well suited."

Naila nodded. "That's an excellent idea." She paused, a moment of doubt. "Do you think people will use a guide like this?"

Raya laughed. "The American heiresses definitely will. It would be invaluable to have all of the information they need about landing a lord in one place."

"I shall make it known to my fellow noblemen that I see this as a worthy endeavor," the duke said.

"And that will make a difference?" Naila asked.

"Your brother-in-law is a duke," Raya reminded her. "People will want to please him. It makes no sense but that is how things work in London."

"And what about you?" the duke asked his wife. "Don't you want to please me?"

Raya blushed and picked up her pen. "I have work to do."

"Do you?" the duke asked in a way that reminded Naila that these two were still newlyweds.

"I must go and write to Kareem without delay." She escaped just as the duke advanced on her sister.

As she closed the door behind her, a servant came down the corridor bearing a tray of sandwiches and desserts. "Excuse me, miss," he said. "I've brought up tea for the duke and duchess."

The duke's deep murmur followed by Raya's laughter sounded through the closed door.

"I think"—Naila tried to hide her smile—"that His Grace would prefer that you return later."

HAWK AND NADINE joined them in London a week after Hind's fall.

"She is recovering," Hawk informed the duke and duchess after he and Nadine were shown to the upstairs sitting room. "She is awake and talking for most of the day."

"Thank goodness." Raya breathed a sigh of relief. "We were worried."

"I knew you would be eager for an update," Hawk said.

Hawk had escorted Nadine to Town to be reunited with her husband and children. He'd brought her directly to Carey House after enduring her ceaseless chatter for the entirety of the journey to London. The woman's husband was a saint.

"I was ready to come to London days ago." Nadine pouted. "But the earl preferred to delay our departure from Briar Hall."

Hawk suppressed a grimace. It was a marvel to him that Naila and Raya were Nadine's sisters. They couldn't be more different from her. "I came as soon as I was assured that Miss Hind was truly well. I wanted to be able to deliver a positive report."

"I was happy to nurse Hind," Nadine said with the air of a long-suffering martyr. "I missed the boys terribly. Being without them for even another hour was unbearable."

"Have you seen the boys yet?" Raya asked.

"Hmm?" Nadine reached for another delicate tea sandwich. "Not yet. I'll go and find them after I finish my tea. I missed them so much."

"Thank you for bringing us good news," Raya said to Hawk, "and for being kind enough to escort Nadine to London."

"It was my pleasure." Not that Nadine had given him much choice.

"Naila will be very happy to hear your news," Raya said.

He wondered where Naila was. She remained out of sight for the next several days, missing all of the entertainments, whether it was a meal at Carey House or a party they all attended. She also skipped excursions to see the sights in London. By the start of the second week, Hawk began to suspect that Naila was avoiding him.

But he did not ask about her. He needed to put his thoughts elsewhere.

Hind was finally considered well enough to travel and arrived in London one week after Hawk and Nadine. Courtesy required that Hawk call on Carey House to check on the girl since she'd been injured on his watch. He expected to see Naila there.

"I hope you are fully recovered, Miss Hind," he said after being shown to the sitting room, where the family had gathered. The two boys were at the round table playing cards, with their parents sitting nearby. Strick, Raya, and Auntie Majida sat in closer proximity to the patient.

"Thank you, my lord." The girl's face had thinned due to some weight loss during her convalescence, but she looked well enough to him. Hind smiled in the direction of her aunt. "The doctor says I am on the mend. Auntie Majida saw to that."

"I am most relieved to hear it." He greeted the scowling older woman. "Mrs. Kassab, I trust you were comfortable at Briar Hall."

"Your house, very big," she told him.

"Yes, it is."

"Very beautiful."

"Thank you." They seemed to have reached a sort of rapprochement, a cessation of hostilities, but they were far from friends. While the women chatted, Hawk and Strick ended up taking their tea near the windows overlooking the street.

"What keeps you in town?" Strick asked,

knowing that Hawk spent most of his time visiting his various estates.

"I am overseeing a renovation of the mews at Trevelyn House," he answered, referring to his London townhome. "I need to be in residence to make certain it is done to my specifications."

"I see. I thought it might be a certain young lady who was keeping you here."

Hawk shot him a surprised look. "You do know that while I find Miss Hind to be charming, I am not interested in her for marriage." He spoke in hushed tones so that the others in the room would not overhear. "She is too young for my tastes."

"I wasn't speaking of Hind," Strick murmured back.

Movement outside the window caught Hawk's attention. It was Naila, accompanied by Kareem, approaching the entrance to Carey House. Her high-necked, close-fitting gown barely contained her curvaceous form. Its vibrant shade of violet suggested that she continued to eschew muted colors. His heart sped up a little. He hadn't seen Naila in weeks. He shouldn't be eager to be in her company, but he was.

"Don't be ridiculous," he said to the duke while straining to hear the pair's muffled voices sounding from the foyer. How much time was Naila spending with Kareem?

He hated the anticipation, the pleasure, that

rushed through his blood at the thought of seeing her again. Suddenly, he was thrust back in time, once again the excited pup who fell so hard he could think of nothing and no one else. He tried not to stare at the door, to pretend he wasn't waiting for her to walk through it.

"Do you think?" Strick asked.

Hawk blinked. "I beg your pardon." What question had he missed?

"You are awfully distracted all of the sudden." Strick glanced toward the door. "One cannot help but wonder why."

Hawk ignored the comment. What was taking Naila so long to make her appearance? Then it hit him. Maybe she and Kareem preferred to be alone together. He shot a look at Auntie Majida, who'd watched him with an eagle eye whenever he'd been with Naila in Philadelphia. But, at the moment, she was perched complacently on the sofa chatting with the others.

Hawk dropped all pretense. "She's avoiding me."

"Who? Naila? No, she isn't."

"How do you know that?"

"She is working on a new project that is taking all her time and attention."

"Is that so?" he replied skeptically. "And is this *project* named Kareem?"

Strick chuckled. "No, but Kareem is helping her. I believe she's titled her project *An American Heiress's Guide to Landing a Lord*."

"What the devil are you talking about?"

"She's writing a guide for American heiresses who want to attract aristocrats."

"What?" he burst out. "That's ludicrous."

"I think it will sell quite well."

"A guide to landing a lord?" he scoffed. "She's hardly an expert on the matter."

"I beg to differ." The duke's eyes glittered. "She certainly knows how to get you all worked up."

"You really are tiresome. How had I not noticed that before?" Hawk stood and addressed the ladies. "Thank you for your hospitality but I must go."

"So soon?" Raya asked.

"I have a building project underway at Trevelyn House that I must oversee."

"Everyone seems to have a project these days," the duke said.

FEELING EXCITED AND energized, Naila left the library to retrieve some notes from her bedchamber. She was spending all her time on the first draft of her guide, which was coming along nicely.

Kareem, who'd arrived in London the previous day, was committed to identifying the historic structures most in need saving, and Strick's sister, Lady Claire, was proving very helpful in sorting out who was who in London society.

Naila spent several afternoons with Guy's sister, Frances, learning etiquette, some of which confounded her. How guests were expected to remove their gloves as soon as they sat down to dinner. And that small talk should never include topics of substance that might lead to genuine discussion. Also, when crossing a muddy street, a lady should lift her skirt with her right hand because using both hands was vulgar.

As Naila crossed over to the staircase, the door to the sitting room opened and Hawk came out wearing a dark tailored suit that was cut to perfection around his strong athletic form.

"Good day," he said, his tone cool and distant.

Her heart leapt, which it definitely had no business doing. "My lord."

"Your cousin appears to be recovering nicely."

"Yes, it is such a relief."

"You seem to be occupied these days."

"I am working on a new project."

"So I have heard." Disdain stamped his face. "Are you really writing a book instructing American heiresses on how to land a lord?"

"It's actually going to be a pamphlet," she told him. "It's an excellent idea, don't you think?"

He bristled. "You must do as you wish."

She registered his rigid stance and the hard set of his mouth. "But you object to the idea."

"It is not my place to object." His expression remained inscrutable. "I have no claim over you or your pursuits."

"No, you don't," she agreed. "But I am still interested in knowing why you seem so agitated."

"You would not appreciate my perspective."

"I assure you that I would."

"Very well. Since you insist, I find monetizing marriage, commodifying it, to be . . . unseemly."

"I am bringing together two parties who need each other."

"Need? It becomes clear to me why I wasn't good enough back then," he said coldly. "I now understand why we didn't work. For you, marriage is all about money."

"How is what I am suggesting any different than what you English have been doing for centuries?" she shot back. "Do you not match people based on their bank accounts?"

"No, not entirely. In society, suitable matches do involve funds but they are based on family lineage, on tradition."

"Tradition? That sounds like someone who is intent on maintaining the status quo."

That certainly explained why now, as an earl, Hawk held himself back from sharing his true feelings, whatever they might be. He kept his emotions so tightly buried, he probably had no idea how he truly felt.

Despite the moments of understanding and connection at Briar Hall, the distance between them again felt unbreachable. The chemistry between them remained strong. But did they have anything else in common anymore?

"What really bothers you is that I am proposing muddying the blood lines," she snapped. "Isn't that right?"

"No." His beautiful mouth twitched with annoyance. "You couldn't be more wrong."

"What's so great about aristocratic blood?" she asked. "Your ancestors didn't even build these palaces. It was the poor, the impoverished, the people who actually worked the land who built these masterpieces."

"What is your point?"

"My point is that these houses can be saved," she shot back, irked by his displeasure. Who was he to judge her? "I don't care who these lords marry. It could be the daughter of a man born in a gutter and why not? At least her father will have worked hard to make his place in society while men like you, who've done nothing to earn your place, wear fancy suits and look down on everyone else."

"Your speech about the poor and downtrodden is very inspiring, but these heiresses are neither," he said dryly. "You've made it clear that marriage is a business transaction that has nothing to do with feelings."

"That is no different from how the English have arranged marriages in the past, based on what each party brings to the match."

"And what does Mr. Amar bring to a match with you?"

She frowned. "Kareem? What are you talking about?"

"He clearly helps you see color in the world again." He cast a look down her body. "The drab gowns are a thing of the past. Do you dress in brilliant shades for him?"

Her cheeks burned at the way he assessed her. And from the jealousy she detected in his tone. Despite doing her best to avoid him since leaving Briar Hall, need for him flared. "I dress for me."

"Do you?" he said softly.

She tipped her head back. "You must leave me alone. We have to leave each other in peace."

"I don't have peace," he growled. "Do you have peace?"

"It's too much." Tears stung her eyes. She hadn't had peace in eight years. She backed away from him, finding herself in an alcove under the stairs. "I can't do this any longer."

He looked stricken. "Don't cry." He used his thumb to brush away the tear that had fallen.

His touch branded her. Instead being a comfort, the skin-to-skin contact ignited a wildfire across her face, down her neck. Sensation stirred in her breasts and deeper still in the lowest recesses of her belly. "Inglese," she whispered, half-terrified by this pull between them.

His gaze burned through her. "Naila." And

then he slammed his lips down on hers, kissing her, hard and demanding. And it was like a huge sigh of relief for her body, as if she'd been waiting for this, for him, forever.

His tongue was in her mouth, entwining with hers. She hugged him closer. She was covered practically from head to toe, as was he, when all she craved was more skin-to-skin contact.

As their mouths took and gave, the kiss deepening, she got lost in the feel of him. Basil was kissing her again. Finally. After all these years, she was a starving woman finally being fed. But she wanted, she needed, more. She clutched at him, bringing him closer still. His member was hard and full against her belly and she relished it. She reached between them to feel his hardness with her fingers, stroking and rubbing, wishing she could free him and feel his member, big and throbbing against her palm.

He gasped at her touch, groaning into her mouth. She felt air around her legs. He was lifting her skirt. She hooked one leg around his and cried out when his fingers found her most private area, spreading the moisture he found there over her folds, until his fingers came to the place that answered her body's call. He moved his fingers around the bundle of nerves that heightened everything. She squirmed from the intensely delicious sensations. She threw her head back. "Oh!"

He continued to apply his fingers in urgent and gentle movements. He watched her now, absorbing the expression on her face.

"So beautiful," he half-groaned, his mouth sucking her throat.

"Oh, oh!" She tried to control her body but she'd completely lost herself. She began to tremble; pleasure seized her legs and rushed through her body. She cried out as the sensation ripped through her, but his mouth found hers, muffling the sound, catching her pleasure.

After, they stood there, draped around each other, their heavy breaths intermingled, faces buried in the crook of each other's neck. Hawk half-held her up because her legs seemed incapable of doing their job. She inhaled him, the scent of his skin, his shaving soap, trying to imprint it in her memory again.

Hawk suddenly pulled away. In her dazed state, she wanted to protest, to pull him back to her so she could continue burrowing into his warmth. She'd waited eight years for this. She wasn't ready for it to end.

His eyes ran over her. Scrutinizing her? He quickly tucked a strand of hair behind her ear and shook out the hem of her dress, straightening the folds of her skirt. Then he turned away and was gone.

Naila blinked. What was that? Had he just used her up against the wall like he might some trollop he found on the street? Impulsively, she went after him. To do what, she didn't know. Maybe to punch him in the face.

She stopped abruptly when she caught sight of the Duke of Strickland standing in the front hall staring at Hawk.

"I thought you'd left," the duke said.

Hawk cleared his throat. "I'm just on my way out now."

The duke's attention darted to Naila. She flushed under his scrutiny, afraid of what she must look like. "Are you well?" he asked.

She could not meet his gaze. "Quite well."

"Hawk," he asked, a warning in his tone, "would you care to explain?"

"No." Hawk held the duke's gaze.

"There's nothing to explain," Naila interjected, her voice a little squeaky.

"Miss Darwish was just on her way to rejoin Mr. Amar to work on her pamphlet," Hawk said.

"Yes. That's right." He'd thrown her a lifeline. She gratefully grabbed it. Even though it meant running out on Hawk yet again. "If you'll excuse me, Kareem is waiting."

Holding her head high, pretending nothing was amiss, Naila escaped.

CHAPTER TWENTY-TWO

Before
Philadelphia

"Intee mejnoona?" Auntie Majida scowled. "You must have lost your senses."

"I love him," Naila said, even as fear shivered through her. "We want to be married as soon as possible."

Majida shot her a suspicious look. "Love? *Shu hadha?* What is that?" She blew a quick raspberry. "There is no such thing."

If auntie really believed that romantic love didn't exist, Naila felt sorry for her. Everyone should have a chance to love someone the way she loved Basil. She was still floating after lying with him. Memories of the way he'd touched her, making her body feel things she could never have imagined, made her cheeks burn.

Auntie Majida narrowed her eyes. "How did you have time to fall in love?" She said the "fall in love" part sarcastically.

Naila avoided her aunt's gaze. "I've seen him at various places . . . assemblies, the bookstore."

She was a terrible liar and Auntie knew it.

"*Kezzaba*." Liar. "When do you see him? *Wain shuftee?*"

"What difference does it make?" Naila asked, instead of answering her aunt's question. "He's been nothing but a gentleman." Not technically true, but Basil was a true gentleman in the realest sense of the word. He treated her like she was the most precious thing in the world. "And now he wants to marry me."

"*Gentleman?*" her aunt repeated sarcastically, making a clicking noise with her tongue. "A respectable boy doesn't sneak around with a girl from a good family. You *are* still a girl?"

Naila flushed. *A girl* meant "a virgin." Once a female was no longer innocent, she became a woman. "Of course," she lied, crossing her fingers in the folds of her skirts.

She told herself that it didn't make any difference because she would soon be married. What did it matter if she and Inglese had anticipated their vows? She didn't regret what they'd done. In fact, she couldn't wait to do it again. Again and again.

"What is that smile?" Auntie Majida growled.

Naila immediately adopted a somber expression. She hadn't realized she was smiling. She couldn't help smiling whenever she thought of her future husband. "He's going to write to Baba and ask to court me."

Auntie shook her head, disbelief all over her face. "*Intee mejnoona*," Majida declared. Holding her hand horizontally in front of her mouth, she clamped her teeth along the side of her pointer finger.

Fear flushed through Naila. Side finger biting was saved for the most serious of offenses, for unthinkable misconduct. Which, of course, Naila was guilty of. Although she'd never admit it to anyone, least of all her aunt.

"You're going to kill your father," Auntie said.

"He might be surprised at first," Naila said. "But once he meets Basil, he will love him."

"*Yee*." A sound that expressed shock, surprise and dismay. "You're too *jahla*. It's your parents' fault."

Naila bit her tongue. She was anything but innocent. Especially after the previous afternoon.

"*Behree*." Auntie's tone grew confidential, which caused alarm to streak up Naila's spine. "You need to know something."

"*Shoo?*" Naila asked. "What is it?"

"*Ihlifee*. Swear that you won't say anything. I'm not supposed to tell you."

"*Wallah* I won't say anything. Tell me."

"Your Baba is sick."

"How do you mean?" Concern welled inside her. "He was fine when we left New York."

"He doesn't want to worry you girls but it's his heart."

"What's wrong with Baba's heart?"

"He has disease in his heart. Dr. Ahmed said your father must be calm. He must not have any upsets."

Naila shook her head. "That's not true, is it?" It couldn't be.

"Why do you think he's working less and napping more?"

"He said he wanted to spend more time with Mama." Baba had suffered a few episodes of chest pain. And he was taking it easier these days. But Naila assumed Baba was easing back so that Raya and Salem, her brother and sister, could step up and learn to run the family linen business on their own. Had he really been preparing them all for a future without him?

Tears stung Naila's eyes. "It can't be true."

"It is true," Majida returned. "So put away this *haki fathee*, this empty talk of marrying this *ajnabee*, this foreigner, because that would kill your father."

Chapter Twenty-Three

Now
England

"Do I need to challenge you?" Strickland spoke lightly but Hawk registered the menace in his friend's voice. "Must Miss Darwish's honor be defended?"

It's about eight years too late for that, Hawk was tempted to retort. But he couldn't get his thoughts in order. He was too full of Naila, of her scent and her skin, the taste of her, the feel of her, the way she cried out when she climaxed.

If only she'd stayed hidden in the alcove. Hawk had barely been able to pull away from her when he heard the door to the sitting room open. He'd hoped to spare her any indignity before she'd emerged, cheeks flushed, mouth swollen from his kisses. With her slightly ruffled hair and gown a bit askew, Hawk knew exactly what Strick correctly deduced.

"Surely," the duke said tightly, "you have not forgotten that you are in my house and that my wife's sister is under my protection."

Hawk adjusted his frock coat, grateful that it hid his aching erection. Still, he angled slightly away from Strick, just in case. "I have not forgotten."

"Then what are you doing?" Strick spoke sharply. "It's one thing to pine away for a respectable woman. It's another to actually lay your hands on her."

Hawk hesitated. To admit to touching Naila would damage her reputation. "I don't know what you're talking about."

"If you're not going to marry her, leave her alone. I cannot, and will not, stand for anything less."

Hawk gave a mirthless huff. "If you'll recall, I did try to marry her."

"Given the circumstances, perhaps you should try again."

"I don't need you telling me how to conduct my life," Hawk bit out, still unable to put his thoughts in order. He needed at least a few minutes to unravel the potential ramifications of those stolen moments in the alcove. What he really wanted to do at the moment was to savor them and replay them over and over in his mind.

"Someone needs to talk some sense into you."

The door to the sitting room opened and Raya came out. She stopped in surprise when she spotted them. "Hawk," she said with a smile, "I thought you'd gone."

Strick kept his focus on Hawk. "As did I."

Her smile faltered as she looked between the two men. "Is everything all right?"

"Of course." Hawk forced an easy tone. "I was just leaving."

"Not so fast." The duke stepped toward him. Hawk braced himself. "I'm not done speaking with you."

Alarm lit Raya's face. "What is going on here?"

"Nothing at all," her husband said smoothly. "The earl and I need to have a word." Hawk allowed himself to be directed into the nearest chamber.

"Strick?" Raya called after them with concern in her eyes.

"There's nothing to worry about," her husband assured her, closing the door on her worried face. He turned to Hawk.

"Are you about to attempt to thrash me?" Hawk asked.

"Do I need to? Or are you going to explain yourself?"

"Are you saying you never touched your wife before marriage?" Hawk snapped back.

Strick gritted his teeth. "That is none of your business. My sister-in-law, however, is my business."

"That's very convenient."

"Raya is my duchess," he ground out. "That's the difference. I married her. Do you plan to do the same?"

"I've always wanted to marry Naila," Hawk said. "You know that."

"Did you just now force her to do something she did not want to do?"

"Of course not!" He spat the words. "How could you even ask that?"

"If she enjoyed your attentions, I suspect she'll embrace a new proposal."

"It's more complicated than that."

"Is it? You want her. She clearly welcomes your attentions. Maybe it's simple. Perhaps you are complicating matters."

Hawk exhaled, rubbing both of his eyes. "It's all very confusing."

"It's obvious to anyone with eyes that you care for her."

Hawk slumped into a chair. "She rejected me when I had nothing."

Strick stared down at him. "So you've repeatedly said."

"Now, if she accepts me as an earl with full pockets, what does that say?"

"What does it matter?" the duke asked impatiently. "You two obviously want each other. And now there is nothing standing in your way."

The duke was correct. Any of the debutantes on the marriage mart obviously wanted Hawk for his fortune and title. He'd accepted that title hunting was part of the London marriage mart.

But when it came to Naila, he wanted, expected, demanded, more. Maybe it was ludicrous but Hawk needed Naila to love him for him and not for the titles and fortune she'd rightfully pointed out that he'd done nothing to earn.

She was the only thing in his life that made Hawk feel out of control. Being with her was always going to feel like walking on the edge of a cliff. When he was in Naila's company, nothing else in the world existed for him. Still. After all this time. Even after the way she'd devastated him.

His hands were clammy, his heart thumping too hard. No one caused him distress like Naila. He'd taken her innocence long ago and even that hadn't stopped her from rejecting him. Their brief rendezvous in Strick's foyer didn't compare to the gravity of actually bedding a virgin. Naila had thrown her honor, and his, aside when she reneged on her promise to marry him. Hawk could barely call himself a gentleman after that.

And now he was supposed to place himself in a situation to repeat that soul-shattering scene. To risk being tossed aside yet again. He struggled to think rationally. It was past time to stop behaving like a young buck ruled by his prick.

He wanted Naila, yes.

Badly.

But those were the carnal desires of the boy

he used to be. He was a man now. He needed to make sound, adult decisions. Hawk let out a long sigh. He knew what he had to do. There was only one way to proceed to resolve matters with Naila once and for all.

ON THE WAY to her bedchamber, Naila asked a footman to inform Kareem that she had a headache and would not be able to work for the rest of the afternoon.

She certainly couldn't focus on her project. Not after what had just happened with Hawk. She wanted to be alone to replay it all in her mind. The taste of him, the sensations, the physical feel of him pressed up against her. Triumph flashed through her. Hawk might pretend not to care but he still desired her and was finally willing to show it.

She closed her eyes and leaned back against the bedchamber door, resting a hand across her chest. Her heart beat wildly against her palm. It hadn't been subjected to this kind of excitement in years.

Inglese definitely had a defter touch now. The things he'd done with his fingers! He knew exactly how to touch a woman. Eight years ago, there'd been the same desire and excitement, terrific pleasure, but ultimately less skill.

A knock at the door startled her.

"Naila?" It was Raya. "Are you in there?"

"Yes, I have a bit of a headache," she answered. "I'm going to take a nap."

"No, you're not!" She rapped more insistently. "Let me in."

Naila rolled her eyes. When her sister got like this, there was no putting her off. She turned and unlatched the door. Raya strode right in. "Are you okay?"

"Of course." Naila shut the door and leaned back against it. "Why wouldn't I be?"

"Strick is worried about you. He asked me to make sure you're well."

Naila's cheeks flamed. How much did the duke know?

"Why are you so red?" Raya demanded to know. "What did the earl do to you?"

"Well." She couldn't help grinning. "It wasn't what he did to me. It was more like what we did to each other."

"What?" Raya's eyes rounded. "I thought you were interested in Kareem!"

"Kareem is a friend. Hawk is . . . is." She searched for the right words. "It's always been Hawk."

"What do you mean *always*?"

"Since Philadelphia."

"You?" Raya slapped her hand over her mouth. "*You're* the girl from America who broke Hawk's heart?"

"Hawk told you about that?"

Raya shook her head. "I get the impression that

Hawk hasn't told anyone precisely what happened. But Strick says Hawk came back a changed man after his trip to Philadelphia. Whatever happened there took a terrible toll on him."

Guilt stabbed Naila. "Auntie Majida convinced me that it was a bad match. That we didn't know Hawk's family and he had no money. She told me about Baba's heart condition and said it would kill him if I went through with marrying Basil. I've regretted my decision ever since."

Raya plopped down on the bed. "I had no idea." She narrowed her eyes at her sister. "That was *years* ago. Why didn't you tell me?"

"I just couldn't." Tears stung her eyes as she thought back to that time, the hardest in her life. "I was afraid I would fall apart if I talked about Hawk and that I'd never be able to put myself back together. Rejecting Hawk was like ripping my own heart out. I had to try to block him out, to pretend he didn't exist. It was the only way I could survive."

"Huh." Raya seemed to still be processing the revelation. "And then . . . the boy of little means and unknown family became an earl."

"I was stunned when I saw him at your pre-wedding ball."

Raya frowned. "But he barely pays you any mind."

"I noticed," she said dryly. "I thought he was completely over me but when he kissed me downstairs—"

"He *kissed* you?" Raya interrupted. "Where? When?"

"I ran into him in the front hallway. We had some words because he is offended by my pamphlet idea and its purpose."

"It's none of his business."

"That's exactly what I told him. Anyhow, before I knew it we were in the alcove under the stairs kissing."

"How was it?"

She sank down on the bed next to her sister. "It made my head spin."

"In a good way?"

"In the very best way. I felt it down to my toes."

Raya clapped her hands together. "This is fabulous! Now you and Hawk can be married and you'll stay in England. Our estates are only a few hours apart."

Feeling giddy, Naila laughed and flopped back on the bed. "I think you are getting ahead of yourself."

"Am I? Strick mentioned that Hawk said something about making things right."

"Did he?" She didn't dare get her hopes up. "I think it's too early to assume Hawk is ready to propose."

"Do you want to marry him?"

Naila took a deep breath and finally admitted, out loud, what she'd dreamed of for eight long years. "I don't think I've ever wanted anything more."

HAWK SENT NAILA a note the following day asking for a moment alone. Excitement bubbled up in her. He was going to propose. She just knew it. Why else would he ask to see her alone?

Obviously, the kiss yesterday had brought it all back. Now neither of them could deny that the pull between them still shone as brightly, and maybe even more intensely, than ever. Time had deepened their feelings, rather than diminishing them.

She took care with her appearance, wearing her thick wavy hair in a half-up style she felt Hawk would appreciate. She selected one of her favorite vibrant dresses, a sparkling emerald-green silk.

Anticipation fluttering through her veins, Naila smiled at her reflection in the mirror. She finally looked like herself again, her eyes bright and shiny, her lips twisted into an expectant smile. The old Naila was back. She was ready to take charge of her life and that meant saying a resounding yes when Hawk came to reclaim her. After eight years, they were finally going to get it right.

It was almost time for Hawk to arrive, so Naila rushed downstairs to be ready to receive him. He made his appearance exactly on time. Like her, he was dressed for the occasion in a handsome mazarine-blue tailcoat over a snowy shirt with a high winged color. His trousers were a gray pinstripe. She almost sighed at how handsome he looked. And how lucky she was that he was finally going to be hers.

Hawk glanced over at her and she swore she saw appreciation there before he averted his eyes. She smiled to herself as he followed her into the back garden where they could speak in private. She'd waited years to have this conversation and wanted no distractions or interruptions.

Naila plucked a gorgeous velvety flower off a bush. Everything was especially beautiful this afternoon. She brought the flower up to her nose and inhaled deeply, savoring its natural perfume. "This feels as if we're coming full circle."

"Does it?" he said stiffly. He kept his distance from her. Strange. Maybe he was nervous? "How so?"

"We first met in a garden. Surely you haven't forgotten," she teased. "I don't suppose you happen to have cigarettes with you?"

He didn't smile. Instead, Hawk cleared his throat. "Thank you for taking the time to see me."

Naila's pulse spiked. This *was* it. He was going to declare himself. She sank on a bench and resettled her skirts to present a pleasing picture. This time, she would accept him as she should have done so many years ago. "Of course. Why would I not?"

He cleared his throat. "It is very important that we speak as openly as possible to settle certain matters between us."

His tone was so cool, so impervious. Disappointment tightened between her shoulder blades.

Where was the old Basil, the man she knew intimately, who spoke easily from his heart?

He was such a remote presence at the moment. Still, she had to be right about their future. After yesterday's encounter, there was no denying what that their future held. Hawk was her *naseeb*, the man destiny intended for her.

She was determined to remind him. "Certain matters?" she said with a coy smile. "Is that what you call our kiss yesterday?"

"Yes, in a manner a speaking. I wish to apologize."

Her brows lowered. "Apologize?"

"Indeed." He stood soldier straight with his hands clasped behind his back. "I took grievous advantage of you yesterday."

Naila scoffed. "We both know that is not true." He said nothing, merely continued to stand there, so she added, "We are both adults and we were both willing. More than willing."

"I am relieved that you feel that way." His manner remained stilted. "We can agree, I hope, that neither of us should feel forced into a situation that neither of us wants."

"Absolutely," she said hesitantly. Where was he going with this?

"I think it's fair to say we both lost our heads yesterday. A temporary lapse in judgment."

Naila blinked. "A lapse in judgment," she repeated dully.

"Precisely. One that will not happen again."

She cocked her head. *"That's* what you came here to say?"

"Yes, of course. What were you expecting?"

She felt lightheaded. Not only was Hawk not proposing, he clearly never had any intention to do so. His words from the alcove reverberated in her mind.

I don't have peace. Do you have peace?

None of this made sense. The way he'd touched her, kissed her. She'd felt how much he'd missed her. How much he wanted her. And now he was claiming it was all just a lapse in judgment?

She narrowed her eyes at him. "Yesterday, when you kissed me, can you honestly say that you felt nothing?"

His expression remained unchanged. "You're a desirable woman. It is obvious there is a physical attraction between us."

"It was more than that," she insisted. "We have an emotional connection." *An unbreakable bond.*

"Once, perhaps. But we were young and that was a long time ago."

Her jaw fell open. "And you have no feelings left for me at all?"

"We are friends, I suppose."

Friends.

Now he was outright insulting her. "You suppose?" She leapt to her feet. "You're lying. You're trying to hurt me because of the way I abandoned you in Philadelphia. You still haven't forgiven me."

"I don't believe you have ever asked for my forgiveness," he said. "And even though some things might be forgivable, they are still impossible to get past."

"You are determined to continue my punishment," she said bitterly. "Even though I was a frightened young girl who knew nothing of the world and faced losing my family, my community and practically everything I held dear."

A muscle ticked in his jaw. "You would have gained *me*. And my unwavering love and devotion until the end of our days. But that wasn't enough."

She blinked back tears. "That wasn't it at all." She almost told him that she'd changed her mind and gone looking for him only to find he'd already sailed for England. But would he even believe her?

"What did you expect when I came here today? A proposal?" His lip curled. "So, I was not good enough for you when I was a man of no position or title. But now that I am an earl, you want to marry me?"

She stiffened. "How dare you accuse me of being some sort of greedy fortune hunter!" she snapped. "My feelings for you have nothing to do with your stupid title or bank account."

He took a deep fortifying breath. "I did not

come to upset you. I am here to rectify any misunderstandings between us after yesterday's unfortunate events."

Misunderstandings.

She sucked in a breath. The pain ripping through her body was so intense she had to resist the urge to double over. "I see."

And she did. He'd come this afternoon not to propose but to hurt her. To remind Naila that she was beneath his notice. His intention was to humiliate her.

She pulled her shoulders back. "I wouldn't want to be your countess anyway."

"Excellent. Then there is nothing further to discuss," he said. "We will put yesterday's regrettable lapse behind us."

"Yes, we will." She stared at him, wishing the agony in her chest would end. What a fool she was to imagine that he might still love her. A man who truly cared about a woman would never speak to her this way. He obviously had waited eight long years for the opportunity to wound her as deeply as she'd hurt him.

"Kareem is waiting for me," she lied. Lifting her chin, she pretended not to care even though it was all she could do not to collapse into a sobbing heap. "I have work to do on my pamphlet. You and I have wasted enough of each other's time."

"By all means," he said tightly. "Go back to

your architect friend." He gave her a quick stiff bow. "Good day, Miss Darwish.

"My lord," she said curtly.

"Well?" Raya said expectantly the minute Hawk reentered the house through the large French doors. She and Strick were seated in the formal salon obviously waiting for happy news.

Hawk suppressed a groan. He should have left via the garden and escaped through the alley. He had accomplished what needed to be done. In the process, he hurt Naila, which he regretted. But they were both better off now that everything was clear. They could go on with their lives, which for Hawk meant finding a suitable wife.

He would use his head this time, not his heart. Allowing emotions to rule his decision was the way to ruination. As for Naila, she already had the architect lined up. Jealousy curled in his stomach at the thought of Naila with another man. He pushed it aside. It was long past time to move on. When they were together, he and Naila catapulted each other's lives into a tailspin. That was no way to live.

"Good day," Hawk said.

"Good day?" Raya repeated. "Good day as in you're leaving?"

Curiosity lit Strick's eyes. "Have you and Miss Darwish come to an agreement?"

"Yes, we have," Hawk ground out. "We have agreed that we do not suit."

"Impossible," Raya exclaimed.

The duke's dark golden brows drew together. "Surely there's been a mistake."

"No mistake," Naila said as she came in behind Hawk. He avoided looking at her. "We have agreed that we do not suit. And never will."

"Agreed," he said.

The duchess looked crestfallen. "But I thought you two would suit beautifully."

"You were wrong," Naila told her.

Now that it was truly over with Naila, Hawk needed to be away from her. "Good day," he said again, marching for the door.

He strode through to the hallway, where a footman opened the door. As he trotted down the stairs to the street level, Strick called out to him.

"Hawk. Wait."

Hawk kept walking. He wanted nothing more than to put this afternoon behind him. Strick caught up. "What happened back there? You asked her to marry you and she said no?"

"She made it clear that she would not accept my proposal. She doesn't want to be a countess."

"But you did offer?"

"No, I did not."

A thunderous look came over the duke's face. He put a heavy hand on Hawk's shoulder, forcing him to stop. "Honor dictates that you make the offer."

Hawk halted and faced his friend. "There is much you do not know."

"I know enough."

"No," he bit out. "You do not. If you did, you would understand that honor does not compel me to offer for Naila."

Strick looked dumfounded. "What the devil are you saying?"

"Honor *does* compel me to say no more."

"Are you insulting the lady's virtue?" Strick asked, a warning in his voice.

"I am telling you that this is over." Hawk gritted his teeth. "Let it go."

He walked away. This time, Strick did not follow.

CHAPTER TWENTY-FOUR

Before
Philadelphia

"I've bought you a ring to match your bracelet," Basil told Naila the next time they met at the park. "It's a promise ring. A placeholder until your wedding band is on your finger." Which couldn't happen soon enough.

He could not believe how fortunate he was. He and Naila were suited in every way. He relished talking to her. Just being in her company made him deliriously happy. And their last meeting demonstrated that Basil could expect a *very* passionate marriage. He'd missed her terribly these past few weeks.

She didn't look well though. Her eyes were swollen and there were dark smudges beneath them. And she did not put out her hand so that he could slip his ring onto her finger. "Are you ill?" he asked. "Come and sit down on a bench."

She didn't move. She just stared at the ground unmoving. Not looking at him.

"Naila." Alarm sparked in the pit of his gut. "What is it?"

"I told you not to love me," she said. "I *told* you."

"As if I had a choice," he said cheerfully, and yet a gnawing sensation began in his chest.

"I am sorry." Her voice broke.

He dropped the ring into its small velvet pouch. "What are you sorry for? Do you regret what happened between us the last time we met?" The words spilled out of him. A part of him already knew what she was going to say but his brain wouldn't allow him to even contemplate it. "You shouldn't feel badly about anything we've done. You are already the wife of my heart and soon we'll be wed."

"I don't regret any of it." Tears filled her eyes. "But we won't be married."

His arm dropped to his side, the ring pouch a leaden weight in his hand. "What are you saying?" This wasn't happening. It couldn't be. "Whatever it is we can fix it, if we stick together."

She shook her head. "This is something that can't be fixed. I cannot do it. I can't marry you."

He stared at her in utter disbelief. "Of course you can. We are meant to be together." Desperation clawed at his chest. "You promised to hold on to me. To us."

"I wanted to, but I cannot."

"You could be with child," he said sharply. "I

cannot abandon you to face that alone. We did things that cannot be undone."

She shook her head. "I am not increasing. I waited . . . until I could be sure. There is no possibility that I am with child."

"Have you had your courses?" Normally he wouldn't discuss something as delicate as a woman's monthly but this was no time to mince words.

She nodded. "I am sorry," she said through quiet tears. "Sorrier than I could ever say."

He stepped back from her. "What are you sorry for?" he asked harshly. "For not loving me enough?"

"No." She shook her head, tears spilling onto her cheeks. "You know that's not true."

"You shouldn't apologize for not loving someone enough." Bitterness crept into his tone. "One cannot control one's feelings."

"That's not true," she protested. "Don't ever say that I don't love you enough."

"Why ever not? It's the truth isn't it?"

"I love you with everything in me. But I told you from the start that this"—she gestured between them—"is impossible."

"If you loved me half as much as I love you, then you would do everything in your power to keep us together."

"You're a man. You can do anything you want."

He gave a bitter laugh. "If only that were true."

The Earl That Got Away

"You will never understand what it is like to be a female."

"Are you are holding out for a better offer? Is that what this is about?"

"If you believe that then you truly don't know me at all."

"Would you like to know what I believe?" he asked, anger accenting each word. "I think you got carried away the other night when you accepted my proposal. But now that you've had time to think about it, you've decided your aunt was correct. That you can do better than tying your future to a man of no discernible fortune."

"Stop twisting everything. You are asking me to risk everything. My family, my community. My fa—" she stopped abruptly. "While you risk nothing."

"If we are speaking plainly, then the truth is that I doubt my family will approve of my marrying an Arab bride from America."

"But will they disown you? Do you risk losing them as I risk losing my entire extended family?"

"Perhaps not." His ears were ringing, his vision hazy. "But I would risk everything for you if it came to that."

"But it won't. The only one of us who risks losing everything is me."

"And it's too much to ask?"

"Yes," she said sadly, quietly. "I suppose it is."

"So this is it? You are able to just leave and never see me again?" He couldn't understand how she could do that. Tearing off his own arm would be less painful than watching her walk out of his life.

"I have no choice." Her cheeks and nose were red from crying.

"Naila." He reached for her hand. "What has happened? Please tell me so that I can take care of everything."

She shook her head, drawing her hand away. "I swore—" Her voice drifted off.

"Swore what?" he asked desperately. "Tell me."

"I swore to be . . . loyal to my family," she said.

"We'll find a way for you to be loyal to us all. I promise."

"There is no way." She finally looked up and met his gaze. "Thank you for giving me the summer of my life."

He shook his head vehemently. "This cannot be the end."

"It has to be. I'm sorry. We're going back to New York."

"When do you leave?" He bit out the question.

"Auntie says tomorrow." She paused, tearful. "I hope we can part as friends."

Disbelief roared through him. "We can never be friends. I can only love you with everything in me or hate you desperately." He felt like he was being skinned alive. "I will never settle for anything as tepid as being your friend."

He could not bear to look at her, but he heard the tears in her voice. "I-I hope that isn't true."

That afternoon, Hawk booked the first passage home that he could find. Taking over his uncle's business was out of the question now. America was ruined for him. It was an abyss of misery and disaster, a black hole through which Naila was forever lost to him.

Naila and her aunt's departure from Philadelphia was delayed for almost a week because Majida came down with influenza and stayed in bed for several days.

Naila spent a great deal of time in bed as well. She was sick to her stomach and it felt like someone was stabbing her brain with an ice pick. Her sleep was restless and plagued by jagged dreams, most of them about Basil. She was beset by doubts. Had she done the right thing in sending Basil away? Had she tried hard enough to stay true to him? She couldn't get Basil's devastated expression out of her mind.

By the third day since her conversation with Basil, Naila knew she could never be happy without him. They would break their news to Baba gently, in a way that would not damage his health. Her father was a loving man who indulged his daughters most of the time. Without Basil by her side, Naila saw only an endless black hole when she imagined what her life would be like now. She'd obviously made a mistake. There had to be a way to make both her family and herself happy.

Basil would help her figure it out. He would forgive her for her momentary lapse. She knew it. He loved her. She rushed to get dressed and slipped out a side door, eager to go to Basil and make things right. She had no idea where Mr. Linton lived, but Basil had once shown her his uncle's factory, so she went directly there. A clerk in the front office regarded her with open curiosity when she asked to see Basil's uncle. The clerk went to get Mr. Linton from the factory floor.

"My dear Miss Darwish," the older man said when he appeared and showed her to a back office. "What can I do for you?"

Everything about Naila's appearing alone at the factory and asking for this man's bachelor nephew was scandalous. But she didn't care. She had to see Basil and wouldn't rest until she reassured him of her commitment and they settled matters.

"My nephew?" Mr. Linton said kindly when she asked about Basil. "I am afraid you have just missed him. He has gone home."

Basil had just been there? She had to follow him. "I am sorry," Naila said, "but I don't know where you live."

Mr. Linton frowned but then his expression cleared. "No, no, my dear girl. Basil isn't at my residence. He has gone home to England."

Her jaw dropped. "No, that's impossible." She shook her head against the possibility that she'd lost her chance at happiness. "He's not supposed to leave for several weeks."

"I was terribly disappointed when he changed his plans. He left two days ago. He is well on his way."

Two days ago. Basil left America one day after she broke his heart. And now he was gone. She had to get to him. But how? England might as well be in another world. There was no way to contact him directly. She'd have to send a letter through his uncle. But that was scandalous. For all she knew, Mr. Linton's sense of honor might compel him to return her letter to her aunt rather than facilitate a clandestine correspondence between an unmarried girl and a bachelor.

The situation between Naila and Basil was no longer fixable. Devastation drummed in her stomach. She'd made a disaster of things. There was no way to make it better.

Naila was condemned to live the remainder of her life knowing that she'd single-handedly destroyed her one chance at true happiness.

Chapter Twenty-Five

Now
England

"It's time for me to return home," Naila announced two weeks later as she and Raya finished lunch. The duke was out and the rest of the family had gone to see the Fish House at the London Zoo.

"Are you sure?" Raya asked.

Naila nodded. "You are married now and must get on with the business of being a duchess, whatever that entails." And she needed to get on with her own life. She'd submerged herself in her work after her last disastrous encounter with Hawk. But it wasn't enough. As long as she remained in England, she'd think of him. She needed to go home.

"But your pamphlet isn't ready yet," Raya protested.

"I have collected everything for it. Now I need to actually organize the information in a way that makes sense."

"Why can't you do that here?"

"Because ultimately I will need to work with an American publisher. The market for the pamphlet is wealthy Americans."

"I understand why you want to leave." Raya sighed. "I will miss you terribly."

"You have a wonderful life here. My place isn't here, as you well know."

"Are you worried about running into Hawk?" Raya asked.

"He doesn't dictate my behavior." Certainly not any longer. She was done moping around because of that man. "I can't believe I wasted eight years pining over him."

Raya sighed. "I was so certain that Hawk would propose."

"Did I hear someone say Hawk's name?" The duke strode into the dining room. "Have I missed luncheon?"

Raya motioned for a footman to set a place for her husband. Naila marveled at how quickly her sister seemed to be adapting to the life of an English aristocrat while still pursuing her business interests. If Hawk had proposed, Naila would be preparing for such a life herself. She'd had a throbbing headache since that scene in the garden.

The duke cut into his lamb. "Hawk has left London."

"Where has he gone?" Raya asked.

"He didn't say precisely. Only that he would not be returning to Town for several months."

Naila understood Hawk's need to get away. She felt it herself.

Thank goodness she had a project. Finishing the pamphlet and overseeing its publication would keep her busy. And after that, she hoped to take on more responsibilities at her cousin's architecture firm. Kareem had promised to try to visit, which she would enjoy.

"So that's the end of it?" Raya asked. "Of you and Hawk?"

Naila ignored the painful throb in her chest. "It was over eight years ago. We both know that now. It's past time we both go our own way."

"If you're sure," Raya said.

"I am," Naila said. "It's time to move on."

PART TWO

An American Heiress's Guide to Landing a Lord

CHAPTER TWENTY-SIX

One year later
London

Naila was strolling along Piccadilly when she bumped into Guy Vaughan coming out of the Fortnum & Mason department store.

"Miss Darwish! The lady makes a triumphant return. Welcome back to London." He tipped his hat, looking dapper in a dark calf-length frock coat over a colorful patterned waistcoat. "What has it been? A year since you last graced us with your presence?"

"Mr. Vaughan, how nice to see you." It was Naila's first time encountering someone she'd met during her last trip to England, which felt like a lifetime ago. "Yes, it's been a little over a year since I was last here."

"You are in my neighborhood," he told her. "I keep apartments at the Albany just there across the street." He pointed in the direction of a handsome brick Georgian structure set back from the main road. "*You* are the true surprise. Your pamphlet is the talk of London."

"Have I created a scandal?" she asked with an amused smile. "Will high society forever shun me?"

"Far from it! The sister of a duchess who has authored the much-talked-about publication of the year is sure to be the most sought-after guest in Mayfair's finest drawing rooms."

"Surely not." Naila still found it hard to believe that so many people knew who she was. After relegating herself to the background for so long, becoming the center of attention took a great deal of getting used to.

Naila had never imagined that her endeavor to save a few architectural masterpieces would make such a splash. But several leading American newspapers had published stories about *An American Heiress's Guide to Landing a Lord*. After that, copies sold swiftly at a scandalously high price. Her American publisher insisted that the heiresses interested in the information Naila had gathered would willingly pay an exorbitant price for it. And he was right.

"Your pamphlet is widely credited with making a match that will save Sherborne House in Berkshire," Mr. Vaughan remarked.

"Actually, that's why I've come to London." Lord Broughton's crumbling Berkshire mansion was slated to receive a huge cash infusion once Miss Phoebe Frost, a wealthy New York oil heiress, wed Broughton's heir in a few weeks' time.

"You are acquainted with the young lady's family?"

"I met them after they purchased my pamphlet. They sought my advice on how to navigate the English aristocracy." Since then, she and the bride-to-be had become friends. "People assume I must know the way of things since my sister is a duchess."

"Your manners have always been impeccable," he said gallantly. "I imagine there will be many more weddings thanks to your efforts. Is it the festivities that bring you to London?"

"That and, of course, I couldn't resist the opportunity to see my sister."

"It is good to have you back among us." He tipped his hat. "Unfortunately, I must leave you because I am late to an appointment. I do hope to see you again soon."

After they exchanged goodbyes, Naila continued down Piccadilly, a bustling street full of shops and activity. She halted when she reached her destination, the shiny dark green frontage of Hatchards bookshop. She stared through the paned windows and caught sight of her pamphlet. There it was on display—*An American Heiress's Guide to Landing a Lord*—in bold gold lettering with navy blue flourishes. She couldn't take her eyes off it.

While she admired her handiwork, Naila

marveled at how different this second trip to England was from her first. She was here now as a respected woman in her own right.

An unwelcome thought intruded on her mind.

Had Hawk seen the publication? Would she run into him on this trip? Trepidation about seeing Hawk again, and potentially churning up the past, had almost kept Naila from accepting the invitation to Phoebe's wedding. Then she'd realized Hawk was the very reason that she had to attend the festivities.

The wound he'd left on her heart was still tender and might always be so, but she couldn't allow the specter of him to dictate how she lived her life. That's why she'd ultimately decided to come. It was a way of proving to herself that she was taking control of her life.

Besides, Raya said Hawk rarely came to London, which was just as well. Naila had written a thing or two in her pamphlet—while in the heat of anger—that he might not appreciate.

With any luck, Hawk would never see it.

"Ahlan wa sahlan." A familiar man's voice greeted her from behind. "Welcome back."

"Salam." Naila turned to greet Kareem. "You are perfectly on time."

She was pleased to see Kareem again after all these months. They'd agreed to meet at Hatchards after Kareem's letter informed her that the venerable bookseller stocked her pamphlet.

"How good it is to see you." He took both of her hands in his. "You are the talk of London."

They both turned to admire the stack of pamphlets in the window. "Sometimes I cannot believe that we actually did it," she said.

"*You* did it," he clarified. "It was kind of you to mention me in your publication. It wasn't necessary."

"Of course it was. I had to acknowledge your contribution," she insisted. "I would never have been able to complete the project without your vast understanding of England's great old houses."

"It was a worthy project and my pleasure to offer any assistance I could," he said. "Have you come back to London alone?"

"As if my mother would allow that," she said. "Auntie Majida and my cousin Hind accompanied me."

He looked delighted. "I must make sure to call on them."

"They'll be very glad to see you."

"Shall we go inside the shop and see how your pamphlet is displayed on the tables?"

"Certainly." She took his proffered arm. "*Yalla*, lead the way."

HAWK RAISED A glass to toast his friend. "To your health and happiness."

The Honorable Charles Brownley, the future Viscount Broughton, dipped his chin. "Which is assured now that Sherborne House is saved for future generations."

The old university friends were sitting at the center bow window in the Savile Club overlooking Piccadilly. It was Hawk's first time back in London since his final break with Naila. He'd avoided society for the past year.

But no more. Yes, he'd come to London for the wedding of one of his oldest friends, but he also intended to find a wife as he'd vowed to do last year. He was finally ready to move past Naila.

"It's fortunate that your American heiress comes with a dowry generous enough to save your family estate," Hawk remarked.

"It is not just her papa's bank account that interests me," Charles said. "It is Phoebe herself. I love everything about her."

Hawk stared at him in surprise. "Are you saying this is a love match?"

Charles grinned. "Deuced convenient, isn't it? She's wealthy *and* I love her." Charles had always been something of a romantic. Unlike most men, particularly Englishmen, Charles wasn't afraid to show his emotions. "I never imagined I would be able to fulfill my familial duty while also following my heart."

"How did you two become acquainted?" Hawk asked.

"Our fathers arranged the meeting. Phoebe's

father, Mr. Frost, found us through that pamphlet that is all the rage."

"What pamphlet?"

Charles laughed. "You have obviously been away from London for too long if you have never heard of this marriage guide that helps pair wealthy American girls with impoverished lordlings like myself."

Hawk blinked, his pulse quickening. Surely, it couldn't be. "What is the name of this guide?"

"An American Heiress's Guide to Landing a Lord," Charles said. "Not exactly subtle, eh?"

So Naila had gone through with her project. "And you say this guide is a big success?"

"An enormous triumph. It's selling swiftly in America as well as here."

Despite the soreness in his chest, pride in Naila for her accomplishment surged through Hawk. Good for her. Not only had she completed her project but it was actually serving the purpose she intended. Charles, whose family home had fallen into disrepair, was proof enough of that. That Naila had had a hand in saving Sherborne House, while also helping Charles connect with a woman he cared for, was an admirable achievement.

There had been many times over the past year when he'd mourned his reluctance to ask Naila to marry him during their encounter in Strick's garden. And then he'd convince himself that he'd made the correct decision and it was all for the best. While he'd wallowed in regret and uncertainty, Naila had taken charge of her life. She'd thrived in his absence, blossomed into an even more admirable woman.

"You say the guide is on sale here in London?" he asked her.

"Yes, I just saw it in the window down the street at Hatchards."

Hawk frowned. "Why would it be popular here in London? Who here would buy it? I thought it was a guide for wealthy American girls looking to marry lords."

"It is. It was, anyway," Charles amended. "The truth is that every lord hopes to be mentioned in the book. These days, it's practically a sign that you've arrived in society."

Why would anyone take pride in having their impoverished status advertised for all to see? It was not a question he could put to his friend, given the depleted bank accounts of Charles's family. Sipping his drink, he peered out the window. And his heart stopped. Surely it couldn't be. His eyes must be playing a trick on him. It was like a replay of what he'd seen through the window of Strick's townhome a year ago.

It was Naila, dressed in vibrant red, striding purposefully along the side pavement. What was she doing here? As she approached the bow window, he noticed her companion was none other than Kareem Amar.

The architect was still sniffing after her. Or maybe, for all he knew, they'd formalized their union. Hawk *had* been out of touch with all his friends for the past year. Would Strick have written to tell him Naila was married? The thought of her being anyone's wife twisted his insides.

He hated the feelings that seeing her again stirred up in his gut.

Joy. Loss. Resentment.

A longing for what could have been.

As she passed the bow window, she flashed a white smile, laughing at something the architect said. It slammed into Hawk like a punch in the gut. Even though Naila would never be his, Hawk would never tire of looking at her. But it was over in a flash; Naila passed the window and was soon out of sight.

Gone yet again.

As he sat there, his chest swelling with the rush of her, Hawk resisted the urge to twist in his seat to watch Naila walk away. He realized that there was something different about her now. It took him a moment to identify what. It was the way she carried herself, with the vigor and confidence of a woman in full control of her destiny.

And—damn it all to hell—it made her all the more attractive.

"Will you do it?" Phoebe asked. "All the girls want you to host salons."

Naila scoffed. "I'm hardly an expert on the aristocracy."

"You know a lot more than we do."

Phoebe joined Naila, Raya and Hind at a Brook Street tearoom, one of the few places respectable young ladies could meet without a chaperone and still maintain their reputation.

"But you hosted salons in New York," Phoebe persisted, "and they were a great success."

"Your family hosted them," she reminded her friend. "Not me."

Hind nibbled on a biscuit. "You are rather skilled at bringing people from different backgrounds together."

"Did you go to the salons?" Raya asked her young cousin.

Hind nodded. "I went to one of them. It was very well attended."

"My father can be intimidating," Phoebe added. "But Naila wasn't afraid to speak her mind."

After Phoebe's ambitious father acquired Naila's pamphlet, he'd reached out for guidance navigating the English aristocracy and paid Naila handsomely for her time.

"I should just write a letter and propose a

deal," Mr. Frost had told Naila back then. "My daughter gets the title and the viscount gets the cash he desperately needs to stay afloat."

Naila had advised Mr. Frost that an English lord might appreciate a more subtle approach. In the end, Mr. Frost had written to Lord Broughton, inviting him to call on them should he ever find himself in New York.

Naila was present at the small dinner party the Frosts hosted a few months later in honor of Lord Broughton and his heir. To the delight of all involved, Phoebe and Charles hit it off immediately and, before long, their fathers were hammering out a marriage agreement.

From there, Naila had advised Phoebe on some of the finer points of English customs, which she'd learned from Guy's sister, Frances, during her short time in England. Some of Phoebe's marriage-minded friends, eager to learn how to land a lord, sometimes joined their sessions.

"I would never know how to behave if you hadn't advised me," Phoebe said. "Charles would have thought me terribly brazen if I had acted as American girls normally do."

"Nonsense." Naila reached for a biscuit. "You are a success in your own right." But she did see the advantages of hosting salons to bring eligible lords and young heiresses together. She'd certainly eased the way for Charles and Phoebe by smoothing any cultural snags that popped up along the way. And now Sherborne Hall was being saved. Satisfaction rippled through her.

"If I am a success," Phoebe insisted, "it is thanks to you."

"Your charms attracted Charles."

"And my dollars," Phoebe said with a laugh. "But having you there to advise me made a tremendous difference. Won't you think about hosting a few salons while you are here?"

Naila bit into her biscuit. "I will seriously consider it."

Raya, who'd listened quietly up until now, set her teacup down. "I think it's an excellent idea."

"You do?" Naila asked.

"Bravo." Phoebe clapped her hands together. "If the duchess thinks it's a capital idea, then it must be. There is no female personage higher than a duchess."

"Yes, there is," Naila reminded her. "Do you remember discussing rank?"

"Of course I do," Phoebe said. "What I meant is that, there is no one higher aside from the royal family. And Her Grace sanctions the idea."

"Not only do I sanction it," Raya said, "but I think you should hold your first salon at Carey House."

Phoebe's eyes widened. "A salon at a duke's London residence? Everyone will want to come!"

Raya directed her gaze at Naila. "Would you like me to host a salon for you?" she asked. "Do you enjoy matchmaking?"

"I'm hardly a matchmaker." Naila hadn't thought of herself that way. "Or if I am, the match I am making is between a great house and an even greater fortune needed to save it."

"How unfortunate that people are a necessary part of your scheme," Raya said dryly.

"If all couples were half as delightful as Phoebe and Charles then yes, I suppose I do enjoy playing matchmaker. I take satisfaction in knowing that Sherborne House will be saved while, at the same time, Phoebe is marrying a man who cares for her."

"Would you like to make more matches?" Raya asked.

"Yes, I suppose I would," Naila said. "But it is rather ironic."

"What is?" Phoebe asked.

"That I should be helping couples come together when I have never managed to make a match for myself."

"You've had plenty of interest," Raya reminded her. "It is not every day that a girl disdains a proposal from a high-ranking lord."

Phoebe's eyes bulged. "A lord proposed to you?"

"What?" Hind asked at the same time. "When?"

"A very handsome, eligible and wealthy lord," Raya added.

"Which lord?" Hind asked.

"And you said no?" Phoebe leaned forward in her seat. "Exactly how high-ranking was this lord?"

"Very," Raya assured them. Naila kicked her under the table but Raya swiftly moved her legs out of the way.

Hind's gaze bounced between the two sisters. "When did this happen?" she asked. "And why have I never heard this story?"

"Because it is nobody's business." Naila glared at her sister. "Raya spoke out of turn. And besides, he never really proposed." At least not when he was a lord.

Phoebe looked scandalized. "Can you speak like that to a duchess?" she half-whispered.

Naila scowled. "You can if she is your sister and if she is being provoking."

"He would have proposed had you been receptive," Raya insisted.

Naila's eyes shot daggers at her sister. "Can we please speak of something else?"

"Don't be angry," Raya said. "If anything your bankability just went up. Not only have you written a pamphlet about catching a lord, you've actually had one who wanted to propose to you."

"That is a private matter," Naila snapped.

"It's unfortunate though," Raya continued, "that you tossed him away."

"Was he a terrible person?" Hind asked.

"No, he wasn't," Naila said. "In the end, we just didn't suit."

"I am sorry that it wasn't a love match," Phoebe said.

"Well, actually—" Raya began.

Naila cut her off. "You've said enough."

Phoebe looked even more scandalized, but Raya just laughed and sipped her tea while Hind continued to give Naila a wondering look.

Chapter Twenty-Seven

"The lady in blue silk is Miss Darwish, the authoress of *An American Heiress's Guide to Landing a Lord*," Charles informed Hawk at they stood in one of the massive receiving rooms in Strick's London townhome attending Naila's first salon. They were with the duke and Guy. "She's bound to be as great a success in London as she is in New York."

"Hawk and Miss Darwish have met," Strick informed their friend.

Charles's eyes widened. "I hadn't realized."

"Yes, we are acquainted." Hawk pretended not to watch Naila glide masterfully around the room introducing the pauper lords to the dollar princesses. She was resplendent in a shimmering gown that skimmed her considerable curves like a lingering lover. Her dark eyes sparkled, her complexion rosy as she smiled.

Success definitely agreed with her.

"I ran into Miss Darwish the other day on Piccadilly," Guy Vaughn said. "She seems very proud of the success of her pamphlet."

"As well she should be." Hawk surveyed the

crowd. "There are quite of number of eligible young ladies here. Charles, did you bring all the New York heiresses back to London with you?"

Charles chuckled. "Quite a number of them. Miss Darwish was very convincing during Mr. Frost's gatherings. She assured a number of the young ladies that there were many grand houses in need of saving."

Guy snorted. "And that interested them?"

Charles grinned back. "The heiresses were much more drawn to the penurious lords that come with the homes."

Guy adjusted his cuffs. "It is peculiar that Miss Darwish has become a successful matchmaker when she herself has never married."

"Oh, she has had offers," Charles told him. "She apparently attracted the serious interest of a lord."

"Has she?" Guy tilted his head. "I wonder who that could be."

Strick stared into his drink. Hawk schooled his features into a neutral expression even as his muscles tensed beneath his dark evening clothes. Was the gossip about him? Or did Naila have a new suitor?

"I've no idea," Charles told him. "According to my betrothed, he was a high-ranking lord."

"How intriguing." Interest lit Guy's eyes. "What happened?"

Charles shrugged. "Apparently it wasn't a love match."

Hawk grabbed champagne from a circulating footman bearing a silver tray of drinks. He bottomed out the entire glass, relishing the burn down his throat and into his chest.

Charles was still talking. "Once all the American heiresses heard that Miss Darwish *had* actually attracted the interest of a lord, they followed her around like she is the pied piper."

Guy chuckled. "I confess that at first I viewed Miss Darwish as something of a plain mouse. But once you become acquainted with her, she is nothing of the sort."

"Plain?" Charles looked at Guy as though he'd taken leave of his senses. "A mouse? Miss Darwish?"

The two men talked on but Hawk didn't follow their conversation. He was far too busy contemplating Naila and the possibility she was advertising her one-time connection to him in order to sell more of her infernal pamphlets.

"I doubt the rumors came from Naila." Strick's voice cut into his thoughts. Hawk realized they were alone; the other two men had wandered away.

"It doesn't matter to me in the least," he lied as he tracked Naila's movements. She appeared to be introducing a marquess's heir to another of her young ladies. "But it is growing rather aggravating."

"What is?"

"Must I always have the damnable misfortune of running into Miss Darwish at every wedding I attend? First yours and now Charles's." It was if the fates were mocking him. Was he destined to always see her at the weddings of other people, a slap in the face when he'd once wanted nothing more than to meet Naila at the altar?

"You are in search of a wife," Strick remarked. "Does anyone here catch your eye?"

He shrugged. "The evening is still young." But he kept his eye on the only woman who had ever really caught his attention. He did not allow himself to regret breaking with Naila. It was the only way to save his sanity, but he still couldn't help admiring her.

Naila was speaking to Raya now, in that confidential way of sisters that makes everyone else feel excluded. He was weary of the turmoil that churned inside him whenever he laid eyes on her. He detested tumult and upheaval. He'd had enough of that last year around the time of Strickland's nuptials. It had to end.

He and Naila had settled their past. Surely neither of them wanted continued awkwardness between them to continue for the entire Season. They were adults.

It was time to call a truce.

MEANWHILE, ACROSS THE room, Naila focused on facilitating suitable matches among her guests.

"Miss Work," Naila said to the fresh-faced Boston department store heiress, "allow me to introduce the Earl of Heresford. His lordship's country seat is an impressive castle in Hampshire."

Which was in danger of collapsing if the earl didn't refresh the dwindling family coffers soon. What Heresford lacked in looks, he made up for with his aristocratic bearing and excellent dress. Most importantly, he possessed a title, which was the primary attribute the wealthy Americans girls looked for.

"Miss Work." Heresford dipped his chin in a supremely elegant manner. "What a pleasure it is to make your acquaintance."

To Naila's relief the two were soon engaged in effortless conversation. That was the thing with American girls. The English nobles were often attracted to their engaging confident manner. She left them to it and turned to find Hawk approaching her. Her skin tightened and grew warmer, as it always did whenever she was around him.

"It's a marvelous feat," Hawk said. "My congratulations."

"Hawk." She feigned surprise, pretending she hadn't seen him coming. As if she hadn't tracked his movements from the moment he first appeared at her salon.

"Welcome back to England," he said.

"Thank you. I did not expect to see you here."

"I do not think we can avoid each other." His manner was almost friendly. "As much as we might like to."

He looked handsome and forbidding in his dark evening clothes. There were more fine lines around his eyes, but they added to, rather than detracted from, his appeal. Why did the annoying man have to grow more enticing every time she saw him?

"I suppose we cannot help but run into each other," she agreed, "since one of your closest friends is wed to my sister."

"It is inconvenient." A smile lurked at the corners his mouth and the memory of how those lips felt against her skin fluttered through her body. Around them, people talked and laughed and footmen weaved among the guests with champagne. But all she saw was Hawk.

"I expected you to give me a wide berth," she admitted, "instead of going to the trouble to actually seek me out."

His steady gaze remained on her face. "We parted on . . . erm . . . less than amicable terms."

Emotion thickened her throat. "I remember." It was seared into her mind.

"But just because we do not suit does not mean we should not be able to be in the same room together. I hope we can try to be friends."

Again, with the friends talk. Even though he'd once told her they could never be friends. That he could only ever feel an intense emotion for her. Love or hate. Nothing as mild as friendship. And yet here they were.

"Of course we can be friends." She forced a cheery tone that sounded false to her ears but she hoped he wouldn't notice. "I would like that."

And maybe one day, far into the future, that might actually be true.

"Excellent." His answering smile seemed a little wistful.

"I didn't realize you were in London," she said. "Raya says you rarely come to Town these days."

His brows lifted. "You are so interested in my whereabouts that asked your sister about me?"

"Ha!" Of course. But she'd never admit it. "I see your sense of self-importance is still firmly in place."

"Ah, but you are the important one here this evening." This time his smile seemed genuine. "What you've accomplished here is truly impressive."

She basked in his praise far more than she should. "The pamphlet has turned out to be a greater success than I ever could have imagined."

"So I have heard." He seemed truly pleased for her. "You must be very proud."

"There is one particularly beautiful old house that is being saved because of a match that was made thanks to the pamphlet."

"Thanks to *you*," he corrected. "Are you speaking of Sherborne House?"

"Yes," she said, surprised. "Do you know it?"

"Very well. Charles Brownley is an old school friend of mine."

She shook her head. "The world really is a small place."

"Particularly the world of the English aristocracy."

"You all know each other, I suppose."

"Something like that."

"We're hosting another salon next week at a tearoom on Brook Street," she said impulsively. "Will you come?"

He paused.

"It is not just American heiresses who will be there." She already wanted to kick herself for taking the conversation down this road. "English debutantes will be there as well."

His eyes rounded. "Miss Darwish, are you trying to matchmake me as well?"

She wasn't, but what could she say now that her impulsive desire to see him again—and to have him witness her successes firsthand—had led them to this point.

"You never know," she said. And then she winked.

Hawk had never seen so much puce in one room. Brownish-purple dresses were everywhere in the tea shop. The establishment was brimming with both American heiresses and London's finest debutantes, a sizable number of whom wore the muddy-colored dresses.

One of the first people he spotted was Frances, Guy's impeccably fashionable sister. "Thank goodness you have the good sense not to wear puce."

Her eyes sparkled. "You've returned to London."

"I could hardly miss the nuptials of the year."

"The wedding of the Honorable Charles Bromley to his American heiress *is* the talk of London." She smoothed a hand down her bodice. "And Miss Darwish deserves all the credit."

"That book of hers is making quite a splash." As he spoke, he spotted Naila going from one table to another, stopping to chat or smile with each attendee.

Frances followed his gaze. "Our quiet friend has come out of her shell."

"She certainly has." He noted that Naila was not dressed like a plum. She wore a soft peach gown that stood out among the sea of unappealing fruit. "Was there a dress code for this engagement?"

"How do you mean?"

"Why does it look like a plum tree exploded in here?"

She looked at him in surprise. "Do you truly not know?"

"I wouldn't ask if I did."

"The puce," she said with an amused expression, "is for your benefit, I believe."

"My benefit?" What the devil was she talking about? "I detest the color. It looks like someone took a particularly sickly shade of pink and soaked it in mud."

"You should ask Miss Darwish," she said with a mysterious smile as she drifted away.

"Why?" he called after her. "What does she have to do with this?" But Frances had already melted into the crowd.

Shaking his head, Hawk scanned the room, seeing many familiar faces, including Strick, Guy and Charles. He was introduced to several young ladies and could not help but notice they were all wearing puce gowns.

Hawk buckled down, determined to engage with each one, to behave like a man in serious pursuit of a wife. He did not expect to care for his future countess in the all-consuming way he had loved Naila. He could never survive such an intense love, but compatibility was important. He hoped to have some interests in common with his wife.

To that end, he chatted and inquired and spoke about the weather with a number of young ladies. However, it wasn't long before he realized that finding a woman with whom he was compatible was going to be far more challenging than he had anticipated.

There was Miss Smith, a real estate heiress from Chicago. "I love puce. It is absolutely my favorite color," she told him shortly after they were introduced.

Lady Madeline was the daughter of a viscount. Her feathered puce hat matched her dress. "What other colors appeal to you, my lord?"

The banal banter continued as he went from group to group until he found himself in company with Naila, her sister, their young cousin Hind and Charles's betrothed, Miss Frost.

"Miss Hind," he said to her. "I trust you have fully recovered from your unfortunate fall at Briar Hall."

"Oh yes, I am completely fine." Naila's young cousin had blossomed in her year away, her bone structure was more defined and she carried herself with more self-assurance.

Miss Frost watched their exchange with great interest. "Miss Darwish," she said to Hind. "May I ask why you are not wearing puce?"

"Me?" Hind flattened a hand against her chest. "Oh, I am not interested in finding a husband in England. I want to live in America."

That was direct. The young lady had obviously overcome the girlish crush she'd once had on Hawk. Then he frowned. Was puce reserved exclusively for maidens intent on landing a husband?

"Not interested in finding a husband in England?" Miss Frost reacted as if she couldn't imagine such a notion. "Why ever not? I think it's lovely here."

Hawk thought that was a good thing considering she was about to marry a future English viscount.

"I am expected to marry a gentleman from our community," Hind answered.

"In New York?" Miss Frost asked.

"Yes," Hind said. "My auntie Majida says a shared background is always helpful in marriage."

"And that is expected of you?" Miss Frost inquired.

Naila's eyes met Hawk's. "Yes," she answered for Hind. "That is what is expected."

Hawk found it interesting, the way she'd looked at him. As if in shared understanding. They seemed to be transitioning into a new sort of relationship, a friendship born of an appreciation for what they'd been through, for what they'd once meant to each other. He was glad they could comfortably be in each other's company. But sadness twinged in his throat for all they'd lost. He shook his head, determined to change the subject before he became too maudlin.

"Miss Darwish," he said to Naila, "is there a dress code for those attending your salons?"

"How do you mean?" she asked. "Anyone who is respectably attired is most welcome."

"I was wondering why so many of the eligible young ladies are in puce."

Someone snorted. He thought it was Miss Frost but when he looked at her she was perfectly composed.

A smile curved Hind's mouth. "It is because of you, my lord." She turned to Naila. "He doesn't know?"

"Well," Naila said, "if you'll excuse me, I must see to my guests . . . my other guests."

"It's in her pamphlet," Hind said and Hawk could see that she was highly amused.

"What is?" he asked as Naila scurried away.

"You are in her pamphlet," Miss Frost clarified.

"Me? Why? I am not in need of an heiress to save my estate."

Miss Frost exchanged a look with Hind before responding. *"An American Heiress's Guide to Landing a Lord* lists every eligible aristocrat, whether or not he is in need of funds."

Hawk blinked. "I beg your pardon?"

"And," Hind added, "the pamphlet lists your yearly income and your likes and dislikes."

"My likes and dislikes?" he repeated. "Such as?"

"Perhaps you'd care to read it for yourself," Miss Frost suggested. "There are a few copies on the table over there."

Hawk immediately crossed over to pick up a pamphlet. He flipped through the pages, reading the various entries.

THE EARL THAT GOT AWAY   269

Marquess of Norbury
    4th marquess
    Entailed estate is Fortworth, but it yields
    a small income, owing to agricultural distress
    Likes: gaming and fencing

Hawk kept thumbing through the pages until he found what he was looking for.

Earl of Hawksworth
    6th earl
    Entailed estate is Briar Hall
    The earl is exceedingly wealthy, having
    inherited all family assets once the previous
    earl and his three sons perished in a
    boating accident
    Likes: Rowing, liver and the color puce

"Did you pay for that guide?" Naila came up to him. "I'm not giving my pamphlets away." The banked smile, the naughty spark in her eye, were so like the young girl he fell in love with that he could only smile.

"I ought to sue you for slander," he said mildly.

"Why? I did say you are exceedingly wealthy and that you enjoy rowing."

"Puce and liver? Two things I absolutely abhor?"

"When word got around that you were likely to attend today's salon, there was obviously a run on puce fabrics at the dressmakers'."

"You find it humorous."

"Don't you? I burst out laughing when everyone started to arrive and I saw so many gowns in your favorite color."

"You, Miss Darwish, are a menace to society."

"You should be flattered."

"I should?"

"Look at how many eligible young ladies want to win you over. I understand that you are in search of a wife."

"And you thought I'd find one dressed in a color I cannot stand?"

"Well, when I wrote your entry, I was rather displeased with you. It was harmless but I found it endlessly amusing."

"And now," he asked, "are you still displeased with me?" What were the new rules around their friendship? Was flirting acceptable? "Or did you encourage the young ladies to wear puce in order to turn me away from them?"

She flushed, looking uncomfortable. Apparently, this new understanding did not include mild flirtation. It was just as well. Nothing about his involvement with Naila could ever be mild. No matter how hard either of them might try.

Chapter Twenty-Eight

"Hawk," Charles said at yet another of Naila's salons the following week. "Have you met Miss Catherine Anne Turner of California? She is a great friend of my darling Phoebe."

Hawk set his features into the polite expression he adopted when meeting any of the eligible young women at Naila's gatherings. By now, he expected them to all bore him as he must bore them. In all honesty, he mostly attended these events in order to witness Naila in all her glory. He relished seeing her get the recognition and admiration she'd always deserved. He'd recognized her exceptionality from the start.

"Miss Turner," he said to the young lady before him. "How do you do?"

"Exceptionally well, thank you." Her answer was crisp and forthright. Her manner no-nonsense. It made him truly take note of her. She was thin, with a long face and even features. He suspected that many would describe her as handsome rather than beautiful.

"Miss Turner's father made his fortune in

ships." Charles turned to Miss Turner. "Hawk is an excellent oarsman. He smashed the competition at university."

"Is that so?" That bit of information seemed to catch Miss Turner's attention. "Did you row on a team of eight?"

"I am a lone rower. My competitions were one-on-one. I prefer to depend upon myself rather than on a team. But that was long ago."

"I'd wager that you could still beat anyone who challenged you," Charles said.

"I wouldn't want to bore Miss Turner with stories about my ancient past. Your father builds ships?" Hawk asked Miss Turner, changing the subject.

"Papa likes to brag that he has made more ships than anyone else in America," she said with an amused smile. "Two hundred wooden sailing ships."

"Your father is the owner of Turner Shipyards?"

"You've heard of it?" She regarded him with slightly more interest. "Most lords here have not."

"As Charles said, I am very fond of rowing and that piqued my interest in ships. I have the highest respect for shipbuilders."

"What do you sail?" she asked.

"It depends," he told her. "Sometimes a scull, other times a skiff."

They continued to talk about rowing and her father's ships and, for the first time since returning to London, Hawk found himself enjoying a conversation with a woman who wasn't Naila.

"I also happen to indulge in a bit of rowing," Miss Turner told him. "Although Mama says it is unladylike."

"I think that is splendid," Hawk said. "There are many women here in England who also enjoy rowing."

"Is that so?" Her eyes lit up. "I do miss it. I haven't been able to indulge since coming to London."

"Then you must come and row with me one afternoon soon," he said impulsively.

She smiled. "I would like that very much."

Naila checked her list to learn the identity of the handsome woman talking to Hawk. Usually she took satisfaction in knowing he was completely bored when talking to heiresses and debutantes at her salons. She could tell by the expression of fixed courtesy he usually adopted.

But this woman was different. Hawk was actually engaged in the conversation and seemed to be enjoying it. He even laughed and bent his head toward the woman as if they were exchanging confidences.

"It looks as if the earl has found someone to interest him." Phoebe appeared next to Naila. "And Miss Turner seems to be taking pleasure in the conversation."

"Miss Turner? That is Catherine Anne Turner, the shipbuilding heiress?"

"Yes, do you know her?"

"Only by name," Naila said. "She was invited, of course. She stands to inherit a great fortune."

"Charles introduced them. He thought they might get along."

"Oh?" Naila made a show of looking at her list in an attempt not to appear too interested. "And why is that?"

"Miss Turner is an avid rower, which the earl apparently indulges in."

Something turned over in Naila's stomach. The shipbuilding heiress shared one of Hawk's passions? The idea of Catherine Anne Turner seeing Hawk rowing in all his topless glory made her teeth clench.

She kept an eye on the two of them chatting until they finally parted ways and Miss Turner made her way over to her and Phoebe. Watching the young lady's approach, Naila noted her tall and slender form, a figure completely unlike her own curvy physique. Was this the kind of woman Hawk preferred?

"I see you're becoming acquainted with the earl," Phoebe said when Miss Turner joined them.

"Yes," Miss Turner said. "He is quite charming."

"Excuse me, ladies." Charles appeared. "But I've come to steal my betrothed. If you will excuse us."

A delighted Phoebe drifted off with Charles.

The Earl That Got Away 275

Naila watched them go, pleased that one of her pairings was also a love match. It was the ideal situation.

"Tell me, Miss Darwish—" Miss Turner began. "Do you know the Earl of Hawksworth well?"

"Please call me Naila."

"I would be happy to. And I am Catherine Anne."

"Catherine Anne it is," Naila said. "What did you want to know?"

"I was wondering how well acquainted you are with the Earl of Hawksworth."

"I know him somewhat well." She tried not to picture Hawk's tender smile whenever he had looked at her in Philadelphia. Or to recall the sensation of his body sliding against hers. Seeing him again had conjured up far too many memories. "Why do you ask?"

"I find him appealing and my parents tell me that I am here to secure a titled husband."

"You certainly are forthright."

"Mama and Papa would say I am too direct but what is the point of beating around the bush?"

"I agree." Naila had to admire a woman who went after what she wanted. "Why waste time equivocating when you can come straight to the point?"

"Exactly," Catherine Anne said. "I admire you greatly, Miss Darwish . . . I mean Naila."

"Me?"

"Why yes! You have a meaningful project. You've written this pamphlet, which will do so much good. It will save many historic places."

"That is my great hope." Naila paused. "You are aware that Hawk is not in need of money?"

"Yes, and that is to his advantage, don't you think? It would be nice to wed a man who isn't after the fortune I will inherit."

"Yes, I can see why you would see it that way," Naila admitted. "But I would be rather sad if your considerable wealth does not go to a property that is in dire need of saving."

Catherine Anne gave a little laugh. "I completely understand your position since that is the point of these salons."

"It is." Naila forced out her next words. "But far be it from me to stand in the way of true love."

Catherine Anne scoffed. "I have only just met the man. We are hardly in love. But I would like to know more about the earl."

"He is kind and decent and smart," Naila said in all honesty. "He feels things deeply and intensely. Any young lady would be fortunate to marry him."

"I shall consider that an endorsement," Catherine Anne said. "We are going rowing tomorrow in order to become better acquainted."

Naila felt a sick drop in her stomach. "Hawk offered to take you out on the water?"

"Yes," she said happily. "I enjoy rowing so we will take a boat that allows for two rowers."

"That sounds lovely." And very intimate and romantic. Naila sighed, swallowing against the ache in her throat when she had no right to be jealous. Hadn't she and Hawk agreed to be friends?

"I hope you both have a wonderful time," she said and tried to mean it.

"What happens next?" Catherine Anne asked Hawk two days later.

They were in a special enclosure along the banks of the Thames waiting for the boat races to begin. Hawk had a boat club membership and was hosting a large party at the regatta.

"There will be a series of races," he explained to her and the rest of the guests, which included Strick and Raya, their young cousin Hind and Naila's architect friend. Charles and Phoebe were also in attendance. Naila had surprised him by coming along with her family members.

Regattas were always lively events. Boats of all sorts dotted the water and spectators were crammed along the water's edge. Drink flowed liberally and a band contributed to the festive atmosphere by playing lively music. The first gun went off and boats of rowers took off down six individual lanes. Spectators cheered and called out the names of their favorite teams.

Hawk mostly stayed by Catherine Anne's side during the competitions. "Each boat must stay in its own water," he explained to her and his other guests. "If any stray into another lane, they are penalized."

They watched several races, with rowing teams of eights, fours and pairs. There was cheering and clapping among his guests, who seemed to be enjoying the races. During a lull in the action, food was laid out on tables in Hawk's enclosure and his guests went over to fill their plates.

By the time Hawk went to get food, most of the guests were already seated at small tables across the enclosure enjoying their meal. He found Naila there helping herself to a second serving.

"What do you think of the regatta?" he asked.

"It's very amusing," she answered. "How are you enjoying spending time with Miss Turner?"

Her directness surprised him. "That is a very personal question."

"Is it?" She spooned some potatoes onto her plate. "It's a friendly question between friends since we are supposed to be friends now, are we not?"

There was something about her attitude that delighted him, a tartness to her tone that sounded a lot like . . .

"Do not tell me that you are jealous!" he blurted out.

She lifted her chin. "Don't be ridiculous."

He took in the radiant color on her face. "Your cheeks have suddenly flushed a beguiling shade of pink."

"We *are* outside," she retorted. "The weather is warm today."

"Is it?" He was enjoying himself immensely. "I hadn't noticed, considering the refreshing breeze that comes off the water."

"Why do you look so amused?"

"Because sparring with you is a delight. We've never done that before."

"That is a good point," she said. "Mostly we are glum and mope around for what might have been."

"Somewhere along the way, we lost the joy, the fun, that we used to have when we were together." The thought saddened him. There was a time when being with Naila was exhilarating beyond anything he'd ever experienced.

"But we are just friends now," she pointed out.

"Shouldn't friends also know fun and joy when they meet?"

She considered that, her face pensive, a little wrinkling of her forehead. He sighed internally. Would he ever not find her completely adorable? "I suppose you are right," she acknowledged. "We used to laugh a lot."

He nodded. "We did."

"So?" she asked abruptly. "Are you courting Miss Turner?"

He blinked, once again taken aback by the question. "I am getting to know her."

"I understand you went rowing together."

Was Naila checking up on him? "We did." His day was improving by the minute. "She is an experienced rower. Her technique is excellent."

"Good for her," she responded. "You are aware that she is very wealthy?"

"Surely you know that I'm not interested in Catherine Anne's money."

"Catherine Anne?" Her brows went up. "You are on a first-name basis."

"Why this interest in who I am courting?" Although he was beginning to have a pretty good understanding of what was going on here. Naila was jealous and barely going to the trouble to conceal her true feelings.

A thrill shot through Hawk. *Naila still cared for him*. Even after all these years. Despite the prolonged lack of contact and ocean-wide distance they'd put between them. Realizing that Naila still had feelings for him galvanized Hawk. Did that mean it wasn't too late for them? Trying to forget Naila certainly hadn't worked. Maybe it was time for Hawk to be honest with himself. To admit that his feelings for Naila were not the boyish yearnings he'd once pretended they were.

The reality was that Naila still appealed to the man Hawk had become.

He released a long breath. What a relief it was to finally acknowledge his true feelings. The question now was whether he was capable of letting the past go. Could he allow himself to be happy at last?

"So you *are* courting her," Naila pressed.

"I didn't say that. But Catherine Anne, Miss Turner, is a pleasant companion." He delighted in watching irritation ripple across Naila's lovely face. "She is smart, enterprising, engaging," he added.

"My purpose in inviting her to attend my salons was not to match her with a wealthy lord," she informed him in an agitated tone. "I want her to wed an impoverished lord with a home of historical significance that needs saving. That is the entire point of this endeavor."

He suppressed an urge to grin. "Maybe Miss Turner has other plans for her future."

"And maybe you do as well."

He shrugged. "Time will tell."

"It certainly will," she shot back.

"What will time tell?" Catherine Anne asked as she approached the food table.

Hawk greeted her with a genuine smile. "Time will tell how many successful matches Miss Darwish's salons will produce." He bowed to both ladies. "If you will excuse me, I must see to my other guests."

Catherine Anne watched Hawk cross over to join a group that included Raya and the duke. "Did he say anything about me?" she asked.

"What?" Naila was busy mulling over the conversation she'd just had with Hawk. The exchange was reminiscent of their interactions in Philadelphia. Clever banter tinged with humor. They used to have so much fun together. She'd missed that part of their relationship a great deal.

"I asked if the earl said anything about me." Catherine Anne regarded her expectantly. "I noticed you chatted with his lordship for quite a while."

"Oh, ah, yes," Naila responded even as acid burned in her chest. "I asked him how your rowing outing went and he said you are an excellent rower."

She beamed. "He did appear impressed by my endurance. We rowed for almost two hours."

"Really?" Naila understood that rowing was hard work because it required the use of every muscle in the body. She herself probably wouldn't last thirty minutes, much less two hours.

"I wonder if I am his type of woman." Catherine Anne kept her eye on Hawk as he circulated among his regatta guests. "Papa says men have types. Do you happen to know of any other young lady he has shown an interest in? Did she look like me?"

"I'm afraid I can't say."

Did men have a type? Maybe Hawk preferred strong, athletic women over someone soft and curvy like her. There were certainly other heiresses at her salons with fuller figures, yet lithe Catherine Anne was the one who'd caught Hawk's attention.

Naila sighed. She shouldn't care but she did. A great deal. Far too much for her own good. After Catherine Anne returned to her table, Guy Vaughan came over. "I hear you can take credit for two more successful matches."

Guy was referring to the recent news that Chicago oil heiress Ellen Goelet had just become engaged to a baron whose Tudor home was in dire need of repair. The two had met because of Naila's pamphlet.

And it was rumored that the father of Boston department store heiress Alberta Work was drawing up a marriage agreement with the Earl of Heresford, whose limited financial resources meant he struggled to upkeep the baroque-style family castle in Hampshire. Naila had introduced Heresford and Miss Work at the very first salon she had hosted in London. Getting Heresford married had remained a top priority for her.

"It is exciting," Naila acknowledged, happy to be talking about something other than Hawk's interest in Catherine Anne. "I am thrilled more structures will be saved."

"It will be interesting to see if Heresford makes it to the altar," Guy remarked.

"Why?" Naila asked. "Is he known to be marriage shy?"

"Heresford is an impulsive sort." Guy sipped his drink. "Scandal often follows the man."

"I certainly hope he won't do anything to jeopardize his future," she said. "Surely he realizes he needs to make a financially advantageous marriage to be able to save his home."

Guy chuckled as he wandered over to get some food. "I see you are all business, Miss Darwish, not unlike your sister, the duchess."

Naila did not see herself that way. But she was grateful she had the pamphlet and her restoration project to keep her busy. She needed the distraction. With each passing day, it became harder to push thoughts of Hawk from her mind.

Chapter Twenty-Nine

Naila plopped onto the sofa. "I think I've made a terrible mistake."

"Why?" Raya looked up from her accounts. She sat at the small round table she used as a desk. "What have you done?"

The two sisters were alone in the family sitting room at Strickland House. "I think I regret not trying harder to make a go of it with Hawk."

"Which time?"

"Very funny." Naila shot her sister a withering look. "At least I was an inexperienced young girl the first time I mucked everything up. But I have no excuse for my idiocy last year."

"I'm not surprised that you have regrets." Raya closed a ledger and put it aside. "Every time you see Hawk again, your old feelings seem to get all stirred up."

"After he kissed me last year, I should have gone after what I wanted with the same focus and drive that I put into writing my pamphlet and getting it published."

"Why didn't you?"

"My pride, my own insecurities, got in the way.

I needed him to declare his undying love for me before I shared my true feelings."

"There is nothing wrong with wanting to be loved," Raya pointed out.

"But I had already broken his heart once." Quiet despair stirred in her chest. "I abandoned him after promising to fight to stay together. Is it any wonder that he was more circumspect when we met again after eight years apart?"

Raya nibbled the back of her pen. "Well, when you put it like that—"

"I immediately regretted my actions in Philadelphia. I tried to tell him that I'd changed my mind but I was too late. He'd already sailed for England."

"What?" Raya threw down her pen. "You never told me that."

"I'm telling you now."

"Does Hawk know?"

She shook her head. "No, he doesn't."

"You've got to tell him."

"Do you think he'll believe me? He'd wonder why I didn't tell him that last year."

"You won't know until you tell him."

"He should hate me. I'd hate me if I were him."

Raya's mouth twisted. "He clearly doesn't hate you. I think it is very clear that he still esteems you."

"He's courting that shipbuilding heiress. And she loves to row just like he does, which makes matters worse. He might actually fall in love with her."

Raya studied her face. "You're jealous of Hawk's friendship with Miss Turner." It wasn't a question.

Naila blew out a breath. "That's what Hawk said."

Raya looked amused. "And is he right?"

"Of course," Naila said glumly. "The thought of Hawk marrying Catherine Anne makes me want to break everything in this house."

Raya put up a calming hand. "Well, let's not do that. Strickland House is full of precious artifacts that go back generations."

"What do you think I should do?"

"Tell him how you feel."

"When he is in the middle of courting another woman? I mean, he says he isn't courting her, but Miss Turner certainly seems to think he is."

"You have to take action if you hope to entice Hawk to ask you to marry him again."

"I might have to propose to him." She sighed. "I doubt he could bring himself to ask me to marry him again. And I can't blame him. He thinks I'm after his title and money."

"You'll have to show him that he's wrong."

"I'm not sure how to do that." But Naila was weary of sitting on the sidelines and letting life happen to her when it came to Hawk. Her most significant achievements, the pamphlet and her salons, had come about because she'd developed a plan and worked hard to make it a reality.

Maybe that should be her approach to love as well.

"I don't know what I'm going to do," she told her sister. "But I'm not going to sit by and do nothing."

"Just be careful," Raya advised.

"What have I got to lose at this point? What's the worst that can happen?" she asked. "Hawk could reject me but I will lose him for sure if I do nothing."

"You're a businesswoman now. You have to consider how your behavior will impact your enterprise."

Naila did not think of herself that way. But Guy had said something similar. Raya had always been the businesswoman in the family. "It's not as though I'm going to tear off my clothes and throw myself at the man during one of my salons."

"If you are perceived as stealing an earl away from one of your heiresses, that could impact your reputation," Raya explained. "That is your entire business model, matching rich American women with poor English lords."

"But Hawk isn't poor. It would be preferable for Catherine Anne to marry a poor aristocrat who can use her money to restore his historically significant property."

Raya chuckled. "All the same, if it looks like you're stealing a lord away from one of your heiresses, that could create a scandal. If I've learned anything since becoming a duchess, it's that the ton abhors scandal. If the very people you are trying to attract, aristocrats and wealthy American heiresses, start staying away from your salons, then your entire scheme to save these crumbling properties will fail in spectacular fashion."

Naila groaned. She couldn't risk ruining any potential matches. The Earl of Heresford was still in the middle of delicate marriage settlement negotiations with Herbert Work, father of the department store heiress. And who knew how many other potential matches were in the works? She could not risk losing both Hawk *and* her passion for saving historic homes.

"What am I supposed to do?" Frustration riled her words. "Just sit back and watch Hawk marry another woman?"

"That, I don't know." Raya picked up her pen. "But I'm confident you'll find a way to win the man and keep your business intact."

SEVERAL DAYS LATER, Charles's family held a gathering at their Richmond house outside London. The house was situated along the Thames and provided extraordinary views of the water. Since the river was placid, several guests took advantage of the rowboats provided by their hosts and went out on the water.

Naila was standing with Hind and Kareem when the Earl of Heresford wandered over with Miss Work on his arm. "I must thank you, Miss Darwish, for introducing me to this delightful young woman."

Naila smiled at him. "It was my pleasure. I thought you two might suit." She'd decided to try matching the two because both had a love for horses and horse racing. Alberta's father ran a prime specimen that had recently won the Belmont Stakes and Heresford owned a gelding he was training to run at Ascot someday.

Alberta Work colored prettily. "I am rather horse crazy but his lordship doesn't seem to mind."

"Far from it," Heresford proclaimed. "It is a pleasure to speak with a young lady who knows so much about horses."

They were distracted by shouting and laughter down near the riverbank.

"Speaking of racing, come, let us go down to the boats," Heresford said. "There's talk of having a rowing competition."

Curious, Naila followed the crowd down to the boats. If there was a rowing race, the chances were high that Hawk would participate.

"Women should row as well," Hawk called out when Naila reached the river's edge.

"Splendid," Charles said. "A man and a lady in each boat. A mixed-pairs rowing competition."

Catherine Anne stepped to Hawk's side. "I shall row with the earl."

Heresford surveyed the crowd. "Which lady will row with me? Miss Work?"

Alberta Work shook her head. "I am a horsewoman not an oarswoman."

The crowd laughed. Heresford turned to Naila. "Miss Darwish, what do you say? Will you partner with me?"

Naila stepped back. "Oh, I don't think so."

"Why not?" Hawk called out. "Has no one ever taught you how to row?"

"Once." She met his challenging gaze. "But my instructor wasn't very good."

"The lady is surely being modest," he returned. "Your pamphlet is proof that you are an exacting woman who would not settle for anything less than the best."

"Do compete, Naila," Hind encouraged her cousin. "You've rowed us at the park before."

"Yes, come and join us," said Phoebe, who'd partnered with Charles. "I'm game to try and I don't know the first thing about rowing."

Naila wanted to argue that it was hardly fair for Catherine Anne to team up with Hawk since both were excellent rowers. But she just said, "Very well," and went to stand beside Heresford.

In all, six pairs joined the competition. As Heresford helped Naila into the boat, she cautioned him about expecting too much from her.

"Not to worry," he said. "I rowed at university. I even managed to beat Hawksworth a time or two."

"I had no idea." The idea that they might actually be worthy adversaries to Hawk and Catherine Anne lifted her spirits.

"And it sounds as if you have rowed at least a little."

"Here and there," she said. She *had* learned from one of the best. Maybe that would help.

"We'll make it a short race," Hawk said as everyone climbed into the boats. "Fifty yards."

"You can do it," Heresford said encouragingly to Naila as they settled in their places. "Stay in rhythm and keep your stroke as smooth as possible."

Naila wiped her hands on her skirts before grabbing hold of the oars. Heresford rowed them into place with the other boats at the starting line. Hawk and Catherine Anne were in the boat beside them. When she briefly met Hawk's eye, he inclined his chin in her direction. She looked away and tightened her grip on the blades.

"I will do most of the work," Heresford assured her. "I can provide most of the power. If you can keep up with the pace, we should be fine."

"I wish I were as optimistic as you," she said. "Miss Turner rows regularly."

"Yes, but I have observed her technique. Her finish is faulty."

"Her finish?"

"When the oar leaves the water. She allows it to drag, which slows down the momentum. Her technique runs in opposition to Hawksworth's."

"Really?" She looked over to where Hawk and Catherine Anne sat straight-backed in their boat, their hands wrapped around their oars. Both wore such serious expressions one would think they were competing to be world champions. Naila sighed. If Catherine Anne's rowing was faulty, Naila could only imagine how bad hers was.

Her heart drummed hard as they waited for Charles's father, Lord Broughton, to shoot the starting gun. A bang sounded and they were off. True to his word, Heresford was a powerful rower. Naila's main task was to keep up with his back-and-forth motion in order not to slow them down. The boat glided through the water, swift and smooth. Spectators cheered them on, some running alongside on the water's edge.

"Go, Naila, go!"

"That's it, Miss Darwish!"

She heard Kareem and Hind yelling her name, encouraging her. She focused on her task, keeping up with Heresford, her pulse blasting in her ears, her muscles beginning to burn from the effort. Before long, she was running out of energy.

"Not much farther now!" Heresford called out from behind her.

In her peripheral vision, she could make out that Hawk's boat was still beside them. A blast of renewed energy flowed through her and she kept powering through even though her muscles were on fire.

They came across the finish line. Out of breath, her muscles trembling, Naila released the oars and looked around. She realized that Hawk and Catherine Anne had won the race, with her and Heresford coming in second.

Kareem and Hind came over as she exited the boat. She practically clung to Kareem's arm because her legs were rubbery from exertion. She sat as someone bought her a glass of lemonade, which she gratefully drank.

Heresford came over to check on her. "Bravo, Miss Darwish. Well done!"

"But we didn't win," she said glumly.

"It was a tight race. We couldn't have expected a better result given Miss Turner's rowing skill." He gazed in the direction of Hawk and Catherine Anne, who were being awarded first place by their host, Lord Broughton. "She is quite accomplished. Miss Turner is a pleasure to watch on the water."

Naila gulped her lemonade to keep from saying anything unkind about Catherine Anne, who did not deserve to be regarded unkindly.

Lightning crackled above. Naila looked up to see formidable gray clouds hanging low from the sky. She'd been so engrossed in the race she hadn't realized that the weather had turned. Lord Broughton's staff began lugging the boats from the water and carrying them off.

"Where will they take the boats?" she asked Heresford.

He pointed to a building up the hill. "That's the boathouse, I believe."

"You were splendid," Kareem said after Heresford wandered over to congratulate Hawk and Catherine Anne.

"I was so proud of you!" Hind exclaimed. "You almost won."

Kareem peered up at the sky. "We should go in. It's about to rain."

"You two go on," Naila said. "I'm just going to sit here for a moment to catch my breath."

"Are you certain?" Kareem asked.

"You don't want to be caught in the rain," Hind said worriedly.

"I won't be," she assured them. "I'll be along in a moment."

After they left her, Naila pretended not to watch Hawk and Catherine Anne accept congratulations all around. She should go and congratulate them herself but at the moment she did not think her legs could carry her. As more and more guests, including Hawk and Catherine Anne, headed indoors, Naila remained seated, absorbing the meaning of that afternoon's events.

Hawk was truly lost to her. He and Catherine Anne had obviously hit it off. It was probably only a matter of time before they announced their engagement. She blinked back tears as the pain of her loss slammed through her. She was truly alone.

She pushed to her feet, but could not bear the thought of rejoining the other guests and watching Hawk and Catherine Anne grow ever closer. She stepped on something in the grass and saw that it was an oar. It must have dropped off one of the boats as the staff carried them to the boathouse.

The boathouse sounded like the perfect place to be alone and get herself together before rejoining the others. She brushed away the tears that spilled onto her cheeks.

Picking up the oar, she headed toward the boathouse. No one could see her cry. How would she explain it? She stepped inside the dimly lit space, where boats were lined up on shelves, one atop the other.

"I was waiting for you to come and congratulate me and Miss Turner on our victory." Hawk's deep, amusement-tinged voice rumbled through her.

She dropped the oar. "Congratulations."

"Thank you. You were magnificent out there."

She turned to face him, hoping the light was

dim enough so that he couldn't tell she was upset. "We lost."

"But you stayed with Catherine Anne and me until the end. No other pair in the competition accomplished that."

She forced herself to meet his gaze even though it hurt to look at him. His hair was wind-blown and rumpled; a ghost of a smile touched his lips.

"I can barely feel my legs. Who knows if I'll be able to walk tomorrow." Outside, the sky rumbled. "What are you doing in here?"

"I saw you walking toward the boathouse. You seemed upset."

"I came to return an oar that I found on the lawn. As you can see, I am fine." She lifted her chin. "You should return to the party."

Concern stamped his face. "Have you been crying?"

She backed away. "Of course not."

"Naila?" He stepped closer. "What is wrong? Did something happen?"

She shook her head, refusing to look at him. "You should return to your Miss Turner. She is surely missing you."

"She is not *my* Miss Turner."

"Isn't she? You two obviously make a great team."

"Do you think so?"

"I still would prefer that she marry an impoverished lord and save a significant house. But, obviously, that isn't up to me."

She felt his intense gaze. "Isn't it though?"

Outside a crackling sound was followed by the pitter-patter of raindrops on the boathouse roof. They stared at each other and Naila was suddenly so hot she felt in danger of catching on fire.

"Catherine Anne is obviously your type."

He advanced on her. "What type is that?"

She backed up. "Tall. Thin. Athletic."

"That is not my type." His voice was a raspy rumble. "I prefer my woman round and soft, with generous curves in all of the right places."

"Oh?" She could barely breathe. Her stays were entirely too tight.

"A woman who feels plush and warm and inviting. A woman I can lose myself in."

She exhaled. "Oh."

"Naila," he whispered. "Why were you crying?"

She bit her lip and shook her head. "It doesn't matter. I am happy for you and Miss Turner. Truly I am. You deserve to be happy."

His eyes flickered to her mouth. "Catherine Anne is a fine person. But no woman compares to you. I enjoy talking to you more than anyone else on the planet." He was so close now that she felt his warm breath on her cheek. "And, by the way, your body is bliss."

They were both perspiring from exerting themselves on the water. "So is yours."

He grabbed her then, urgently and without restraint, and she went willingly, gratefully. He kissed her hard, sucking her bottom lip, nibbling on her upper lip. He tore off the scarf at her neck and sucked the sensitive flesh there. "Tell me to stop if you don't want this."

She tilted her head to give him better access to her nape. "I do," she said desperately, clutching him closer to her. "I want you."

He groaned and his hands went to her jacket, which she urgently shrugged out of with his help. He unbuttoned the high-collared white shirt she wore beneath it. She worked on unfastening her skirt and allowed it to drop to the ground. Thank goodness she was wearing sporting clothes so she wasn't encumbered by a bustle. She stood before him in just her combinations, a thin camisole with attached knee-length drawers worn beneath a confining corset. By cinching in her waist, the stays emphasized her generous bosom and round hips.

"Look at that body," he said reverentially, unfastening her corset one hook at a time. "You are a goddess." With each hook that he undid, she breathed a little easier. The corset fell away and she was left wearing only her undergarments, which left little to the imagination. His hand went to her breast, squeezing and massaging.

"Since you, I've never truly looked at another woman." He sucked her nipple through the frothy fabric. She clutched his head to her breast. His other hand went to the place between her legs, where her drawers were not sewn at the crotch.

They groaned in unison when he touched her intimate flesh and his fingers were immediately coated with her dampness.

"You're very ready," he said against her breast.

"For you? Always," she half-cried, so full of need for him that she could barely stand it.

His fingers played with the delicate nub that seemed to have a million different nerve endings. And the tension ratcheted up in her. He fell to his knees and hiked her leg over his shoulder and put his tongue where is fingers had been.

"Oh!" she cried out, the sound guttural because she could not have formed a coherent word even if her life depended on it.

He sucked at her and flicked his tongue hard and flat against the sensitive point between her legs. She lost all reason. She could think of nothing but wanting more. *More.* Until the tension reached a breaking point and bliss rippled through her and her body throbbed with relief.

He rose to his full height, tearing off his jacket. He reached for his trousers and she helped him free his member. She took it against her palm.

"Harder if you please," he rasped. "Stroke firmly."

"I do please." She did as he instructed, feeling the power of having this man in the palm of her hand. He was thick and hard, steel encased in silk. Instinctively, she dropped to her knees to kiss it. He made a sound deep in his throat. She rubbed her lips against the side of his shaft, pressing firm kisses up and down the length of him. "Tell me what to do."

"In your mouth," he rasped. "If . . . you want—"

"I want," she said before closing her lips around him.

"Deeper," he gasped. "If you'd like."

"I'd like." She took him as deep as she could manage without gagging. His hand was on her head and she stared up at him as she sucked on him.

"Enough," he said, pulling her to her feet.

"Was I doing it wrong?"

"No, you were doing it too well. I want to be inside you."

"I want that, too." She'd dreamed of this moment for nine years. She wanted to make him hers. Forever.

Hawk was her *naseeb*. The mate that fate and destiny meant for her. She had no doubt. She wasn't a naive little girl anymore. She knew they had something she could never hope to find with anyone else.

"Are you certain, Naila?" he asked. "This time there can be no turning back."

"I don't want to turn back." She knelt on the ground and lay back. "I want it all with you. Only you."

He stared down at her. "Open your legs for me. I want to see you."

She opened her legs so he could look his fill. His eyes blazed. "You are mine now."

"I am," she said. "And you are mine."

He knelt between her legs.

"Are you going to do more than look?" she finally asked.

He was on her so fast that she could not help but laugh. And then he was entering her and she stopped laughing. Instead, tears leaked from her eyes. Joy and need filled her in equal measure. She was finally where she was always meant to be, joined with Hawk. With Basil.

"My love," she sighed.

He stroked in and out of her with firm measured strokes. "Move with me, sweetheart," he urged, helping her find her rhythm. And then her hips were rising up to meet his thrusts and she felt him so deep inside her that relief poured through her. She felt her climax coming again, the pressure and the promise of bliss and blessed relief.

Outside a storm raged, the rain pounding so hard on the roof that Naila did not hear herself cry out even though she knew that she did.

Chapter Thirty

Afterward, Hawk couldn't stop running his hands over Naila's gorgeous body. He could hardly believe he was here with her. That she was naked and he could look and touch his fill.

"Mmm." She stretched under his touch, purring like a cat. "That feels so good."

"You had better get used to me touching you always." He ran a hand over her breast. Cupping it, weighting it in his hand. "Beautiful." He bent forward to kiss the soft brown tip and couldn't resist a quick taste.

She pulled his face up to hers to kiss him fully on the mouth, her bold tongue lazily exploring his. Outside the rain slammed against the roof.

"I am sorry I didn't offer for you at Strickland House last year," he said impulsively. "I should have. I wanted to."

"Why didn't you?"

"I suppose I was still angry with you for rejecting me in Philadelphia. I truly thought it best that we parted. I couldn't survive losing you again."

"I suppose I deserved that." She feathered a finger lightly over his chest, exploring the landscape of his body.

"You did not. I am profoundly sorry for the way I treated you that day."

"I am the one who owes you an apology for Philadelphia. And an explanation."

He caught her hand and brought her fingers to his lips. "It's unnecessary. I have forgiven you. You were young and afraid. I understand that now."

"It was more than that. My father was ill. His heart was weak. Auntie Majida said my running away with you might be too much for his heart. I truly believed my desertion could kill my father."

"Your father was ill? Why didn't you tell me?" It would have explained so much about Naila's shocking desertion.

"Auntie Majida swore me to secrecy. My father didn't want anyone to know."

"Was it true? Was he ill?"

She nodded. "It was. He survived for several years afterward but his heart grew even weaker over time. That's what eventually killed him." A tear slipped down the side of her face.

He kissed her softly. "I'm sorry, my love. I'm sorry you lost him."

"I did love my father very much." She held his face in her hands. "But not enough to desert you."

He turned his face to kiss her palm. "I don't understand."

"I came back for you," she said and he heard the emotion in her voice. "But I was too late. You were gone."

He stared at her. "What do you mean?"

"In Philadelphia, three days after our last terrible meeting, I realized I couldn't live without you. I rushed to find you to tell you." She looked stricken. "But then your uncle told me you'd sailed for England. I'd lost my chance."

He was stunned. These revelations upended everything he thought he knew about their breakup. "If only I'd known."

"I don't blame you for hating me."

"I could never hate you. I detested myself for not being able to get over you, but I never hated you. How could I when I love you more than anything?"

She gave him a watery smile. "Still?"

"More than ever."

"We haven't lost our chance?"

He nibbled her shoulder. "I cannot live without you. I fear you are stuck with me."

"I could get used to having you around all of the time."

He was growing hard for her again but this was no time to get carried away. "We should go into the house before they miss us."

"Before your Miss Turner misses you," she said tartly. "Is that what you mean?"

"I barely remember her name." He couldn't resist passing a hand over her mound, toying with the dark patch of curls there. "As I said, it's always been you."

That seemed to satisfy her because she pulled him to her for another long, lingering kiss. "You are right. We should go," she said when their lips parted.

He sat up but not before pausing to admire her one more time. "You are without a male relative in England. I guess I should speak to Strickland."

"Wait." She stood up and reached for her combinations. "We need to think about how to go about this."

"What do you mean?" He enjoyed watching her bend over as she put her undergarments on.

"Everyone thinks you are courting Catherine Anne Turner."

"So?" He rose and reached for his trousers. "I'm not."

"She seems to think you are."

"I never asked Catherine Anne's father for permission to court her."

Naila hooked herself into her corset. He preferred her naked but she still looked like a dream. He made quick work of shrugging into his clothes, topping his shirt and waistcoat with a blazer.

"I cannot be perceived as stealing the lords right out from under my clients."

He tied his neckcloth. "Catherine Anne is a client?"

"It is an informal arrangement, but her father has been generous with his thanks."

He paused. "Just how much money have you made as a result of this endeavor?"

"Enough for you to be reassured that I don't have to marry you for money or position."

He flushed. "I never thought you did. Not really. That wasn't my proudest moment."

"Let's forget the past and only look forward."

He pulled her up against his body. "I definitely look forward to the future with you." He kissed her hard and fast.

"And to answer your question about my finances," she said proudly, "I have earned enough to support myself indefinitely."

Hawk knew she was marrying him for him. He didn't require proof. "You're going to make me hard again."

She playfully evaded his grasp when he tried to pinch her plump bottom. "And it would be ruinous if I angered the heiresses and their fathers by marrying a man that the daughter of a very wealthy and powerful American magnate has set her sights on."

Dread tickled his gut. "What are you saying?"

"And you must admit that you did encourage her."

"Naila," he demanded. "*What* are you saying?"

"We need to take it slow. Our relationship must be a secret for now."

"You think to keep me a secret? Like you did in Philadelphia? I will not stand for that," he said roughly. This could not be happening. Not again. "You are either proud to stand beside me or you are not. It is that simple."

She reached for his hand. "It's not that—"

Her words were interrupted by banging on the boathouse door. "Is anyone in there?" Charles's voice sounded outside.

"Did you lock the door?" Naila asked Hawk.

"Of course. I didn't want to be interrupted." He started for the door. "You'd better hide yourself."

He pulled the door open to find Charles, accompanied by a Broughton footman.

"Hawk," Charles said with surprise. "What are you doing in the boathouse?"

"I came to return an errant oar I found on the lawn," Hawk said easily. "And then I got caught in the rain."

Charles looked past him. "We are looking for Miss Darwish. She promised to come indoors before it rained but no one has seen her. Her cousin is worried about her."

"Miss Darwish?" He shook his head. "No, I haven't seen her. If she isn't in the house maybe she took refuge from the rain elsewhere." He stepped outside and firmly pulled the boathouse door closed behind him. "Come on then, I'll help you look."

Two DAYS LATER, Naila still couldn't get images of making love with Hawk out of her mind. Which was fine with her. She enjoyed reliving the boathouse scenes over and over again.

"How is 'Operation Get Hawk to Propose Again' going?" Raya asked when she entered the sitting room where Naila was finalizing plans for her next salon.

Naila smiled. "I have reason to believe that everything will work out."

Raya studied her face. "Did something happen?"

"You could say so, yes. But I'd like to be quiet about it, just for now."

"Come on," Raya cajoled, "you can tell me."

"You'll just run to the duke and tell him everything."

"Well, not everything."

They were interrupted by the appearance of Strickland and Guy Vaughan. "Guy has stopped by to have tea with us."

There were greetings all around while Raya rang for the butler to have a tray brought up. A few minutes later, Phoebe arrived to visit with Naila and was invited to join the group for tea.

Guy turned to Naila. "I heard you put on quite a show at Broughton's Richmond house."

Raya turned to her. "You did?" She and the duke had not attended the party.

Naila flushed. "We had a boat race."

"You raced a boat?" Raya asked, incredulous.

"In pairs," Guy explained.

"Miss Darwish raced with Heresford," Phoebe said. "She was magnificent."

"Oh," Raya said, losing interest so quickly that Naila almost laughed out loud.

She hadn't seen Hawk in two days. She assumed he was respecting her desire to be discreet. She and Hawk were finding it harder and harder to be restrained around each other. She told herself it was a good thing that he hadn't immediately come around. If he had, she might have blushed just looking at him and remembering what they'd done.

"I hear congratulations are in order," Guy said to Naila.

"For what?" Naila asked. Surely Hawk hadn't said anything to Guy.

"You have another successful match on your hands."

"I do? Who?"

"It's something of a scandal. The earl eloped with Miss Catherine Anne Turner."

Naila's stomach dropped. The room spun. She must have heard wrong. She *had* to have.

"What?" Raya exclaimed.

The duke frowned. "I had not heard anything of the sort. When did this occur?"

"Just after Broughton's boat race party," Guy said. "Apparently after the race, the earl was so taken with Miss Turner's performance on the water that they were caught *in flagrante* shortly after the storm that sent everyone indoors."

"Impossible!" Raya said.

"I assure you that it is true. They were found in one of the unused drawing rooms. Discretion dictates that I not elaborate further."

"Yes, that is quite enough," the duke warned. "Given that there are ladies present."

Naila couldn't breathe. There had to be some mistake. Hawk would never go directly from bedding her to playing around with Catherine Anne. And eloping with her.

He *had* been upset when she told him they had to hide their involvement. *Not again*, he'd said. She twisted her fingers in her lap. She hadn't had time to explain that it was just for a little while. What a fool she'd been not to make sure he understood.

"I shall say no more," Guy said. "But scandal or no, it's quite the success for you, is it not Miss Darwish?"

"Yes," she said faintly, not knowing what else to say.

Phoebe studied her. "I thought you would be

more jubilant that Lord Heresford's castle will now be saved."

She blinked. "Heresford?"

"That's right," Guy said. "Who did you think I was referring to?"

"The Earl of Heresford has run off with Miss Catherine Anne Turner?" Naila repeated to make sure she comprehended the situation.

"Quite so," Guy said.

Phoebe sat on the edge of her seat, happily chipping in to the latest gossip. "Her father caught them and quickly carted them off to Gretna Green to seal the union."

"Oh." Intense relief poured through Naila, leaving her weak in the limbs. "How wonderful."

"Very, very wonderful," Raya added. "What a huge success for my sister."

"Yes," Naila said. "I had hoped to find Heresford a suitable heiress."

"And so you have," Guy said. "But I thought he was interested in the department store heiress."

As had Naila. She fervently hoped Alberta Work wasn't disappointed. The young woman had seemed hopeful for a match. "I did think Miss Work and Heresford had bonded over their shared love of horses."

"Heresford is apparently fonder of rowers than riders," Guy quipped. They proceeded to talk of other matters as the tea was brought in. Naila barely followed the conversation. She was still trembling from the terrible scare she'd had. She needed to see Hawk and clear everything up.

She wanted no more misunderstandings between them. She could not risk losing Hawk again. She couldn't bear it. To hell with her enterprise. Her business and reputation were far less important to her than Hawk. She could not risk losing him again. She'd made that mistake as a young girl. She would not repeat the same colossal error as a grown woman. This time, she would not be afraid to take what she wanted, the consequences be damned. The next time she saw Hawk, she would bare her heart to him.

"Miss Darwish?" The butler's voice cut into her thoughts.

She blinked. "Yes?"

"Mr. Amar is here to see you."

"Kareem is here?" She wasn't expecting him. "Please show him in."

Kareem arrived and greeted everyone in his usual pleasant and polite manner. But Naila knew the man well enough to detect that something was wrong. He seemed nervous and on edge.

"Is everything all right?" she asked.

"Yes." His gaze met hers. "But I need to speak with you privately regarding a matter of great importance."

"I DO HOPE you are not too disappointed about Miss Turner's defection," Charles said to Hawk after they'd exercised their horses in Hyde Park. They'd met for an early morning ride and were preparing to depart, each to their own homes.

"Not at all." Hawk suppressed an urge to grin. Catherine Anne's elopement with Heresford was the best news he'd heard in a long while. "I hope they'll be very happy."

"I'm sure Miss Darwish will be thrilled that Heresford's castle will be saved."

"Undoubtedly." Hawk's body hummed with anticipation. The last obstacle to him being with Naila was conveniently gone. He'd kept his distance since the boathouse, as Naila had asked. But now she had no reason to keep their relationship a secret. Now was the time to court her openly and lavishly. He could not wait.

"You're looking awfully cheery," Charles remarked.

He patted his mount's nose. "Am I?"

"What is going on?"

Hawk grinned. "I may soon have news of my own."

Charles's brows shot up. "You?"

"Why are you so surprised? I'm an earl. It is my duty to marry."

"Well, yes, but after you returned from America, it seemed like you intended to remain a bachelor forever. Who is the lucky lady?"

"I think I shall wait until she officially accepts my offer before divulging her identity."

"That's very mysterious of you. Love certainly seems to be in the air these days."

"Why? Who else is getting married?"

"Haven't you heard? Miss Darwish is betrothed to that architect."

Hawk almost dropped the reins. "I beg your pardon?"

"Miss Darwish is engaged to that Kareem Amar fellow."

He frowned. "There's obviously been a mistake."

"No, no mistake. Phoebe was there when it was announced."

The blood rushed to Hawk's ears. "What?" It couldn't be. "Impossible."

"I assure you it is all done. Phoebe heard about it from Miss Darwish herself. She was visiting at Strickland House when the architect made a dramatic appearance."

"When was this?"

"Just yesterday afternoon. The betrothal is quite fresh."

No. *No.* "How did that come about?"

"The architect went around to Strickland House yesterday afternoon and asked to speak to her in private. Once she accepted his offer, they informed the family of their decision."

"How did the family react?" he asked numbly, still in complete disbelief.

"The old aunt was thrilled apparently. She made this high-pitched noise that is supposed to be celebratory. And everyone laughed and applauded afterward."

An ululation. Hawk remembered it well from Strick and Raya's wedding celebrations. The trilling howl that expressed joy and happiness at Arab celebrations.

"When is this wedding supposed to take place?"

"I believe they hope to marry next month."

Hawk's gut cramped. Why would Naila accept the architect's offer? It couldn't be. There had to be some mistake.

And yet.

He'd been cold to her after they made love. Told her he would not keep their love a secret. And then he'd stayed away for two days because he thought that's what she wanted. What if she'd misunderstood his absence? What if she'd taken his subsequent nonappearance as a rejection?

Or did she think she actually loved the architect? Maybe she realized her attraction to Hawk was purely physical. Sexual. Carnal. She'd collaborated with the architect on her pamphlet. They shared a love of architecture. They were like-minded in many ways.

"You're awfully quiet," Charles remarked.

"I'm just thinking of everything I have to do today."

"Are you attending Miss Darwish's salon tomorrow?" Charles asked. "You can congratulate the betrothed couple there."

"I will try." He had, of course, planned on seeing Naila there. An earl in search of a wife would draw no suspicions by appearing at one of Naila's salons. But now he didn't know what to think. There'd obviously been some mistake. Or misunderstanding.

Confused thoughts ricocheted inside his skull. What the devil was Naila up to? Was this a diversion? No, it couldn't be. He immediately dismissed the notion. Naila would never toy with the architect's emotions. Unless the man was in on whatever scheme she'd concocted.

"I must go." Charles interrupted his thoughts. "I am meeting Phoebe later."

Taking his leave of Charles, Hawk's immediate instinct was to race right over to Strickland House to clear up this obvious misadventure. But then he thought better of it. He didn't always manage to express himself as eloquently as he hoped in his conversations with Naila.

No, talking with her might not be the most effective way to achieve his aim. He would put it all down on paper. He would show her everything in his heart. And this time, if she turned him down, there could be no doubt, no wondering if he'd said something wrong.

He was going to propose to Naila again. This

time he intended to write her a letter that laid bare all of his feelings, put everything on the line. He was going to deliver the note himself. He would leave nothing to chance this time.

And then he would wait to hear from Naila.

CHAPTER THIRTY-ONE

Two days later, Naila still hadn't seen or heard from Hawk.

She'd been so certain that he'd attend her latest salon that she would have bet a year's worth of pamphlet sales on it. Her heart had skipped a beat with each new arrival but Hawk was never among them. She hadn't had the chance to tell him that she was ready to go public with their betrothal, no matter what the consequences.

"I wonder where Hawk is," she'd finally said to Charles and Phoebe, unable to stop herself from asking about him.

"I asked him just yesterday if he would attend," Charles informed her. "He said he was unsure."

Why would Hawk question coming to her salon? He'd attended the few others she'd hosted. Now, as she stared out the window of the upstairs sitting room, she couldn't help wondering what was going on with Hawk.

"*Shoo malitch?*" Auntie Majida asked.

She looked over at her aunt, who was working on her *tatreez* needlework. "What do you mean? There is nothing wrong with me."

"You keep staring out the window." She dipped another stitch, red thread on black fabric, creating an intricate pattern. "Are you waiting for someone?"

"Who would I be waiting for?"

Auntie Majida made a skeptical humming sound deep in her throat. "Yes. Who."

"Why do you think I'm waiting for someone?"

"You get that look when you think about *il ajnabi*."

She did? "I don't know what you're talking about."

Her aunt looked at her with dark beady eyes. "You still want him, even after all these years." It was a statement, not a question.

Naila looked away but she didn't bother to deny the truth of Auntie's words. It wouldn't be long now before she and Hawk told the family that they intended to be together.

"He left you a letter," Auntie said.

"Who did?" Naila asked absently, turning back to gaze out the window.

"The boy from Philadelphia."

Naila swung around to stare at her aunt. "Hawk sent me a letter?"

Her aunt nodded.

Her heart beat a little faster. "When?"

"Two days ago."

"What?" Excitement bubbled up in her. "Where's this letter?"

"*Fa ibbee*," the aunt answered, reaching into the hidden breast pocket of her traditional thobe where women often kept money and other valuables.

"Why didn't you give it to me before?" she demanded to know.

"You know why."

Her chest burned. "Because you're still against my marrying him."

"It is always better to marry your own kind."

"You accepted Raya's marriage to an *ajnabi*."

The older woman fixed her with a sharp look. "You know why."

Naila was aware of certain extenuating circumstances surrounding Raya's marriage to Strick. But she didn't care about any of that now. She reached for the letter, snatching it up like precious gold. "Why are you giving this to me now?"

"You are old," Auntie Majida said matter-of-factly. Aunties never worried about hurting anyone's feelings. "Who else will marry you?"

Naila let out a joyous half-laugh. "Who else indeed?"

And she went away to read the letter in private.

My dearest Naila,

How to begin? I have torn up a fortune in paper while trying to tell you what is in my heart.

And, put quite simply, it is you. It is your laugh, and the way you look at me, it is your pleasure in drinking a cup of mint tea, and how you row a boat or single-handedly save a crumbling mansion. It is how you exist as your incomparable self.

I have heard of your engagement to Mr. Amar and I confess to being deeply confused. I believed we had reached an understanding. What have I done to turn you away so quickly? I am convinced there's been some mistake, but then I am petrified when I contemplate that perhaps word of your betrothal to another man could be true.

You once accused me of not speaking plainly about matters of the heart. That is why I am writing to you now. I cannot let you go away from me until I am convinced that you understand how deeply I cherish you. I have loved you since we first met in the garden in Philadelphia. I now believe my soul became forever intertwined with yours the moment we met.

I am not a man of many words, but just know that I love you to the depths of my being. I will never love another as I love you. In all of these years, I have never met a woman who compares to you. As much as I've tried to drive you from my mind these last nine years, it's an impossible task.

And so, yet again, I offer you my heart. What

of you, my love? Am I firmly lodged in your heart and mind the way you are forever entrenched in mine? Will you still have me?

Yours now and always,
Basil

Tears gathered in Naila's eyes as she read and reread the note. Hawk loved her and wanted to marry her. Breathless with excitement, she folded the letter and tucked it under her pillow. She had to find him right away. Auntie Majida had held on to his letter for two days. What must he be thinking?

She changed quickly and quietly let herself out through the garden entrance. She didn't want to contend with Auntie Majida asking her where she was going. She dashed over to Hawk's London residence, half running, bursting into a smile every few minutes when she thought of their reunion. She couldn't wait to tell him that she too had loved him from the beginning, that there could be no other for her.

By the time she arrived at his townhome on Grosvenor Square, Naila was out of breath. She ran up the front steps, not caring who saw her, an unmarried woman, pounding on the front door of a known bachelor.

The heavy front door opened to reveal a disdainful-looking footman in full red-and-black regalia. "May I help you?" he intoned, peering down his nose at her.

"Lord Hawksworth," she managed to say as she gulped in breaths of air. "I must see him."

"His lordship is not at home to visitors."

"He will be at home to me. Tell him it's Naila and that I've just read his letter and my answer is yes." She erupted in happy laughter. "A thousand times yes."

"His lordship sent you a letter?" He regarded her more carefully now. "To which he required a response."

"Yes, yes, that's right." She was beginning to catch her breath. "My name is Miss Darwish."

"Darwish? The author of *An American Heiress's Guide to Landing a Lord*?"

"Yes, that is me," she said. Now that Hawk's footman knew who she was, he would surely admit her.

He frowned. "With respect, Miss Darwish, his lordship is not at all fond of liver or puce."

It took her a minute to understand his point. "I realize. Please, I must speak to his lordship regarding a most urgent matter."

"I'm afraid that's not possible."

She couldn't bear the thought of Hawk going another minute thinking she'd chosen not to respond to his letter. "Kindly go and tell him that I'm here."

"I cannot. His lordship is not at home."

Her face fell. "Where is he?"

"I'm afraid I'm not at liberty to say."

In her desperation to reach Hawk, Naila lost all patience. "If you value your place in this house, you will tell me where Hawksworth is. He would want my response to his letter in all haste, which you are preventing."

"Very well," he relented. "His lordship is out rowing."

"Where?" she demanded to know. "Where does he row when he is in London?"

"He takes his scull out at Philips Boat Club. It's just a few blocks from here."

He directed her on how to get to the boat club. But she was so excited and flustered that she couldn't remember whether to go left or right at the last turn. Thankfully, a passing washerwoman pointed her in the correct direction.

When she finally arrived at the boat club, Naila was out of breath again. Her cheeks burned and her heart thumped hard. She imagined Catherine Anne Turner would not be winded in the slightest had she undertaken the same journey on foot. But there was no reason to think of Catherine Anne now. Miss Turner had landed her earl and now it was long past time for Naila to do the same. She would not let her earl get away again.

She stood on the water's edge searching all of the boats for Hawk's familiar form. And there, in the distance, finally, she spotted him.

Hawk rowed as hard as he ever had before, his skiff barreling down the Thames.

His muscles burned but he barely noticed. His thoughts churned. Where was Naila? Why hadn't she responded to his letter? He'd delivered the note to Strickland House himself. He'd stopped short of placing his message directly in her hands but surely Philips, Strick's butler, would have given it to her. A servant, even the highest servant, would never disobey an earl's direct order.

He pulled up at the boathouse after more than two hours on the water. Boathouse attendants rushed over to see to his boat. Out of breath and perspiring profusely, Hawk stepped onto dry land.

"How dare you!"

He turned at the sound of Naila's indignant words, a voice he'd been waiting to hear for what felt like an eternity.

"How dare I what?"

She had her hands on her hips, and her cheeks were flushed, as if she'd run a long distance. "How dare you believe I would contemplate marrying another man?"

A smile touched his lips. He knew it couldn't be true.

"We'll put the boat away, your lordship," one of the attendants said. "Do you require anything else?"

That's when Hawk realized they were drawing attention from the attendants and other boaters. "That will be all." He turned his attention back to Naila. "Let's go somewhere a little more private."

He led her into the boathouse.

"Boathouses are not exactly where we do our best talking," she noted.

The words shot straight to his prick. "I remember."

After a quick word with the boatkeeper, he led Naila upstairs to the boatkeeper's private lodgings, a two-room space with a narrow bed on at the far end. A worn wooden table with three chairs and a tattered sofa were the primary furnishings in the main room.

"This is scandalous," she said as he closed the door. "Are you trying to ruin me?"

"Too late for that," he quipped. "Although I would not mind ruining you again and again."

"If the boatkeeper tells anyone that I was here with you, my reputation will be ruined. People will avoid my salons."

"I know the boatkeeper. And I will pay him handsomely for his discretion. If he values his position, he won't say anything to anyone."

Her cheeks flushed even more. "How dare you

believe that I would get engaged to Kareem? He is just a friend."

"What the devil took you so long to respond to my letter?"

"Auntie Majida held on to it for a couple of days. She only gave it to me this afternoon."

"You won't let her come between us again." It was a statement. Not a question.

"Never." Her dark eyes blazed. "I don't care how that impacts my reputation or my matchmaking enterprise. I want you and I intend to have you."

His eyes flashed. He took a step toward her. "You have no idea how long I've waited to hear you say that."

She set her hand flat against his chest, stopping his advance. "Now, you tell me what your excuse is for believing I would agree to marry another man the day after we . . . you know . . . in the boathouse."

"I was told by Charles that you were betrothed. That the architect visited you at Strickland House to declare his undying love."

She shook her head. "You *do* know that I am not the *only* Miss Darwish currently staying at the ducal residence."

"Are you saying . . . ?" Hawk felt like a fool. "The architect is marrying Miss Hind?"

"Yes, you idiot!"

"How did that come about? All this time, I thought the man was pining for you."

"We have always been friends, nothing more," she explained. "Hind and Kareem developed feelings for each other during Hind's convalescence at Briar Hall."

"Hmm." Hawk was floating on air. "He did visit every day."

"And it never occurred to you that he did so because he was interested in Hind?" she asked. "I believe Hind is the reason he stayed behind and didn't come to London with the rest of us."

"I am an idiot." He advanced on her, pushing her up against the door with his body. This time she allowed it. "A very happy idiot." He bent down to kiss her even though he was in desperate need of a bath. She kissed him back with equal parts irritation and passion.

He broke the kiss. "Charles said that Kareem came to Strickland House and specifically asked to speak with you in private."

Her hair was slightly askew and she was breathless from his kiss. He resolved right then to keep Naila as breathless as possible as often as possible. He pressed his open mouth against hers, tangling his tongue with hers.

After an arousing clash of lips and tongue, she turned her head to the side so she could speak. "After he talked with Hind, he came to ask to speak with me."

"Why?"

"On account of our friendship, he and Hind

wanted to tell me first before informing the rest of the family."

"That was thoughtful of them." He cupped her breast and her breath caught. "It saves me the trouble of calling him out."

"Don't be ridiculous." She brushed a hand against the hard ridge of his prick. "Does anyone still duel?"

Hawk sucked in a breath. He liked it when Naila took what she wanted. "I would absolutely resurrect the practice if required."

She rubbed more insistently against his prick. "Or you could just believe in me."

"Oh, I believe in you." He started to hitch up her skirt. "More than you know."

She adjusted her stance, widening her legs to better his access. "What are you doing?"

"Do I really have to explain it to you?" His seeking fingers found her sweet moist pussy. "Or should I just show you?"

She hitched up one leg and he took firm hold of it, giving himself license to touch her more liberally. "Showing me . . . will . . . be sufficient," she gasped.

"Good." He slid a finger inside her.

"Oh!" she panted.

He added a second finger. "You could be carrying my child right now. We weren't careful."

She moved against his fingers, her plush lips

open, her eyes locked on his. "We didn't need to be."

"Does this mean that you accept my proposal?"

She hesitated. His fingers stilled.

"Don't stop," she protested.

"Answer my question," he demanded.

"Keep going and I will."

He resumed his exploration, feeling the tightness of her sheath, relishing how she was practically dripping for him. "Well?"

She moaned with pleasure. And he couldn't stop himself from bringing her off. He sped up the movement of his fingers, thumbing her clit the way he knew she liked. It didn't take long before she tensed and cried out. He covered her mouth with his, swallowing her orgasm, kissing her hard and rough.

"Oh my," she said when her body was so relaxed he thought she might slide to the ground.

"Now answer the question." He held her up. "Do you accept my proposal?"

Her lazy satisfied smile made his aching prick jerk. "Should we take care of you?" she asked, brushing the back of her hand against the placket of his trousers.

"Later." He stilled her exploration, not wanting to come against her hand. "Answer the question."

"Well," she said, yawning and stretching, "accepting your proposal will ruin my plans."

"What plans are those?" he growled.

"I came here to propose to *you*. It seemed only fair, considering that you had to ask the last time."

He smiled. "I should turn you down. Turnabout is fair play."

She pretended to pout. "I could always see if Kareem would agree to marry me instead of Hind."

"Don't you dare," he snarled.

"Well," she asked. "What do you say? Will you marry me?"

"Hell yes!" He scooped her up in his arms and set her on the table.

"What are you doing?" she asked.

He undid his trousers, taking his aching prick into his hand. "We're going to take care of me now."

She lay back, spreading her legs. "Mmm," she said. "I cannot think of a better way to celebrate our engagement."

He pushed into her, seating himself as deeply as he'd ever seated himself in any woman. "Neither can I."

"I suppose this means we are definitely getting married."

"Until death parts us."

"No." She shook her head. "That's not good enough."

"It isn't?" He stroked into her. "What is?"

"In Arabic we say, *fil dunya wal akhra*."

"And the translation?"

"It means in this world. And the next."

"I had no idea that Arabic is so poetic." He kissed her gently. "Exactly so, my love. May we be together always—in this world and the next."

Chapter Thirty-Two

The line dancing at their engagement celebration was a bit of a mess on account of there being too few Arabs and too many non-Arabs trying their hand (and feet) at it for the first time.

"We're messing up the tempo," Hawk said to Naila while they kicked and dipped their way through the dance. They moved to the beat of the throbbing *tabla* drum the architect had brought over for this evening's party.

She squeezed his hand as they moved shoulder-to-shoulder. "Nonsense, it's the spirit of the *debke* that matters and everyone seems to be having a good time."

She was laughing and out of breath. He was breathless, too, but mostly from looking at her and being filled with wonder at being able to publicly claim Naila as his.

"I cannot believe I had to wait nine years to be able to dance in line next to you," he said loudly over the music, remembering the time Naila's male cousins very pointedly kept him from holding Naila's hand.

"Was it worth the wait?" she asked.

"It would have been preferable to be able to do it years ago," he grumbled. "I don't see how we gained anything from being miserably apart all those years."

The music swelled, the beat growing more insistent. The *debke* dancers at the head of the line, those who set the tempo, picked up the pace. Kareem and Ghassan were at the lead, followed by Strick, Guy and a handful of other men. Hawk was happily at the end of the men so that he could hold his love's hand. Naila was first in line for the women, followed by Nadine and Hind and several American heiresses trying to follow the steps with varying degrees of success.

When the music ended, the fatigued dancers broke away to rest their feet and get something cool to drink. Strick's footmen served a refreshing icy lemon mint drink.

"This is delicious," he said, bottoming out the glass.

Naila, flushed and radiant, sipped her drink. "We must grow *na'na* at Briar Hall so that we can make *limonana* whenever you like."

"*Na'na*?" he repeated.

"Mint," she translated. "Every self-respecting Palestinian household grows their own mint."

"If it means I can have this drink . . . what is it called?"

"*Limonana*. It's a combination of the words lemon and *na'na*. Basically, it's a mint lemonade."

He reached for another full glass. "We'll need to direct the gardener to plant mint right away."

Charles and Phoebe wandered over. "I never imagined we'd be celebrating your betrothal before Phoebe and I made it to the altar," Charles said.

Hawk grinned. "I need to lock the lady in before someone else does."

Phoebe sidled up to Naila. "Everyone is agog that you've captured an earl."

"*I* captured her," Hawk corrected. "And it wasn't an easy task."

Naila's cheeks colored. "I don't think they need to hear the entire story," she interrupted.

"I wouldn't mind hearing it," Charles said.

Fortunately for Naila, Strick and Raya came over, and Charles and Phoebe excused themselves, leaving the four of them on their own.

"Congratulations you two," Raya said. "I'm thrilled Naila will be here in England with me."

"Everyone is excited for you," Strick added.

Hawk scanned the room, his gaze landing on the scowling older woman sitting on the perimeter of the dance floor. "Not everyone, apparently. Auntie Majida looks less than thrilled."

"Nonsense," Raya said. "Auntie always looks

mad but she's relieved that all three Darwish sisters will now be married. Finally."

The older woman suddenly started wailing. Hawk froze. Was she about to cause a scene? He looked to Naila but she was smiling, her focus on her aunt. Strick and Raya also acted as if nothing was amiss.

It took Hawk a moment to realize the old lady wasn't wailing. The high-pitched rhythmic sound was an ululation. "Isn't that an expression of joy and celebration?" he asked.

"Yes." Naila laughed. "I told you she was happy."

To finally be accepted by Auntie Majida was a validation Hawk didn't realize he'd been waiting for. "Well"—he smirked in Strick's direction—"it looks like you are not the only foreigner husband Auntie Majida approves of."

"You never know," Strick said with a twinkle in his eyes. "Didn't Naila ever tell you that ululations can also be an expression of sorrow?"

Hawk's smile slipped. "Is that true?" he asked the sisters.

"Don't listen to the duke," Naila said. "Come on. I want to waltz with my future husband."

"It would be my pleasure." Hawk offered his arm. When he took her into his arms, all was right with the world.

"Hawk," Naila said. "There is something I've been meaning to ask you."

They took a twirl. "And what is that, my love?"

"Do you remember that ring you tried to give me the first time you proposed, the one that matched the bracelet you gave me?"

"Yes," he said slowly. "What of it?"

"I would like for that to be my wedding gift from you."

"I'm afraid that won't be possible."

"Why not?"

"Because it's in Philadelphia."

"You left it there?"

"I actually tossed it into the river when I was rowing," he said apologetically. "I was a little upset."

"That's a shame."

"I'll have twenty different rings made to replace it."

"Don't be silly," she returned. "As long as I have you, that is all I need."

"*Ya rohee*," he said.

She blinked. "What?"

"Did I say it wrong? Your aunt taught it to me."

Her expression grew misty. "Not at all. You said it correctly. *Ya rohee*."

"My soul," he said. "You are my soul. You've always been. I cannot wait to marry you."

"*Fil dunya wal akhra*," she said softly.

"Absolutely." This time he remembered what those words meant. "In this world and the next."

He'd spent an eternity waiting for this woman, biding his time until he could claim her as his own in front of the world. He would never hide his love for her again. That is why, in full view of their guests and not caring who saw them, he kissed his bride-to-be with a smile on his lips.

AUTHOR'S NOTE

The journalist in me can't help being inspired by true-life events and, therefore, sprinkling them into my manuscripts.

In the case of *The Earl That Got Away*, the manual Naila writes was inspired by a real periodical, *Titled Americans: A List of American Ladies Who Have Married Foreigners of Rank*. Like Naila's manual, *Titled Americans* listed the names of eligible peers, their estates and incomes. You can read the highly entertaining eligible bachelor entries in the book *Titled Americans: The Real Heiresses' Guide to Marrying an Aristocrat*.

While Naila's motive for writing her pamphlet—to save grand English homes because of their archeological significance—is fictional, the purpose of the real manual was the same: to help wealthy American girls marry European men with titles. In real life, dozens of English lords did wed American heiresses with generous dowries in the late 1800s and early 1900s in order to finance the upkeep of their struggling palatial estates.

Many people contributed to the development

of this novel, including the talented authors who attended the Kiawah Island writing retreat in the spring of 2024. Thank you to Sarah MacLean, Sophie Jordan, Louisa Darling and Adrianna Herrera for helping me brainstorm the finer elements of this story. Louisa deserves a special shoutout for coming up with the perfect title, *The Earl That Got Away*, to match the energy of *The Duke Gets Desperate*, the first book in my Sirens in Silk series.

Mostly, though, I need to thank *you*, the readers, reviewers, Bookstagrammers and BookTokers for reading my books and spreading the word about them. I know you have limitless titles to select from and I'm honored whenever you choose to spend a few hours with me, through my books.

Discover more from
DIANA QUINCY

SIRENS IN SILK

CLANDESTINE AFFAIRS

DISCOVER GREAT AUTHORS, EXCLUSIVE OFFERS,
AND MORE AT HC.COM.